# GRENDEL KENTUCKY

written by
**JEFF McCOMSEY**

illustrated by
**TOMMY LEE EDWARDS**

lettered by
**JOHN WORKMAN**

chapters 3 & 4 colored by
**GIOVANNA NIRO**

logo and design by **CHRIS FERGUSON**

variant covers by **MIKE DEODATO JR. & DAVE JOHNSON**

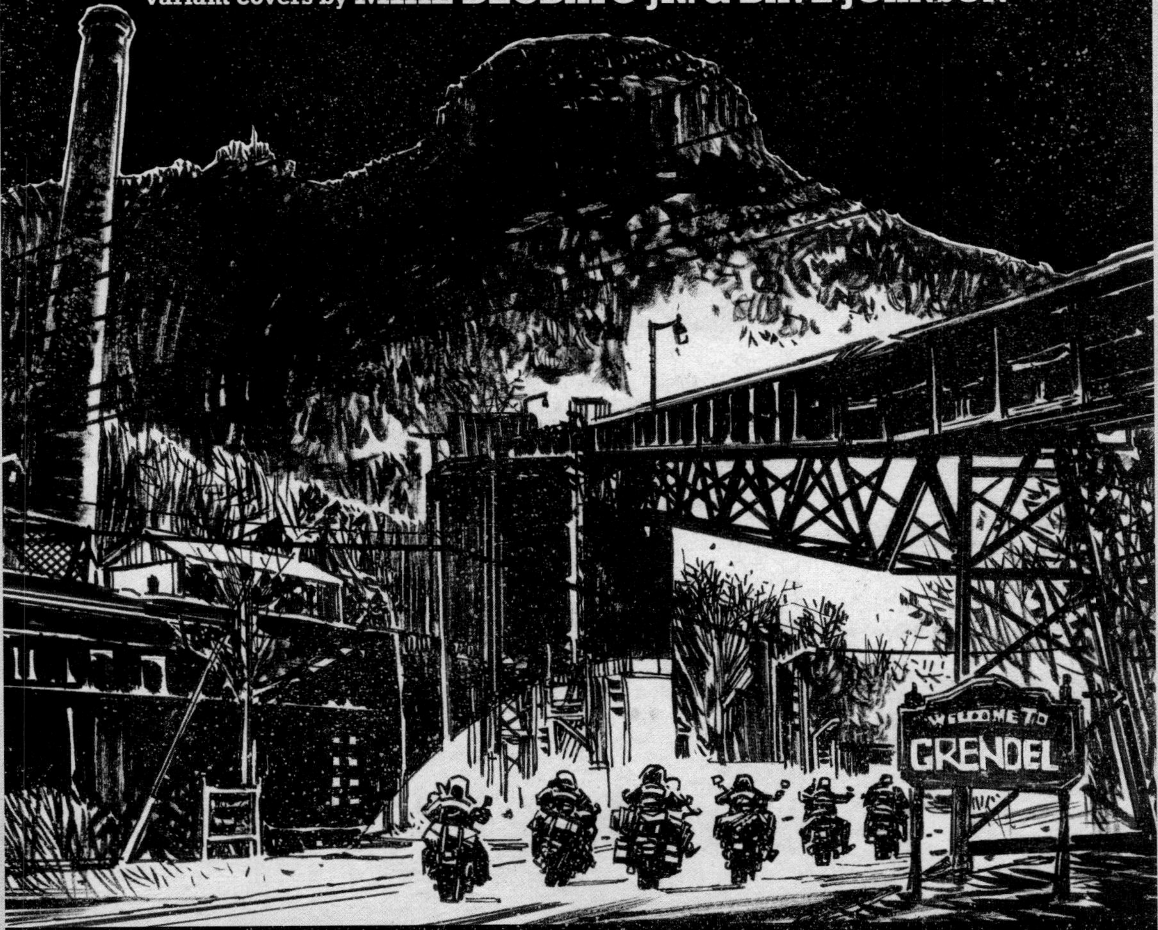
WELCOME TO
GRENDEL

AWA UPSHOT AWA_studios AWAstudiosofficial UPSHOT_studios UPSHOTstudiosofficial

**Axel Alonso** Chief Creative Officer
**Chris Burns** Production Editor
**Stan Chou** Art Director & Logo Designer
**Michael Coast** Senior Editor
**Jaime Coyne** Associate Editor
**Ariane Baya** Accounting Associate
**Frank Fochetta** Senior Consultant, Sales & Distribution
**William Graves** Managing Editor
**Bill Jemas** CEO & Publisher
**Amy Kim** Events & Sales Associate
**Bosung Kim** Production & Design Assistant
**Allison Mase** Executive Assistant
**Dulce Montoya** Associate Editor
**Kevin Park** Associate General Counsel
**Lisa Y. Wu** Marketing Manager
**Jackie Liu** Digital Marketing Manager

**GRENDEL, KENTUCKY, VOLUME 1. March 2021.** Published by Artists Writers & Artisans, Inc. Office of publication: 150 West 28th Street, 4th Floor, Suite 404, New York, NY 10010.  **Printed in Canada.**

10 9 8 7 6 5 4 3 2 1

AWA UPSHOT

$3.99
MATURE

#1 of 4

# GRENDEL, KENTUCKY

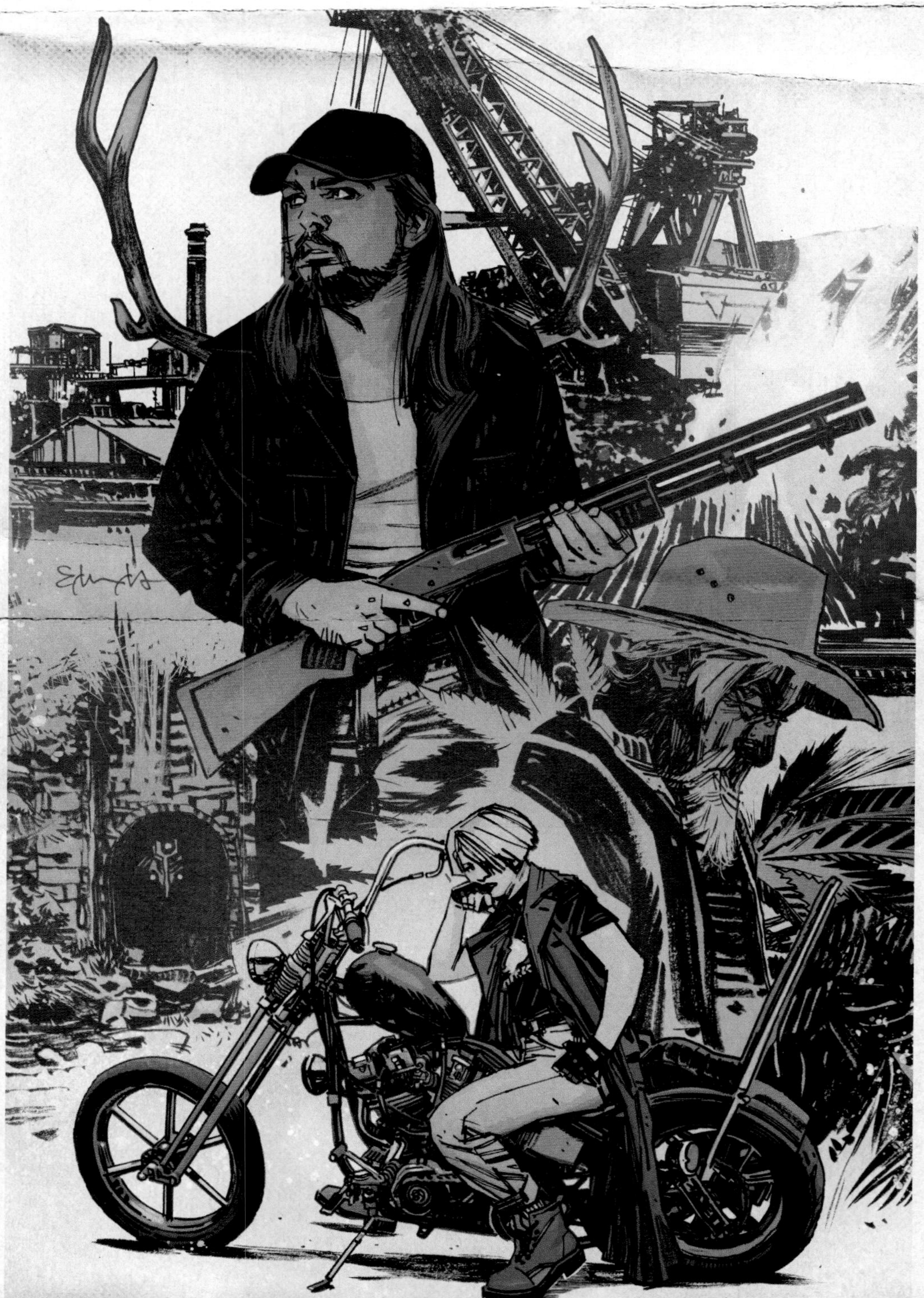

written by
**JEFF McCOMSEY**

illustrated by
**TOMMY LEE EDWARDS**

lettered by
**JOHN WORKMAN**

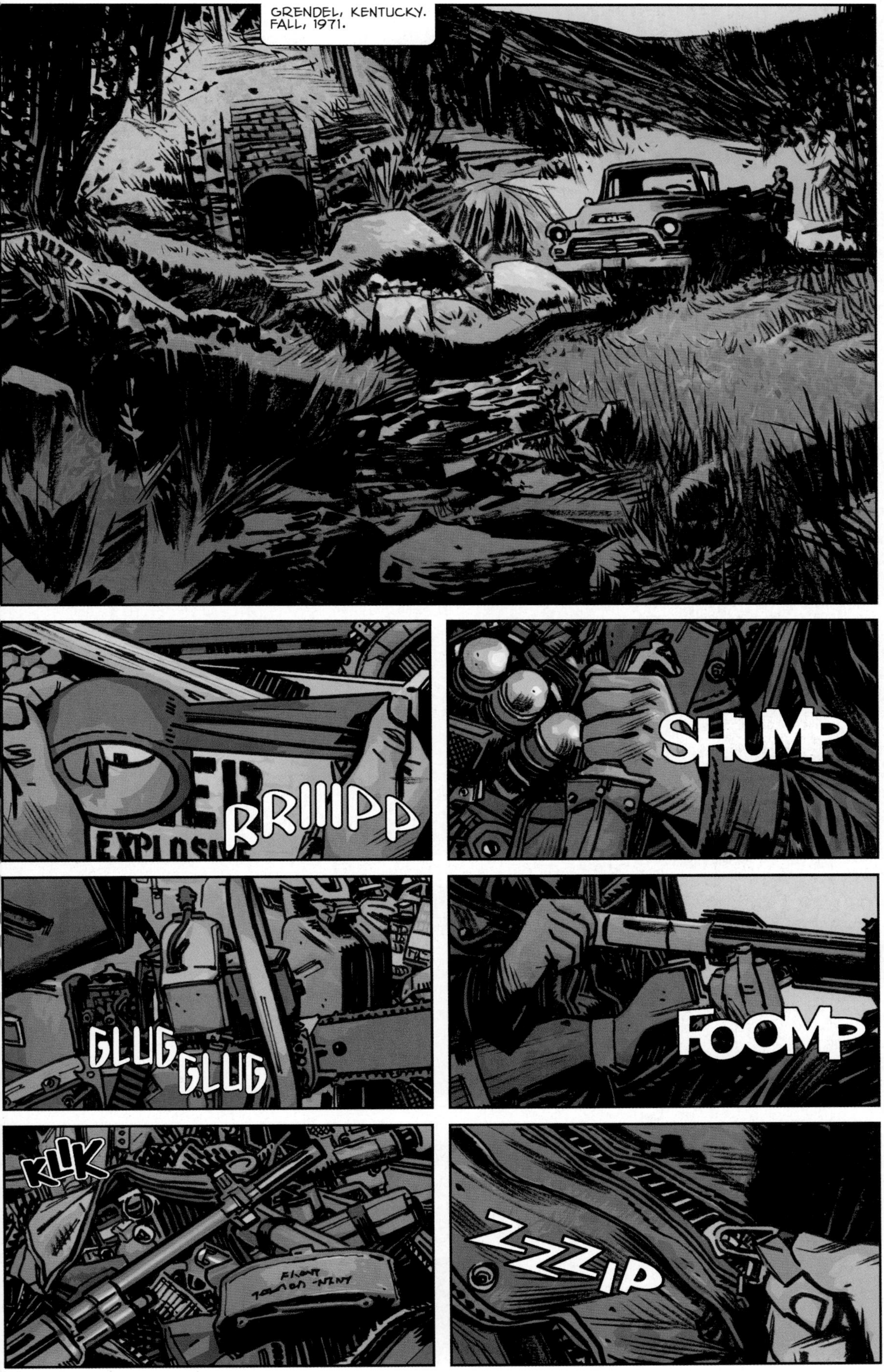
GRENDEL, KENTUCKY.
FALL, 1971.
RRIIIPP
SHUMP
GLUG GLUG
FOOMP
KLIK
ZZZIP

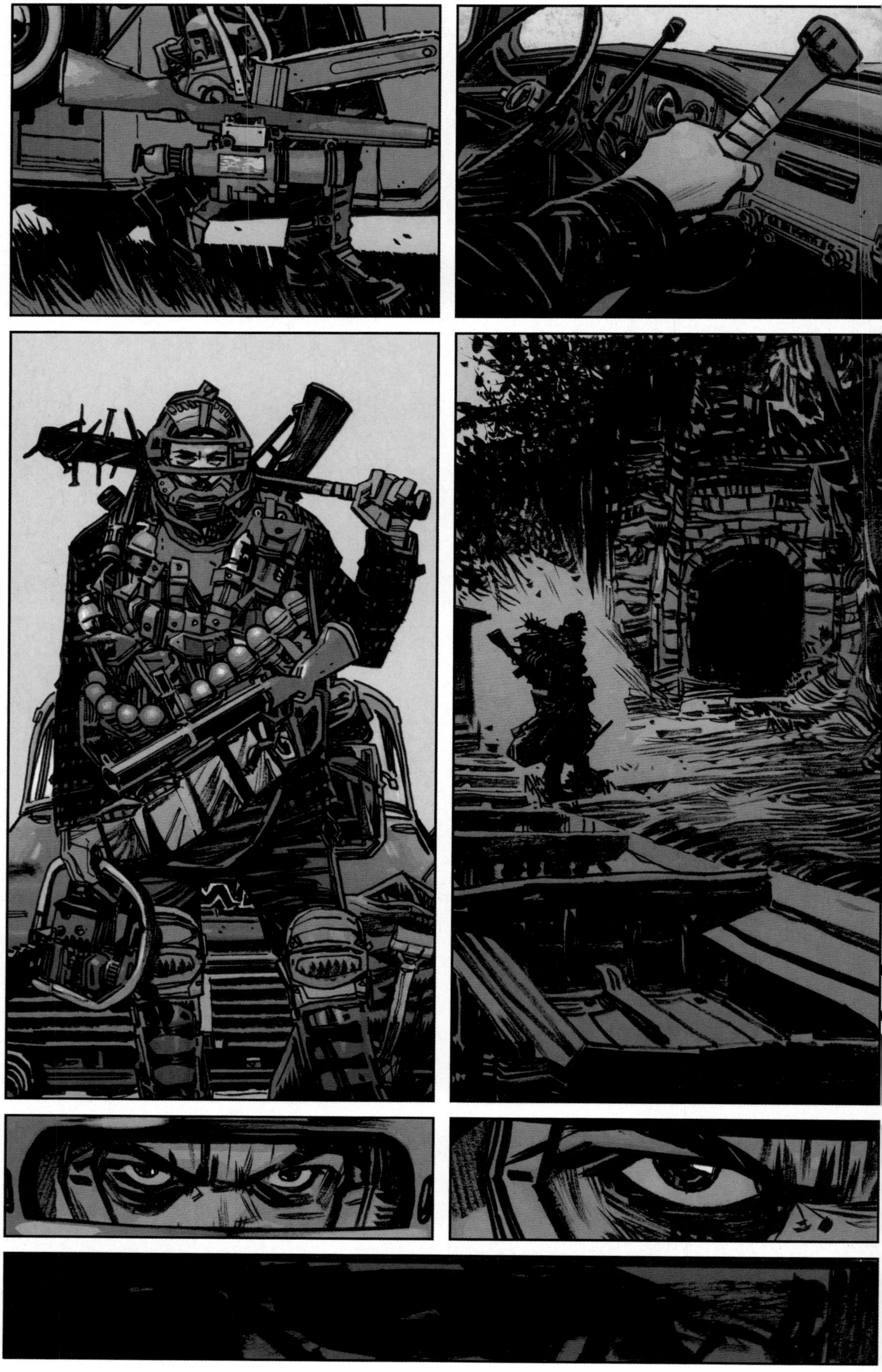

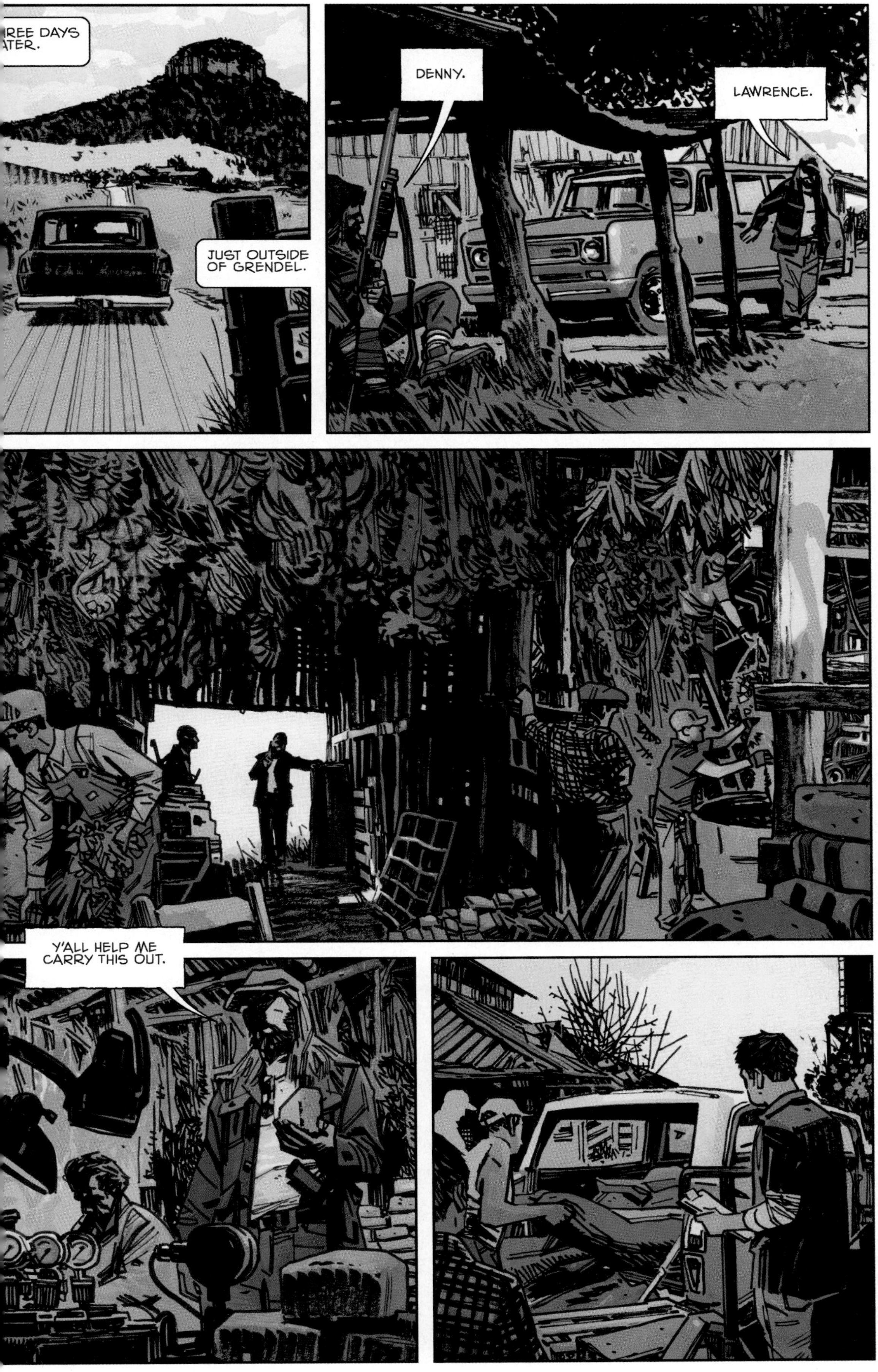

REE DAYS
ATER.
JUST OUTSIDE
OF GRENDEL.
DENNY.
LAWRENCE.
Y'ALL HELP ME
CARRY THIS OUT.

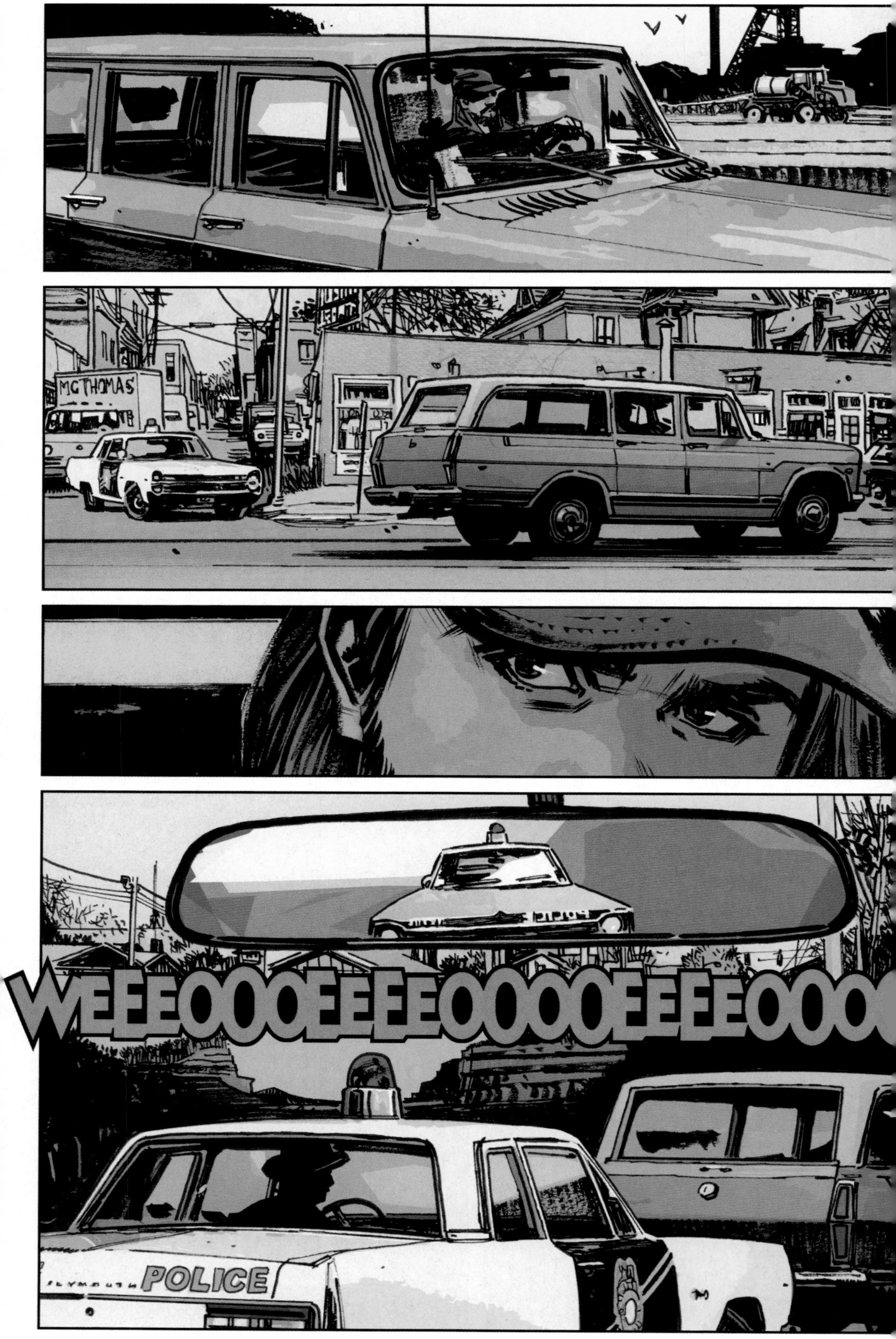

MCTHOMAS
WEEEOOOEEEEOOOOEEEEOOO
POLICE

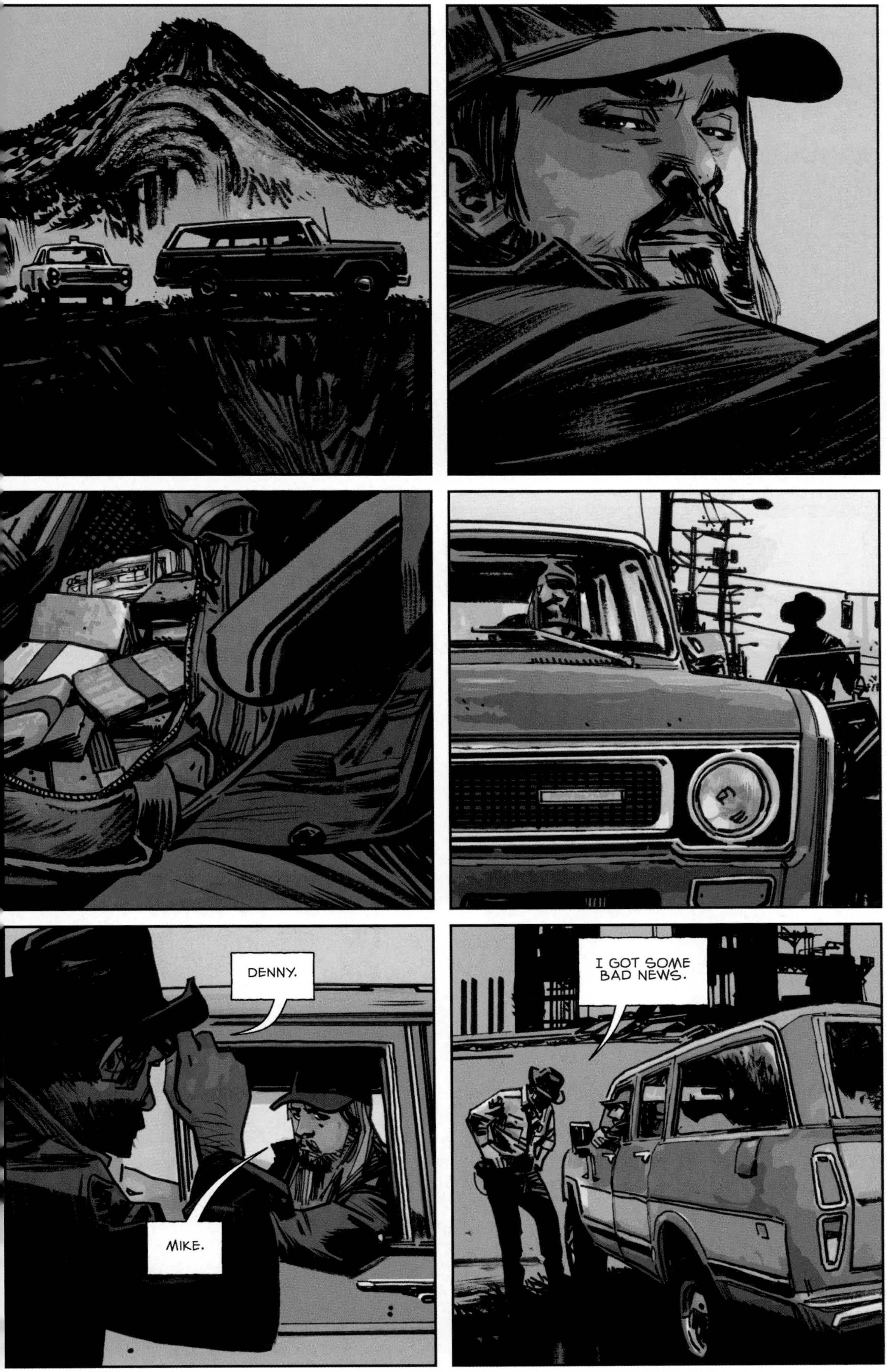
DENNY.
MIKE.
I GOT SOME BAD NEWS.

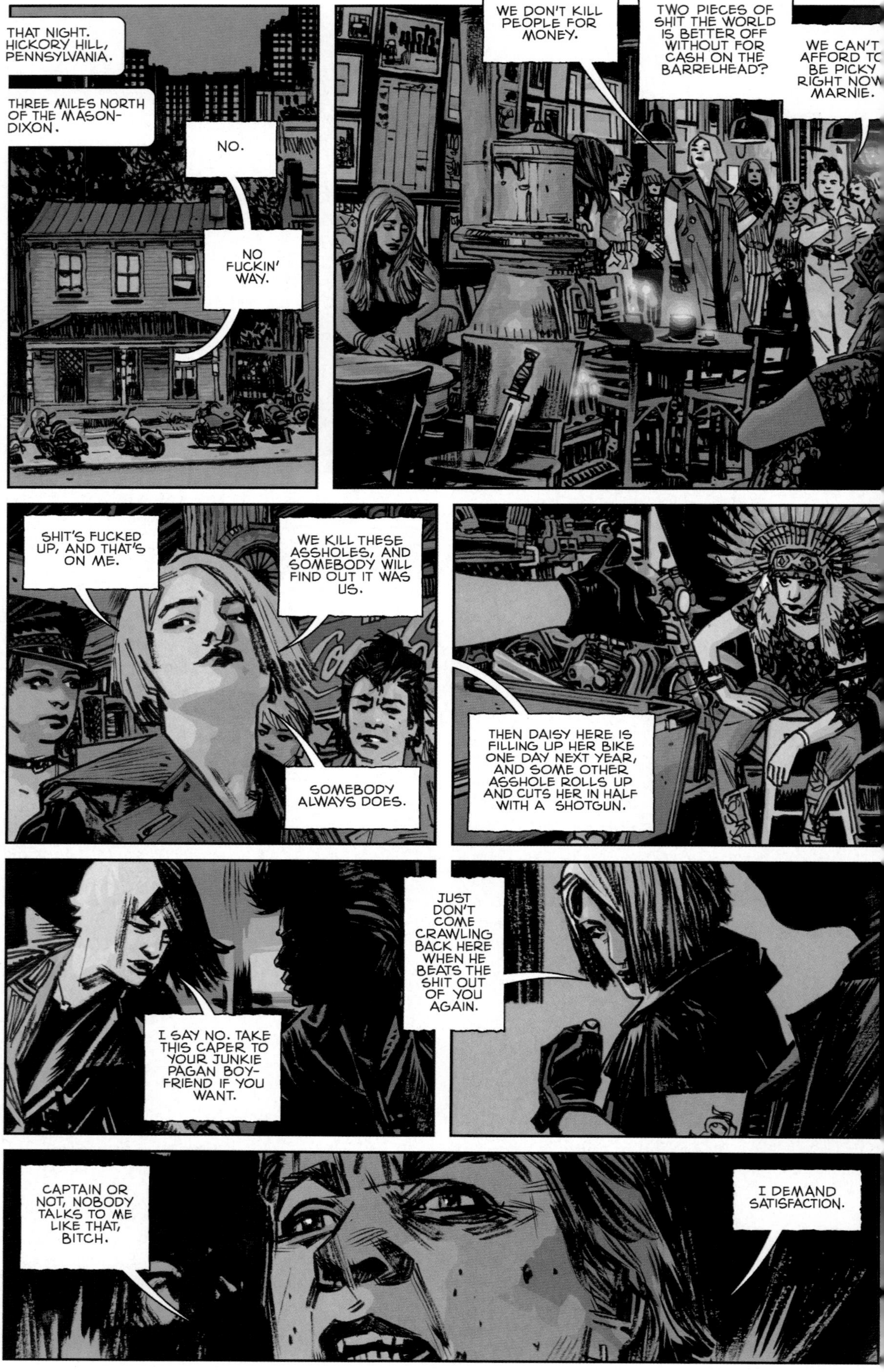
THAT NIGHT. HICKORY HILL, PENNSYLVANIA.
THREE MILES NORTH OF THE MASON-DIXON.
NO.
NO FUCKIN' WAY.
WE DON'T KILL PEOPLE FOR MONEY.
TWO PIECES OF SHIT THE WORLD IS BETTER OFF WITHOUT FOR CASH ON THE BARRELHEAD?
WE CAN'T AFFORD TO BE PICKY RIGHT NOW MARNIE.
SHIT'S FUCKED UP, AND THAT'S ON ME.
WE KILL THESE ASSHOLES, AND SOMEBODY WILL FIND OUT IT WAS US.
SOMEBODY ALWAYS DOES.
THEN DAISY HERE IS FILLING UP HER BIKE ONE DAY NEXT YEAR, AND SOME OTHER ASSHOLE ROLLS UP AND CUTS HER IN HALF WITH A SHOTGUN.
I SAY NO. TAKE THIS CAPER TO YOUR JUNKIE PAGAN BOY-FRIEND IF YOU WANT.
JUST DON'T COME CRAWLING BACK HERE WHEN HE BEATS THE SHIT OUT OF YOU AGAIN.
CAPTAIN OR NOT, NOBODY TALKS TO ME LIKE THAT, BITCH.
I DEMAND SATISFACTION.

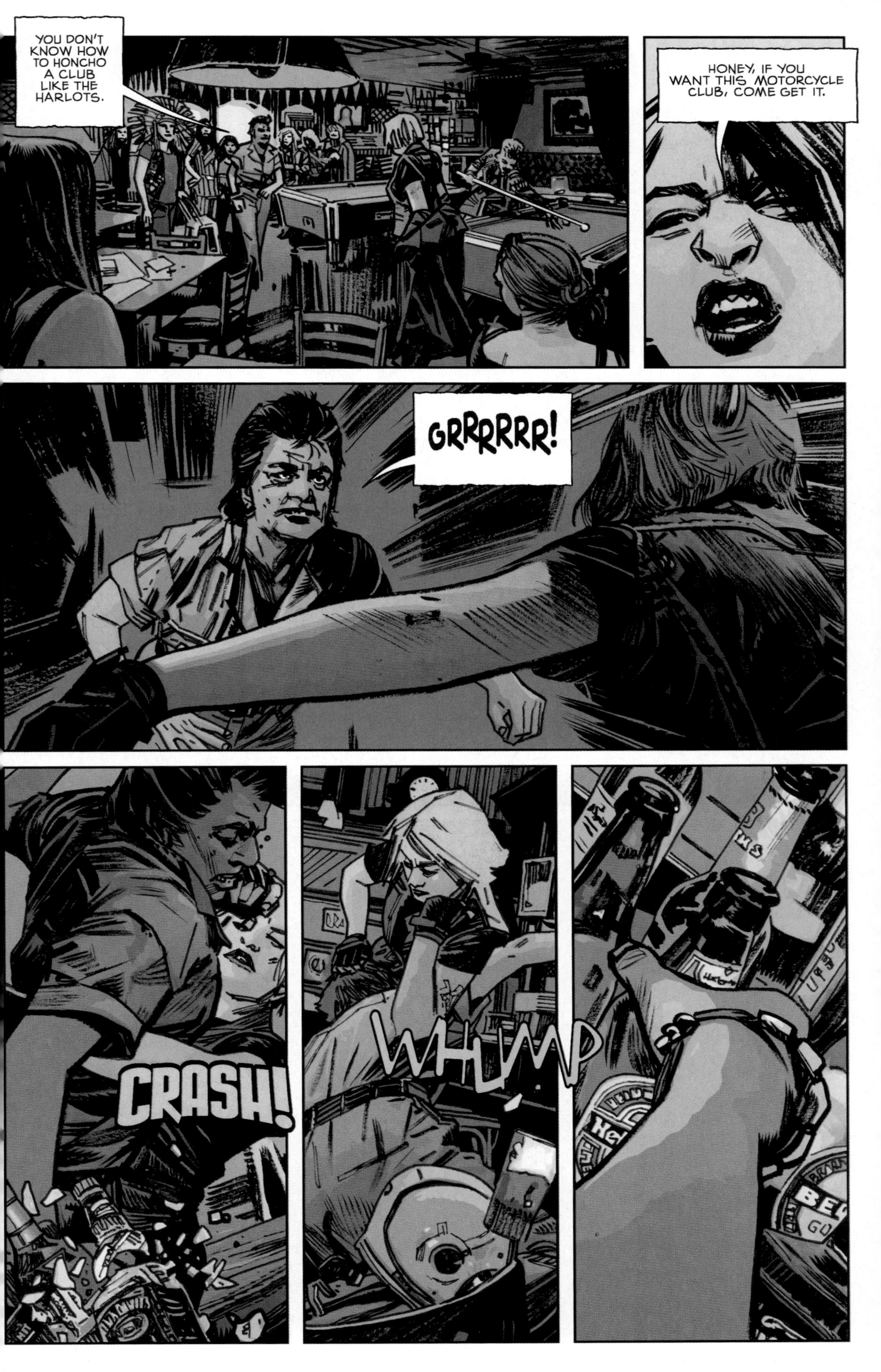
YOU DON'T KNOW HOW TO HONCHO A CLUB LIKE THE HARLOTS.
HONEY, IF YOU WANT THIS MOTORCYCLE CLUB, COME GET IT.
GRRRRRR!
CRASH!
WHUMP

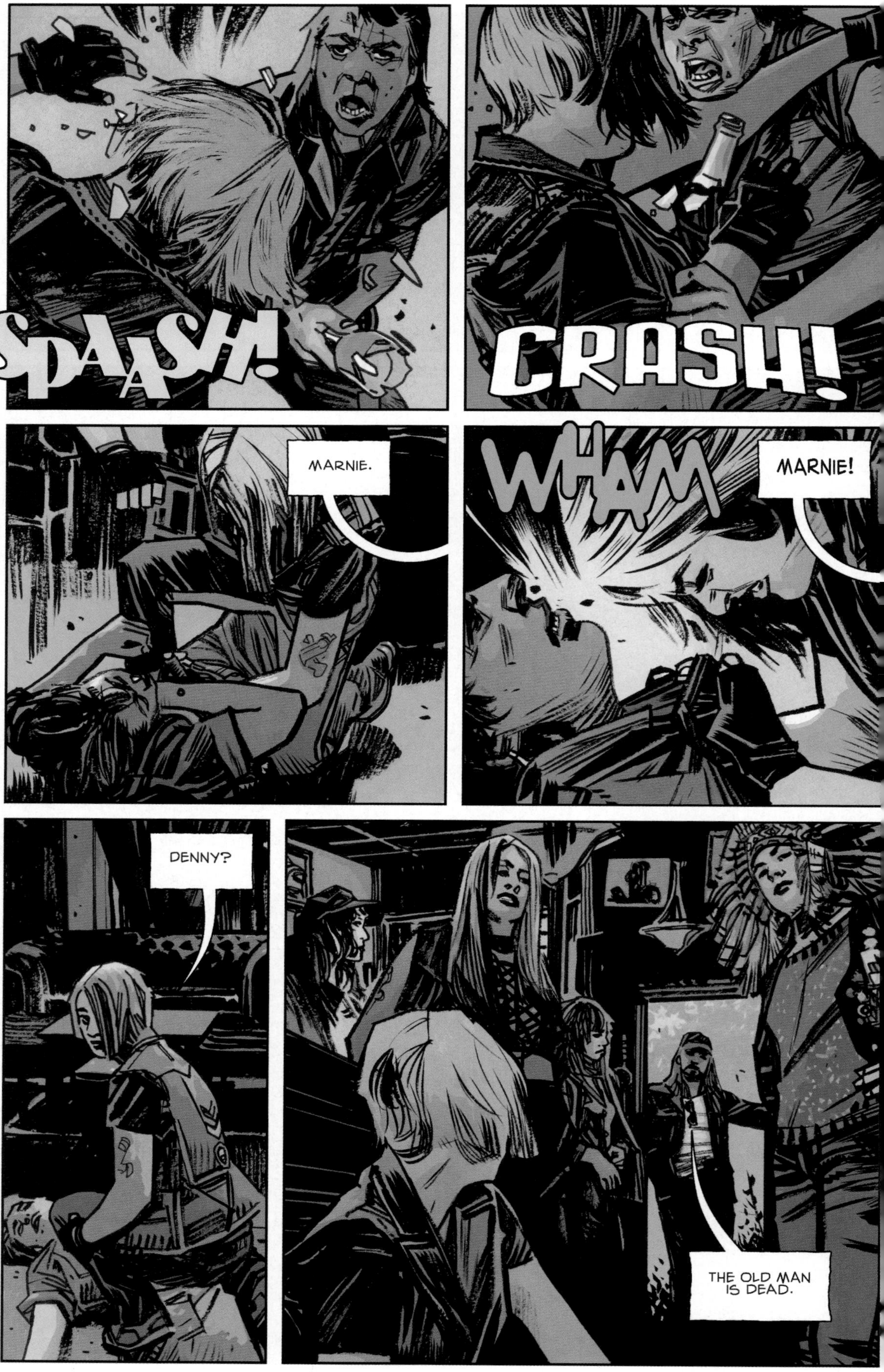
SPAAASH!
CRASH!
MARNIE.
WHAM
MARNIE!
DENNY?
THE OLD MAN IS DEAD.

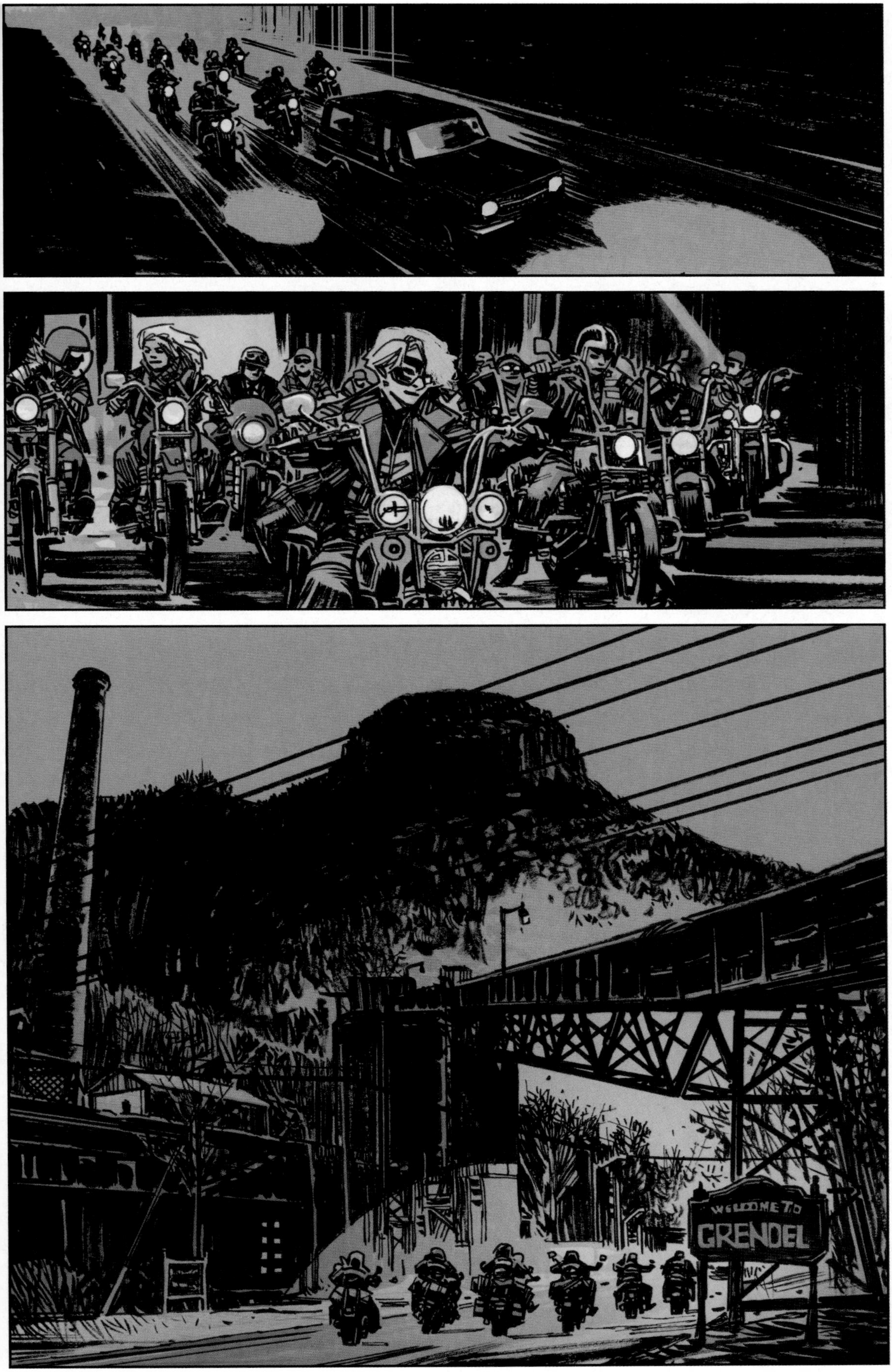
WELCOME TO
GRENDEL

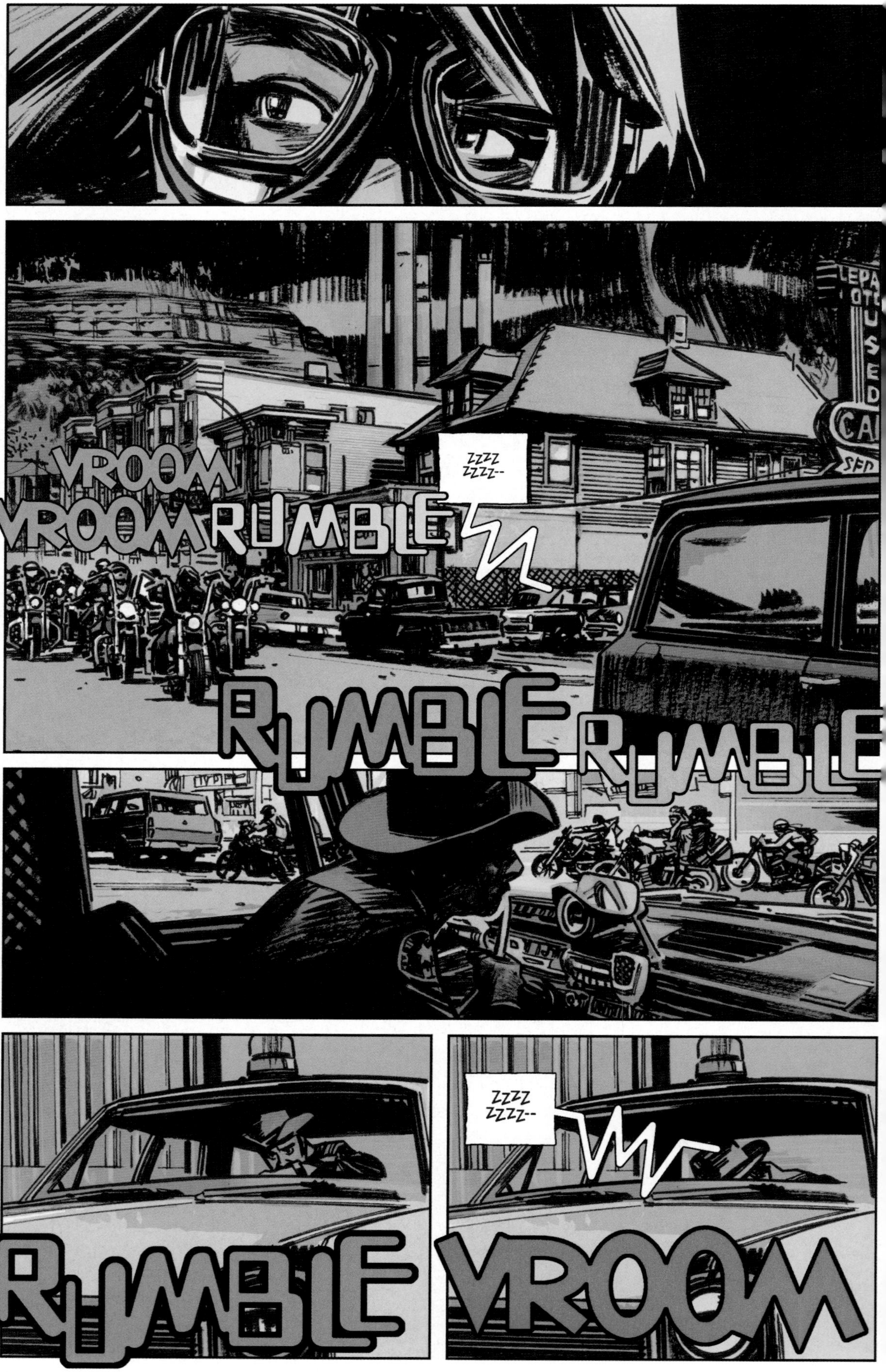
VROOM
VROOM
RUMBLE
ZZZZ
ZZZZ--
RUMBLE
RUMBLE
RUMBLE
ZZZZ
ZZZZ--
VROOM

--HE WHIPS THE CAR OFF THE ROAD AND INTO THIS CORNFIELD.

HE KILLS THE LIGHTS AND THE ENGINE.

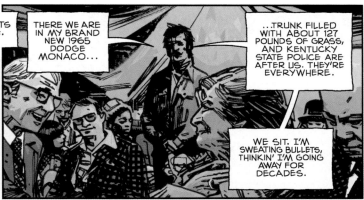

THERE WE ARE IN MY BRAND NEW 1965 DODGE MONACO...

...TRUNK FILLED WITH ABOUT 127 POUNDS OF GRASS, AND KENTUCKY STATE POLICE ARE AFTER US. THEY'RE EVERYWHERE.

WE SIT. I'M SWEATING BULLETS, THINKIN' I'M GOING AWAY FOR DECADES.

I LOOK OVER AT CLYDE, AND THAT FUCKER IS ASLEEP.

HAHAHAHAHAHA!

STAYED THERE 'TIL THE SUN COME UP. NO MORE COPS.

CLYDE WOKE UP. WE DROVE THE SHIT TO DEKE'S. WENT HOME.

THANK YOU, WAYNE.

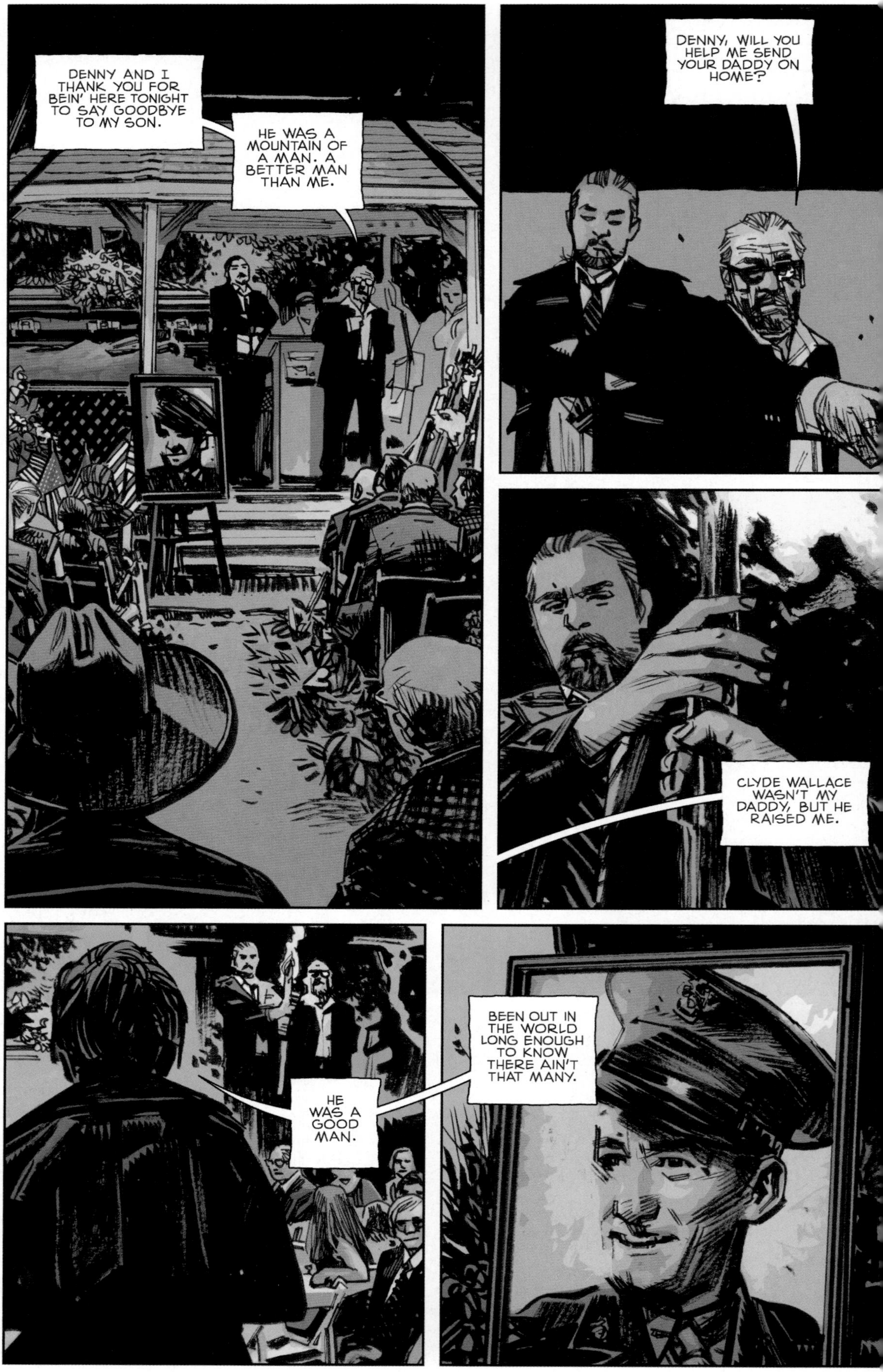
DENNY AND I THANK YOU FOR BEIN' HERE TONIGHT TO SAY GOODBYE TO MY SON.
HE WAS A MOUNTAIN OF A MAN. A BETTER MAN THAN ME.
DENNY, WILL YOU HELP ME SEND YOUR DADDY ON HOME?
CLYDE WALLACE WASN'T MY DADDY, BUT HE RAISED ME.
HE WAS A GOOD MAN.
BEEN OUT IN THE WORLD LONG ENOUGH TO KNOW THERE AIN'T THAT MANY.

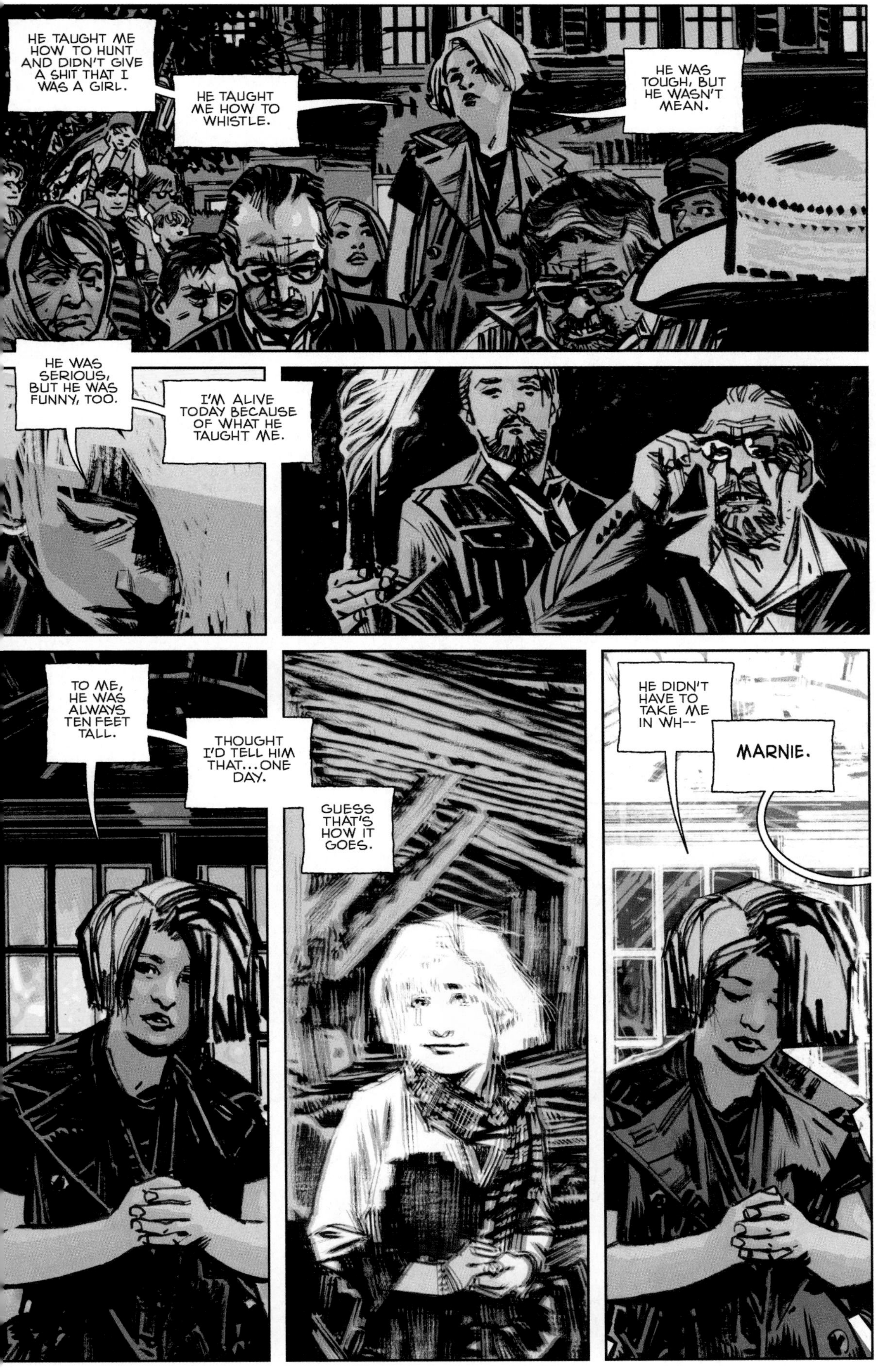
HE TAUGHT ME HOW TO HUNT AND DIDN'T GIVE A SHIT THAT I WAS A GIRL.
HE TAUGHT ME HOW TO WHISTLE.
HE WAS TOUGH, BUT HE WASN'T MEAN.
HE WAS SERIOUS, BUT HE WAS FUNNY, TOO.
I'M ALIVE TODAY BECAUSE OF WHAT HE TAUGHT ME.
TO ME, HE WAS ALWAYS TEN FEET TALL.
THOUGHT I'D TELL HIM THAT...ONE DAY.
GUESS THAT'S HOW IT GOES.
HE DIDN'T HAVE TO TAKE ME IN WH--
MARNIE.

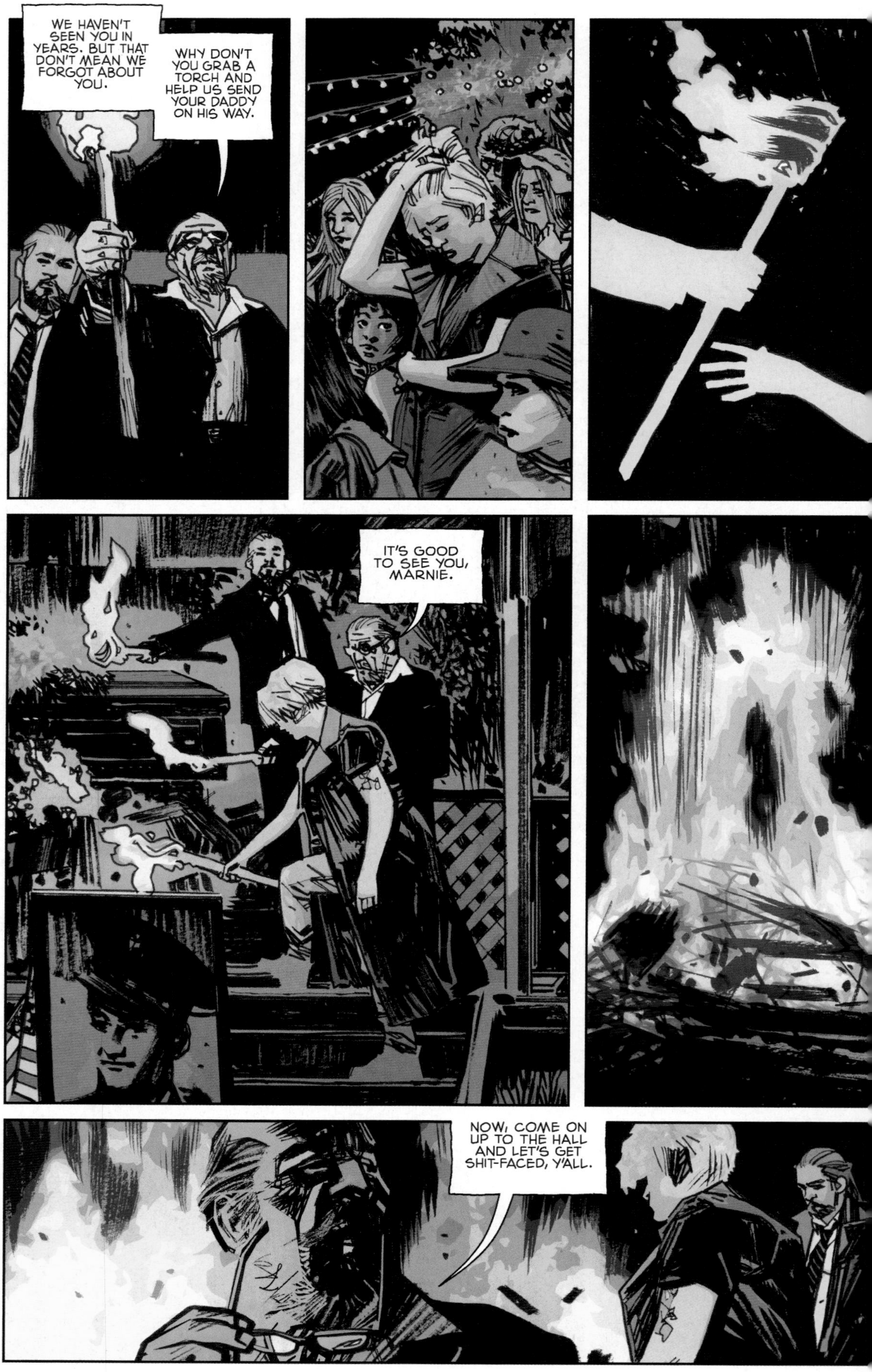
WE HAVEN'T SEEN YOU IN YEARS. BUT THAT DON'T MEAN WE FORGOT ABOUT YOU.
WHY DON'T YOU GRAB A TORCH AND HELP US SEND YOUR DADDY ON HIS WAY.
IT'S GOOD TO SEE YOU, MARNIE.
NOW, COME ON UP TO THE HALL AND LET'S GET SHIT-FACED, Y'ALL.

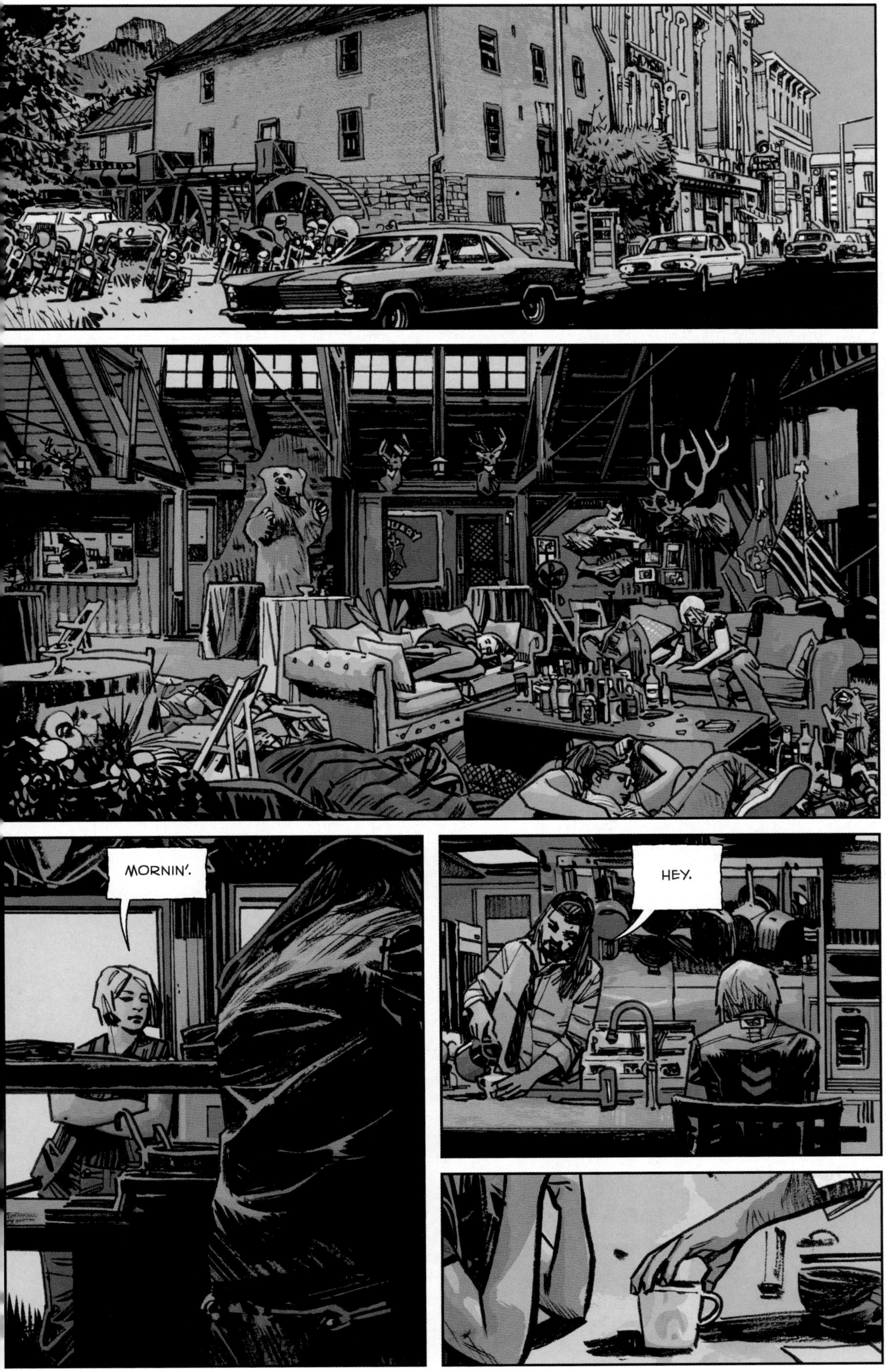
MORNIN'.
HEY.

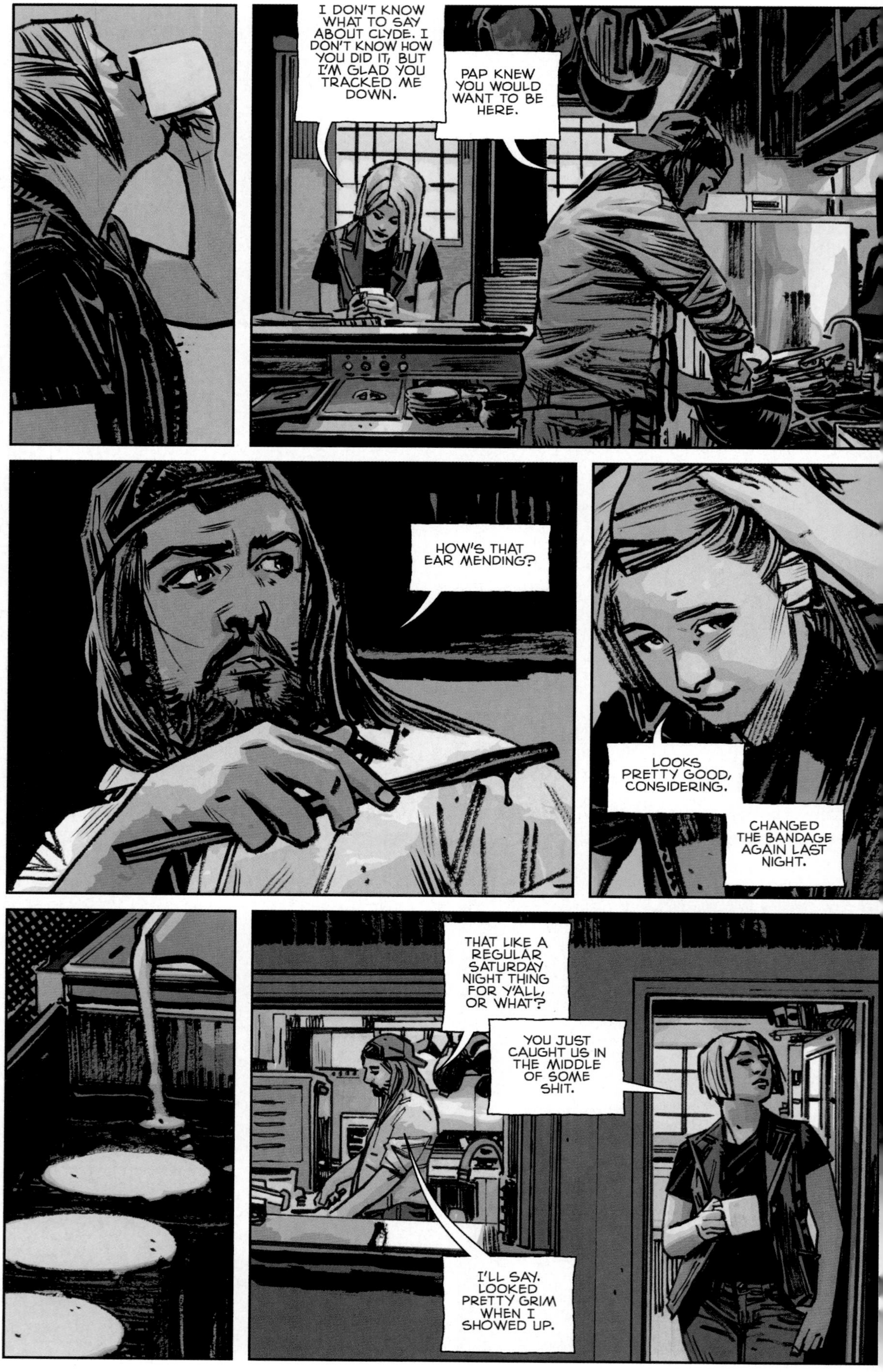
I DON'T KNOW WHAT TO SAY ABOUT CLYDE. I DON'T KNOW HOW YOU DID IT, BUT I'M GLAD YOU TRACKED ME DOWN.
PAP KNEW YOU WOULD WANT TO BE HERE.
HOW'S THAT EAR MENDING?
LOOKS PRETTY GOOD, CONSIDERING.
CHANGED THE BANDAGE AGAIN LAST NIGHT.
THAT LIKE A REGULAR SATURDAY NIGHT THING FOR Y'ALL, OR WHAT?
YOU JUST CAUGHT US IN THE MIDDLE OF SOME SHIT.
I'LL SAY. LOOKED PRETTY GRIM WHEN I SHOWED UP.

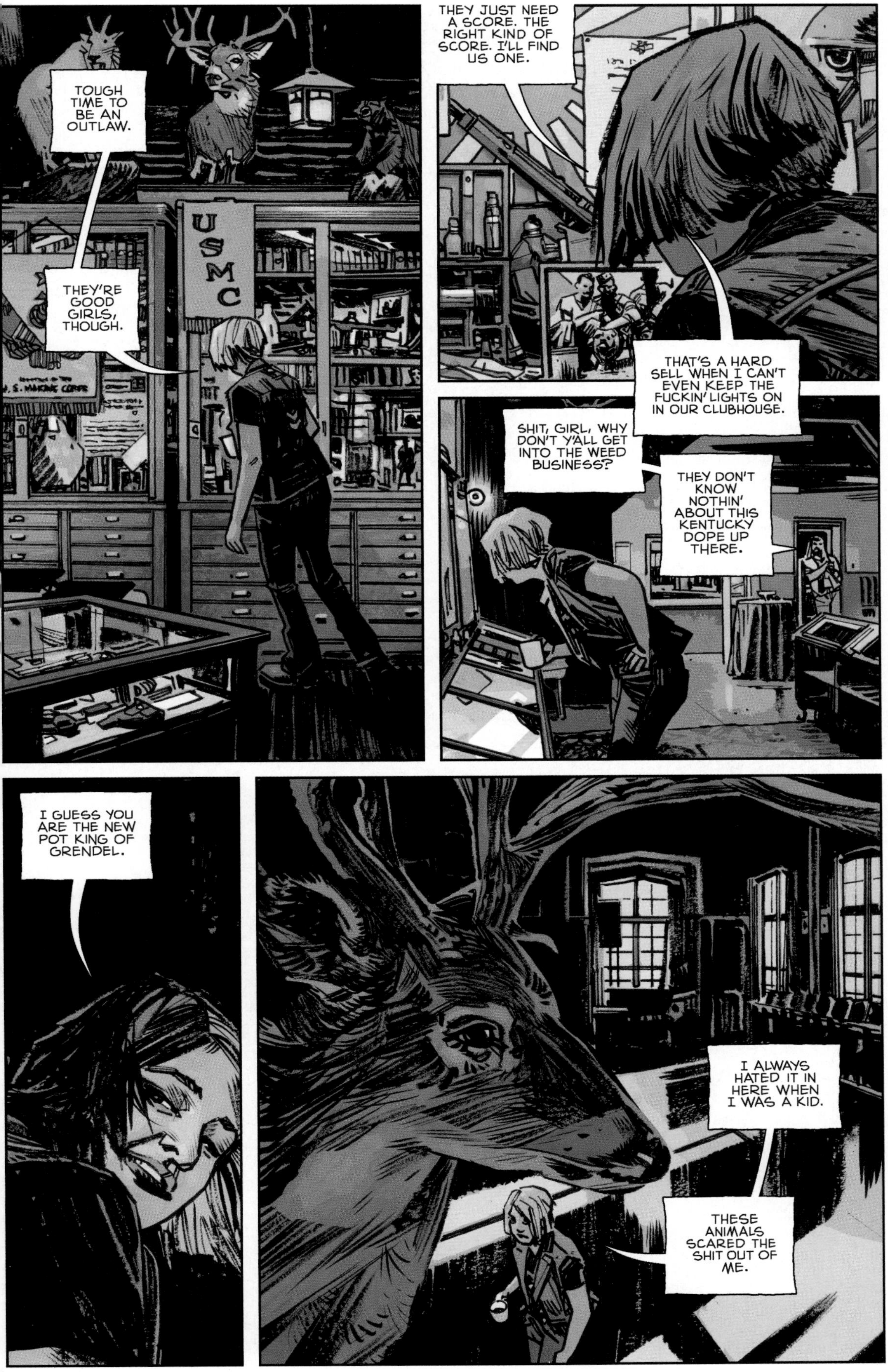

TOUGH TIME TO BE AN OUTLAW.
THEY'RE GOOD GIRLS, THOUGH.
USMC
THEY JUST NEED A SCORE. THE RIGHT KIND OF SCORE. I'LL FIND US ONE.
THAT'S A HARD SELL WHEN I CAN'T EVEN KEEP THE FUCKIN' LIGHTS ON IN OUR CLUBHOUSE.
SHIT, GIRL, WHY DON'T Y'ALL GET INTO THE WEED BUSINESS?
THEY DON'T KNOW NOTHIN' ABOUT THIS KENTUCKY DOPE UP THERE.
I GUESS YOU ARE THE NEW POT KING OF GRENDEL.
I ALWAYS HATED IT IN HERE WHEN I WAS A KID.
THESE ANIMALS SCARED THE SHIT OUT OF ME.

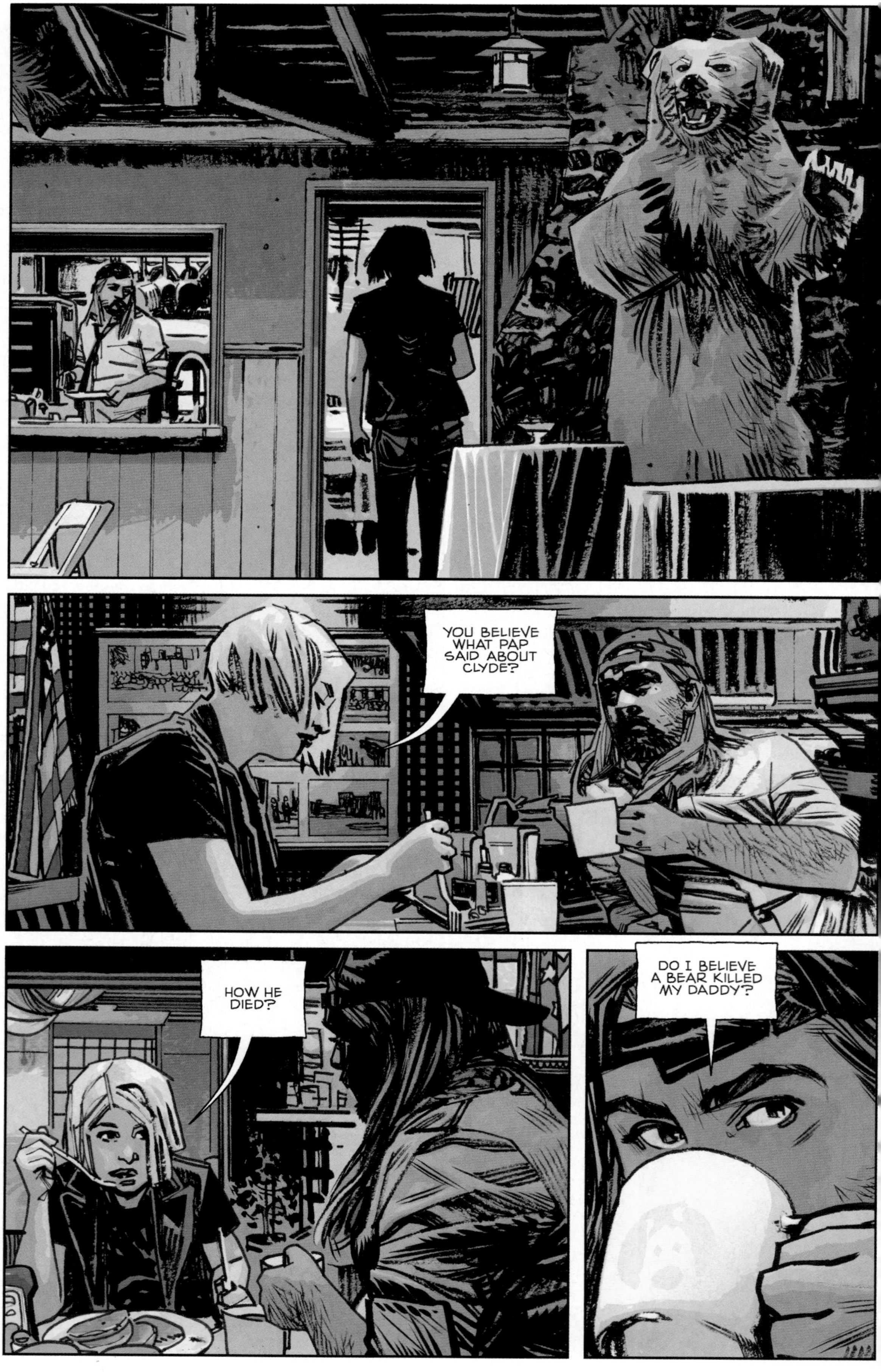
YOU BELIEVE WHAT PAP SAID ABOUT CLYDE?
HOW HE DIED?
DO I BELIEVE A BEAR KILLED MY DADDY?

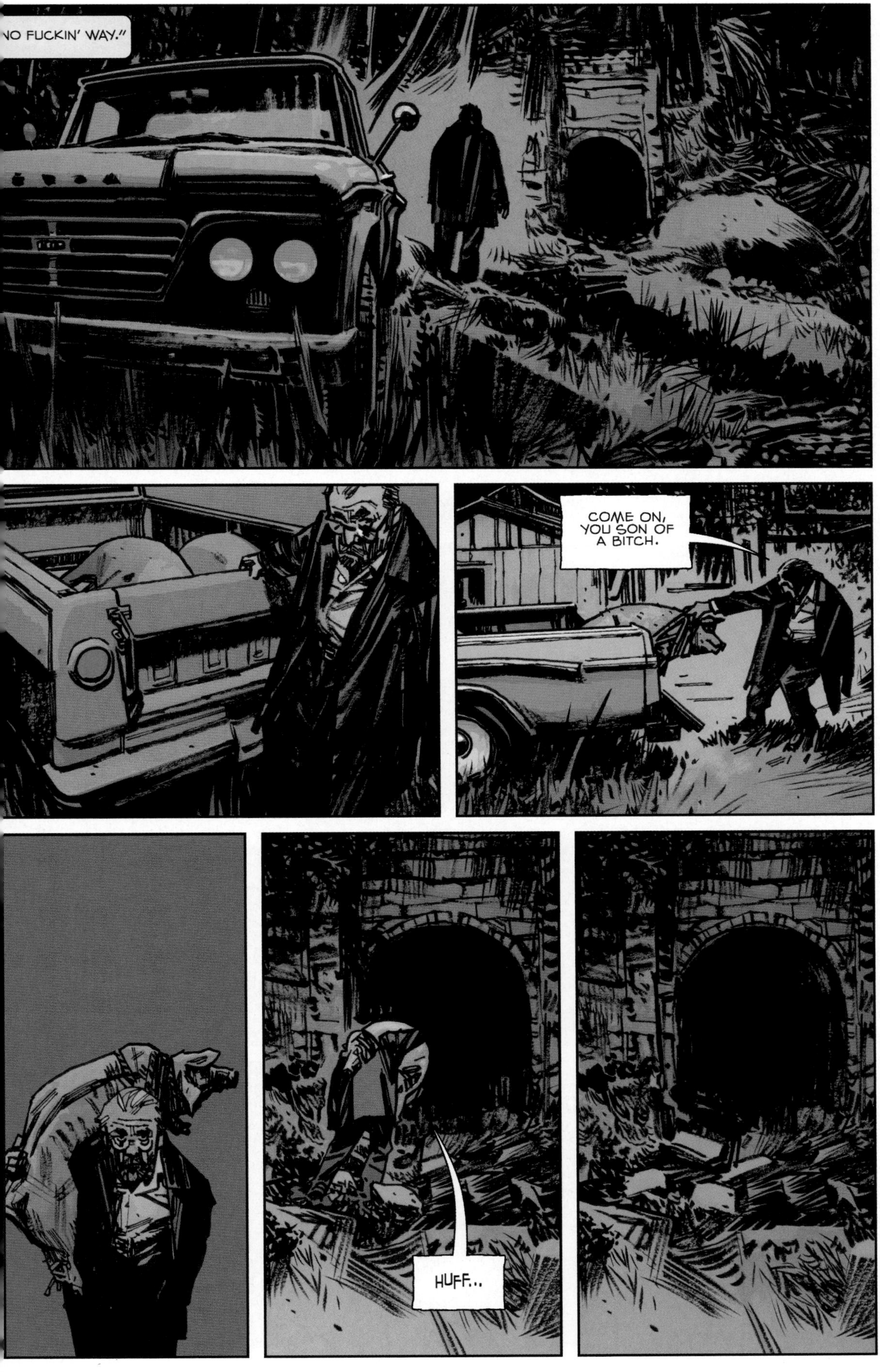
NO FUCKIN' WAY."
COME ON, YOU SON OF A BITCH.
HUFF...

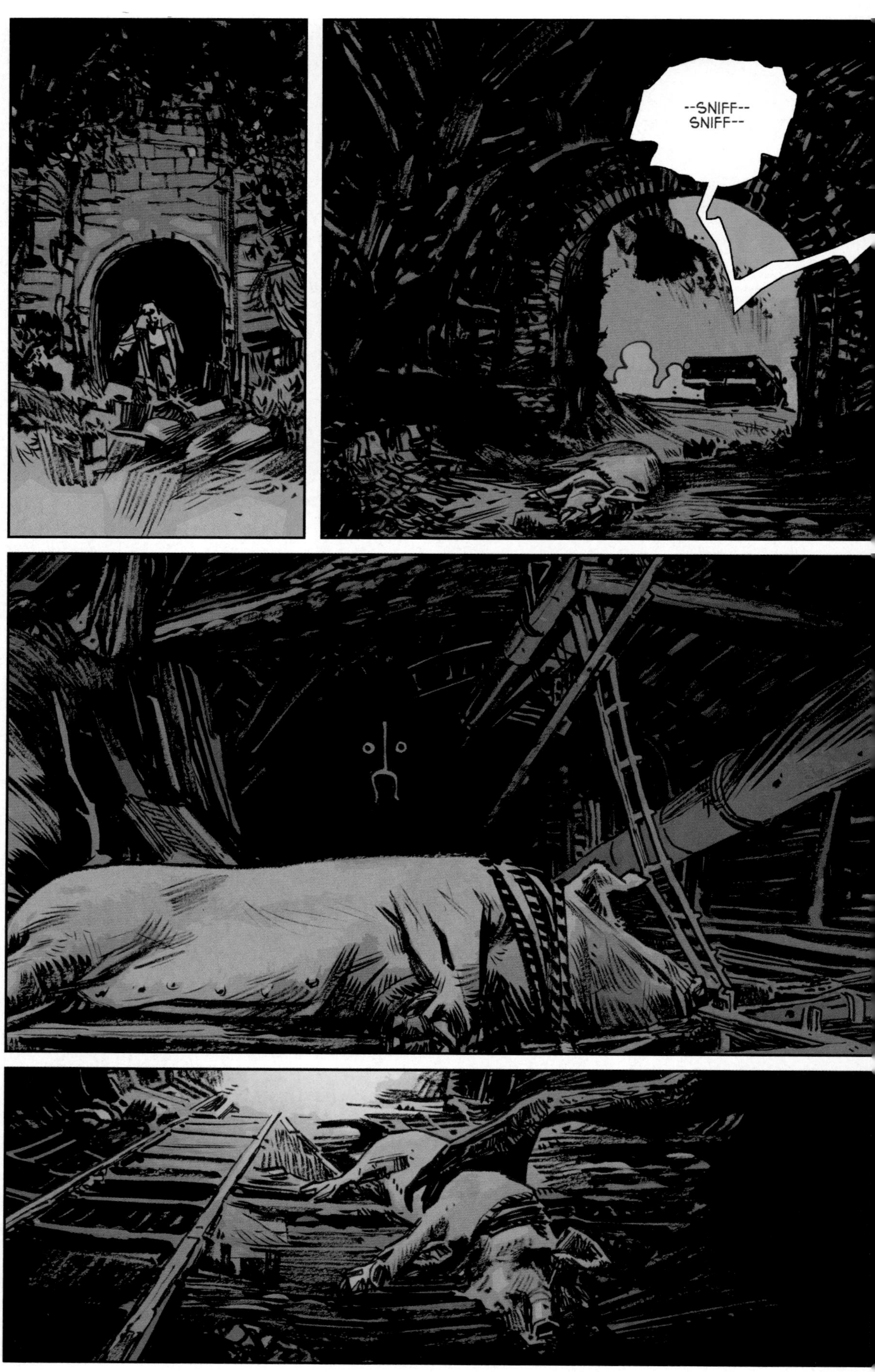
--SNIFF--
SNIFF--

# Obituary Notices

## Clyde Wallace, farmer, killed in bear attack

Special to the Kentuckian

GRENDEL, Ky.—Clyde Wallace, 48, of Grendel, died Thursday in the Hage County General Hospital at Grendel.

Officials from the Hage County sheriff's department ruled the death a result of a bear attack. Wallace was last seen in the vicinity of the old mountain coal mine just outside of Grendel.

He was a farmer, part of a generational agricultural legacy, that started with his father and continues with his son, Denny. Wallace was well-regarded in the Grendel community, where he was born and raised.

Funeral services will be held Sunday at 2 p.m. at the Gerads Funeral Home chapel in Grendel with the Revs. E. D. Shaner and Jeffrey Parker officiating.

Burial will be in the Grendel Town Cemetery by Gerads Funeral Home.

Pallbearers will be Randall "Pap" Wallace, Denny Wallace, Sheriff's Deputy Mike Scalera, Wayne Cipes, Jimmy O'Barr, and Christopher Ryall.

He is survived by his father, Randall "Pap" Wallace, Grendel; one son, Denny Wallace, Grendel; and one daughter, Marnie Wallace, Hickory Hill, Pa.

Friends will be received at Grendel town square after 5 p.m. today.

CLYDE WALLACE

## Grendel-area deaths and funerals

**Mrs. Edward E. Barnes**, 46, of 711 E. Washington, a native of Taylorsville, Ky. Funeral, 11 a.m. Friday, Neurath Funeral Home, 725 E. Market.

**Mrs. Mabel Board**, 53, of 8214 Dixie Highway. Funeral, 2 p.m. Friday, W. G. Hardy Valley Funeral Home, 10807 Dixie Highway.

**Mrs. Cleo Albert Kern Bronner**, 44, of Jeffersonville, Ind., formerly of Louisville. Funeral, 11 a.m. Friday, St. Raphael Catholic Church, 2900 Bardstown Road.

**A. Gordon Cheschew**, 57, of Spring Garden Lane, Anchorage, Ky. Memorial services, 11 a.m. Friday, St. Luke Episcopal Church, Anchorage.

**Mrs. Margy Coakley**, 42, of Elizabethtown Rt. 3, a native of Green County, Ky. Funeral, 2 p.m. Thursday, Perry & Alvey Funeral Home, Elizabethtown.

**Reese D. Cooke**, of 606 Virginia in Lyndon, Ky., a native of Corbin, Ky. Funeral, 11 a.m. Friday, Ratterman's, 3711 Lexington Road.

**Mrs. Lillian C. Hibbs**, 76, of 5298 Euclid. Funeral, 1 p.m. Friday, W. G. Hardy Valley Funeral Home, 10807 Dixie Highway.

**Mrs. Daisy Golladay Jeffries**, 76, of Big Clifty, Ky. Funeral, 1 p.m. Friday, Little Clifty Memorial Church, Big Clifty.

**James F. Jones**, 48, of Anchorage, Ky. Funeral, 2 p.m. Thursday, Winston Funeral Home, Russellville, Ky.

**Mrs. Mary Sophia Nibbley**, 78, of Woodhaven Medical Services. Funeral, 11 a.m. Friday, Nanadley Funeral Home, 4337 Taylor Blvd.

**Robert D. Kinchelor**, 96, of 222 S. Birchwood Ave. Funeral, 2 p.m. Thursday, Herbert C. Cralle Funeral Home, 2428 Frankfort Ave.

**Marvin Louis Lawson**, 44, of Anchorage, Ky., a native of Fayette County, Ky. Funeral, 2 p.m. Thursday, Foreman Funeral Home, 10600 Taylorsville Road.

**Mrs. Ruth Young Watkins Meacham**, 75, of the Medicenter, a native of Lawrenceburg, Ky. Funeral, 11 a.m. Thursday, Highlands Funeral Home, 3331 Taylorsville Road.

**Mrs. Harold B. Mitchum**, 69, of 7808 Circle Crest Road. Funeral, 10 a.m. Thursday, Pearson's, 149 Breckinridge Lane.

**Dr. John Frank Noel**, of Lawrenceburg, Ky., formerly of Louisville. Funeral, 11 a.m. Friday, McAfee Funeral Home, 3920 Bardstown Road.

**Mrs. John Reed**, 55, of Bardstown, Ky. Funeral, 2 p.m. Thursday, St. John A.M.E. Zion Church, Bardstown.

**Henry J. Rothman**, 79, of 1207 Hull. Funeral, 9 a.m. Friday, St. Aloysius Catholic Church, 1129 Payne.

**Taylor B. Smith**, 72, of 1222 S. 41st, a native of Lebanon, Ky. Funeral, 2 p.m. Saturday, Rowan & Grevious Mortuary, 1400 Beech.

**Charles Andrew Spurgeon**, 55, of Old Zaring Road, Brownsboro, Ky., a native of Fayette County, Ky. Funeral, 2:30 p.m. Friday, R. A. Stoess & Sons Funeral Home, Goodwood, Ky.

**Mrs. Mamie Coffey Woods**, 66, of Shelby County. Funeral, 2 p.m. Thursday, Hall-Taylor Funeral Home, Shelbyville, Ky.

### Kentucky deaths

GREENSBURG—Mrs. Sarah Ellen Pickett, 78, died here Wednesday. Funeral, 10 a.m. (CDT) Friday, Cowherd & Parrott Funeral Home here.

SOMERSET—Mrs. Lennie Dauhan, 61, of Nancy, Ky., died here Wednesday. Funeral, 2 p.m. Friday, White Oak Baptist Church, Nancy. The body is at the Pulaski Funeral Home here.

## Heroic efforts fail to save fire victim

SITKA, Ky. (AP)—An 81-year-old woman died despite the heroic efforts of a young neighbor when fire gutted her house in this Johnson County community.

Mrs. Mattie Fire was burned to death in an early morning fire Friday, but her invalid daughter, Audrey, was saved from a fiery death by Russell Selvan, police reported.

## Livestock markets

Federal-State Market News Service (Quotations are in cents per pound)

| | | | |
|---|---|---|---|
| HOGS | LOU. | INDPLS. | E. ST. L. |
| Receipts | 2,500 | 3,700 | 3,900 |
| Price Trend | [illegible] | [illegible] | [illegible] |
| [illegible] | [illegible] | [illegible] | [illegible] |
| [illegible] | [illegible] | [illegible] | [illegible] |
| [illegible] | [illegible] | [illegible] | [illegible] |
| CATTLE | LOU. | OMAHA | E. ST. L. |
| Receipts | 2,000 | 9,000 | 3,500 |
| Slaughter Steers | | | |
| Price Trend | Steady | Steady | Up ¼-½ |
| Prime | [illegible] | [illegible] | [illegible] |
| Choice | [illegible] | [illegible] | [illegible] |
| Heifers | | | |
| Price Trend | Off ½ | Steady | Up ¼-½ |
| Prime | [illegible] | [illegible] | [illegible] |
| Choice | [illegible] | [illegible] | [illegible] |
| Good | [illegible] | [illegible] | 27-30 |
| Cows | | | |
| Price Trend | Off ½ | Steady | Up ¼ |
| Utility | [illegible] | [illegible] | 20-23 |
| Cutter | [illegible] | [illegible] | [illegible] |
| Canner | 17-19 | [illegible] | [illegible] |
| Bulls | | | |
| Price Trend | Steady | Weak | Off ½ |
| Utility & Comm. | [illegible] | [illegible] | 24-26 |
| FEEDERS | LOU. | OKLA. CITY | SIOUX CITY |
| Steers | | | |
| Receipts | 1,800 | 4,000 | 1,200 |
| Price Trend | Steady | Steady | Steady |
| Choice [illegible] lbs. | [illegible] | [illegible] | |
| Choice [illegible] lbs. | [illegible] | [illegible] | |
| Good | [illegible] | [illegible] | 33-36 |
| Heifers | | | |
| Price Trend | Steady | Steady | Steady |
| Choice [illegible] lbs. | [illegible] | [illegible] | 30-32 |
| Good | [illegible] | [illegible] | |
| VEALERS | LOU. | SO. ST. PAUL | E. ST. L. |
| Receipts | 150 | 100 | 200 |
| Price Trend | Steady | | Steady |
| Choice | [illegible] | | [illegible] |
| Good | [illegible] | | [illegible] |
| Standard | [illegible] | | [illegible] |
| LAMBS | LOU. | SAN ANGELO | E. ST. L. |
| Receipts | 135 | | 400 |
| Price Trend | Steady | | Steady |
| Prime | | | [illegible] |
| Choice | 31 | | [illegible] |
| Good | 26 | | |
| Ewes | 4-8 | | 3-5 |

## Student is accused of picking marijuana

LEXINGTON, Ky. (AP)—Three students from Marshall University, Huntington, W. Va., have been arrested here, one accused of harvesting marijuana in a field on a county road, police said yesterday.

County Patrolman Kenny Jones said he was answering a trespassing complaint when he discovered James Campbell Wall III, 22, of Huntington, W. Va., in a field. He was charged with possession of marijuana, the officer said.

Arrested in a nearby car were Richard F. Flynn, 21, and Joseph A. Ramella, 20, both of Huntington, on minor charges not related to drugs.

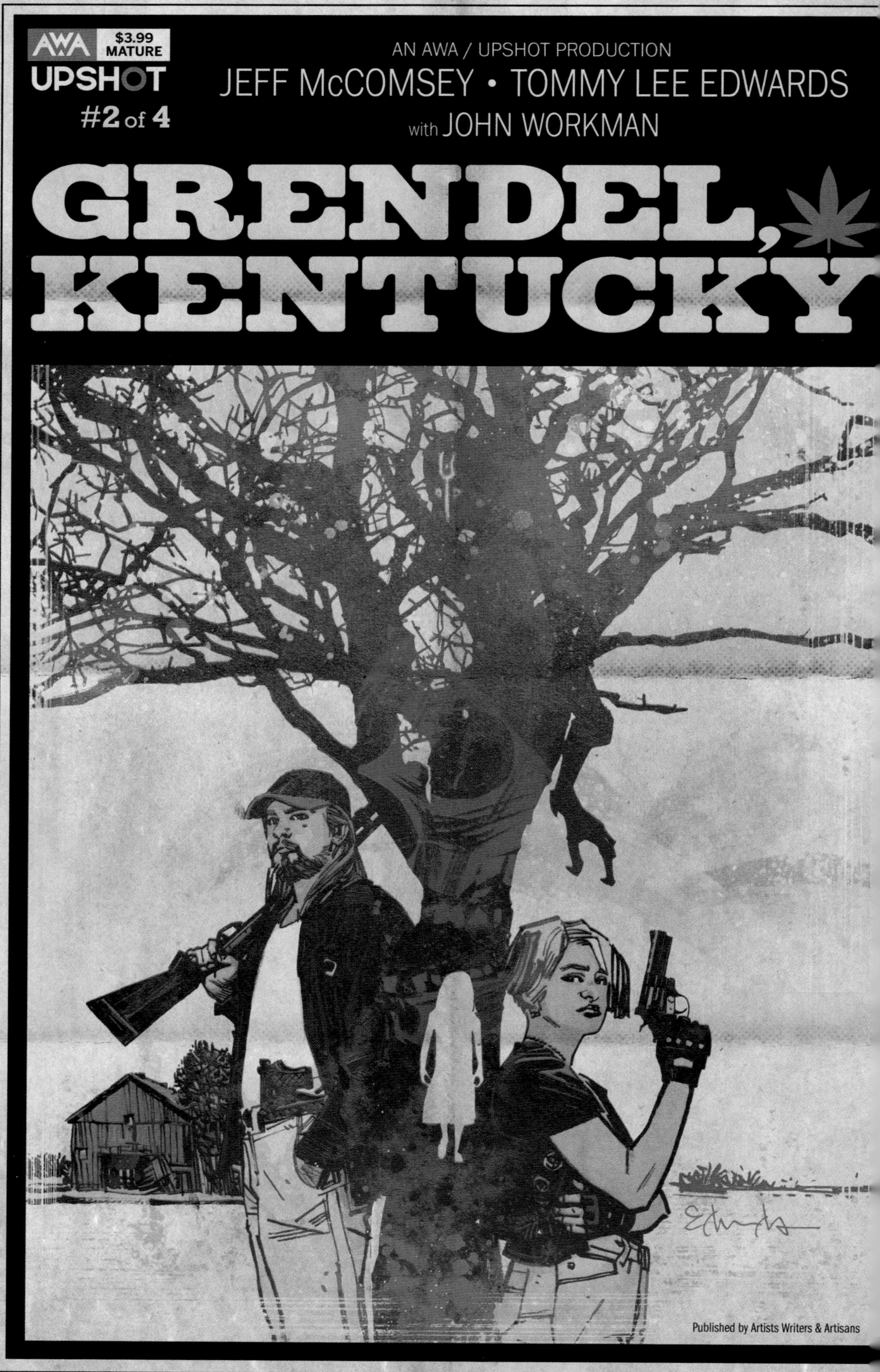
AWA
$3.99
MATURE
UPSHOT
#2 of 4
AN AWA / UPSHOT PRODUCTION
JEFF McCOMSEY • TOMMY LEE EDWARDS
with JOHN WORKMAN
GRENDEL, KENTUCKY
Published by Artists Writers & Artisans

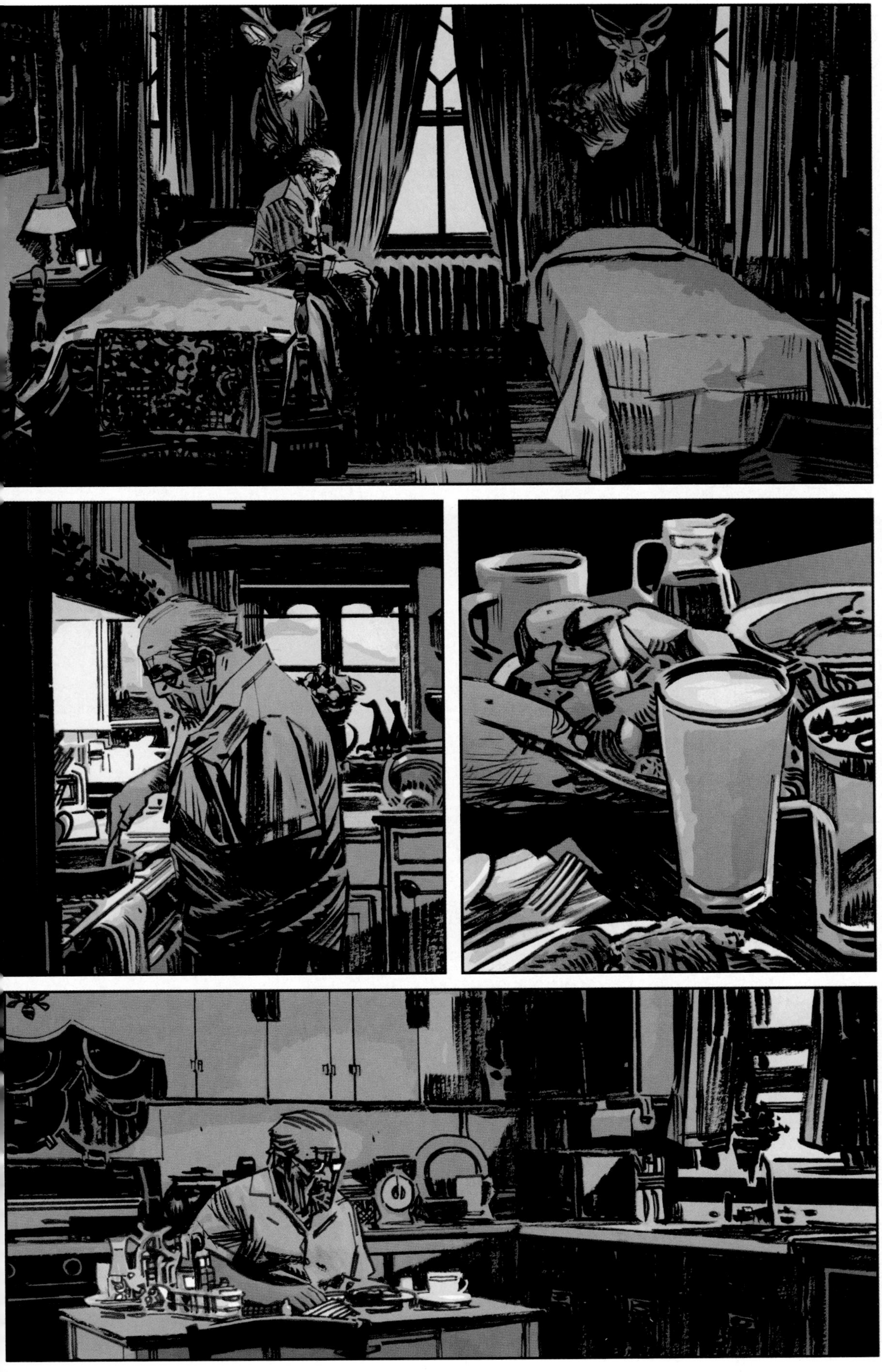

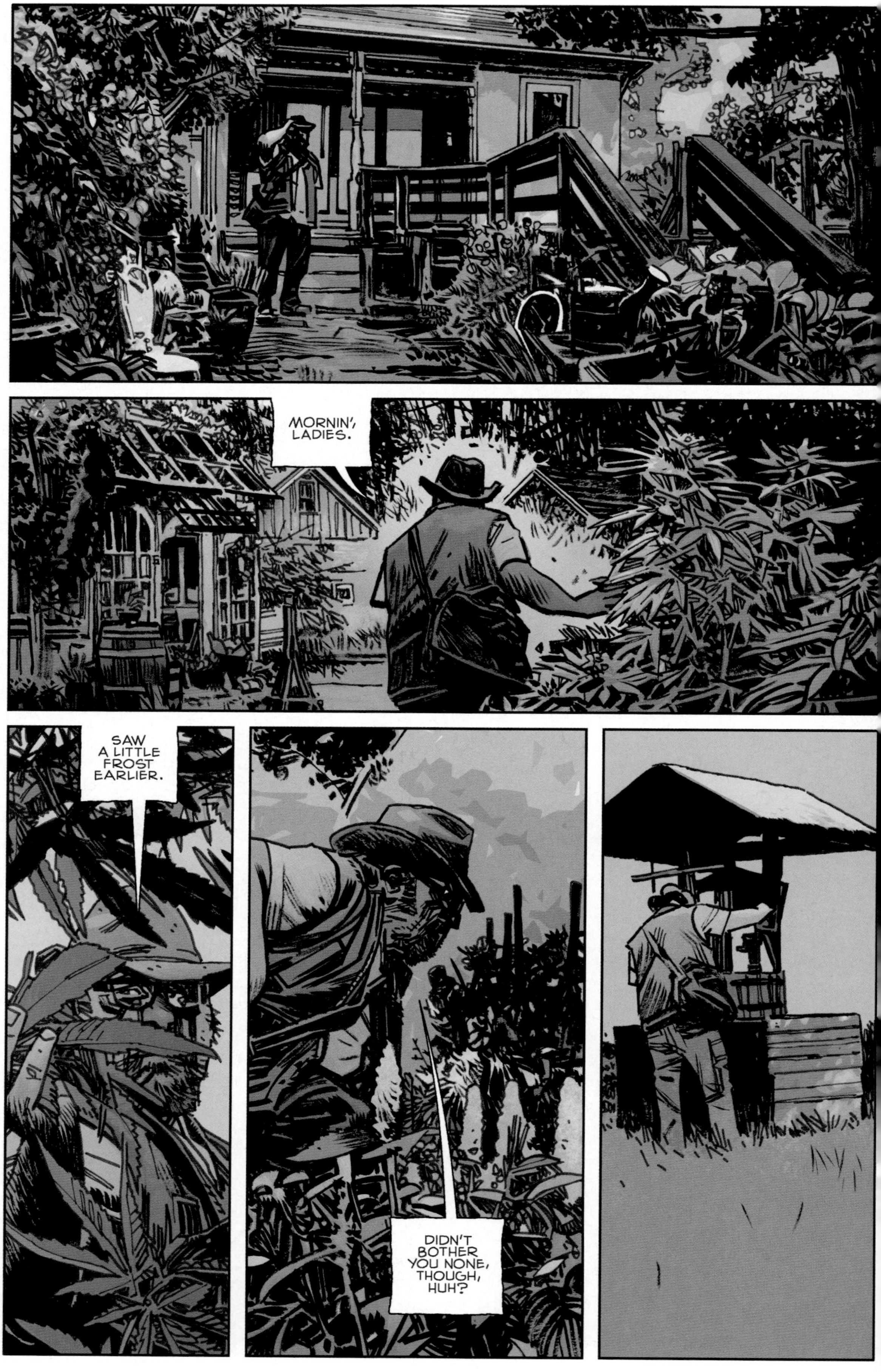
MORNIN', LADIES.
SAW A LITTLE FROST EARLIER.
DIDN'T BOTHER YOU NONE, THOUGH, HUH?

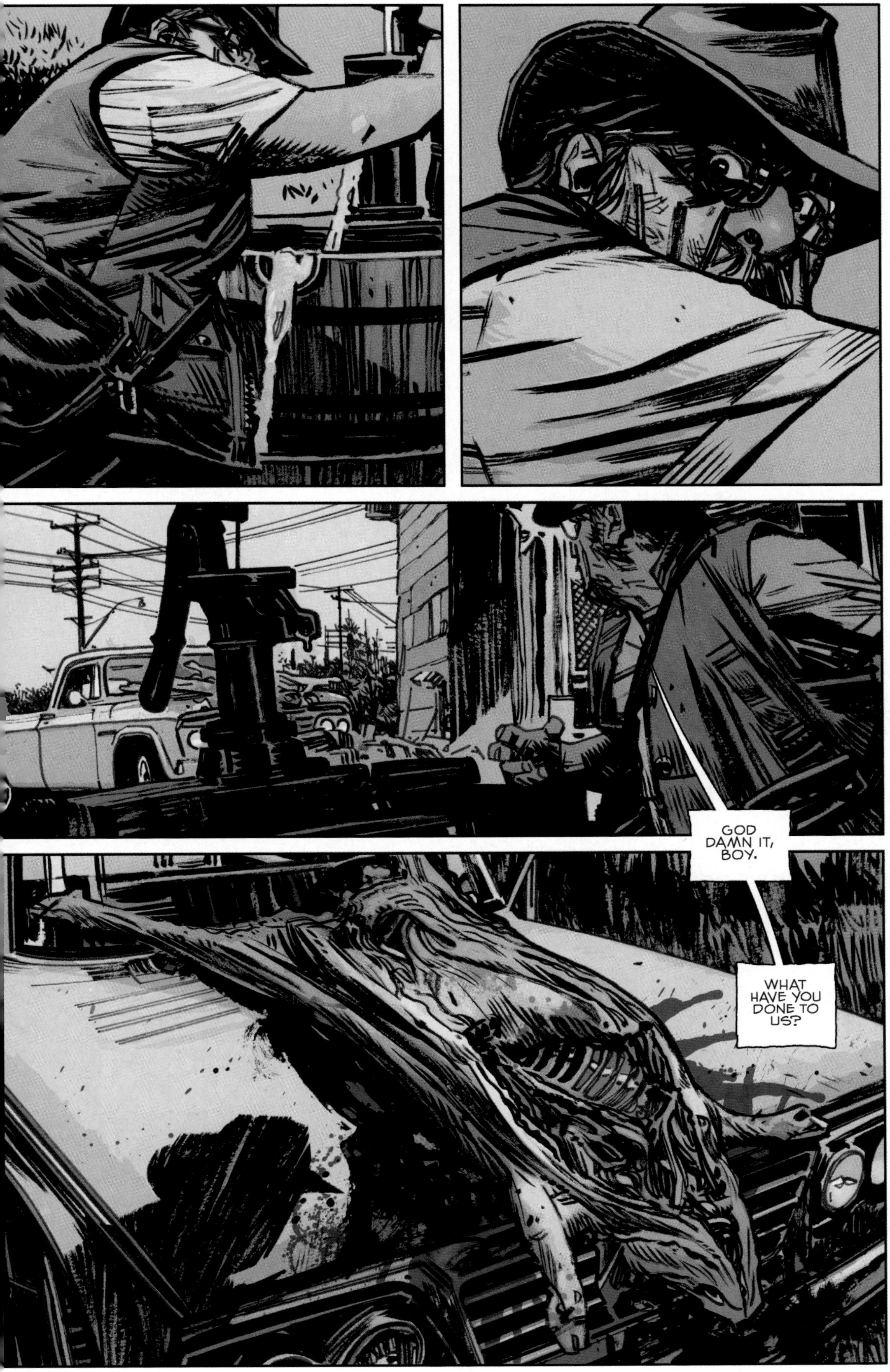
GOD DAMN IT, BOY.
WHAT HAVE YOU DONE TO US?

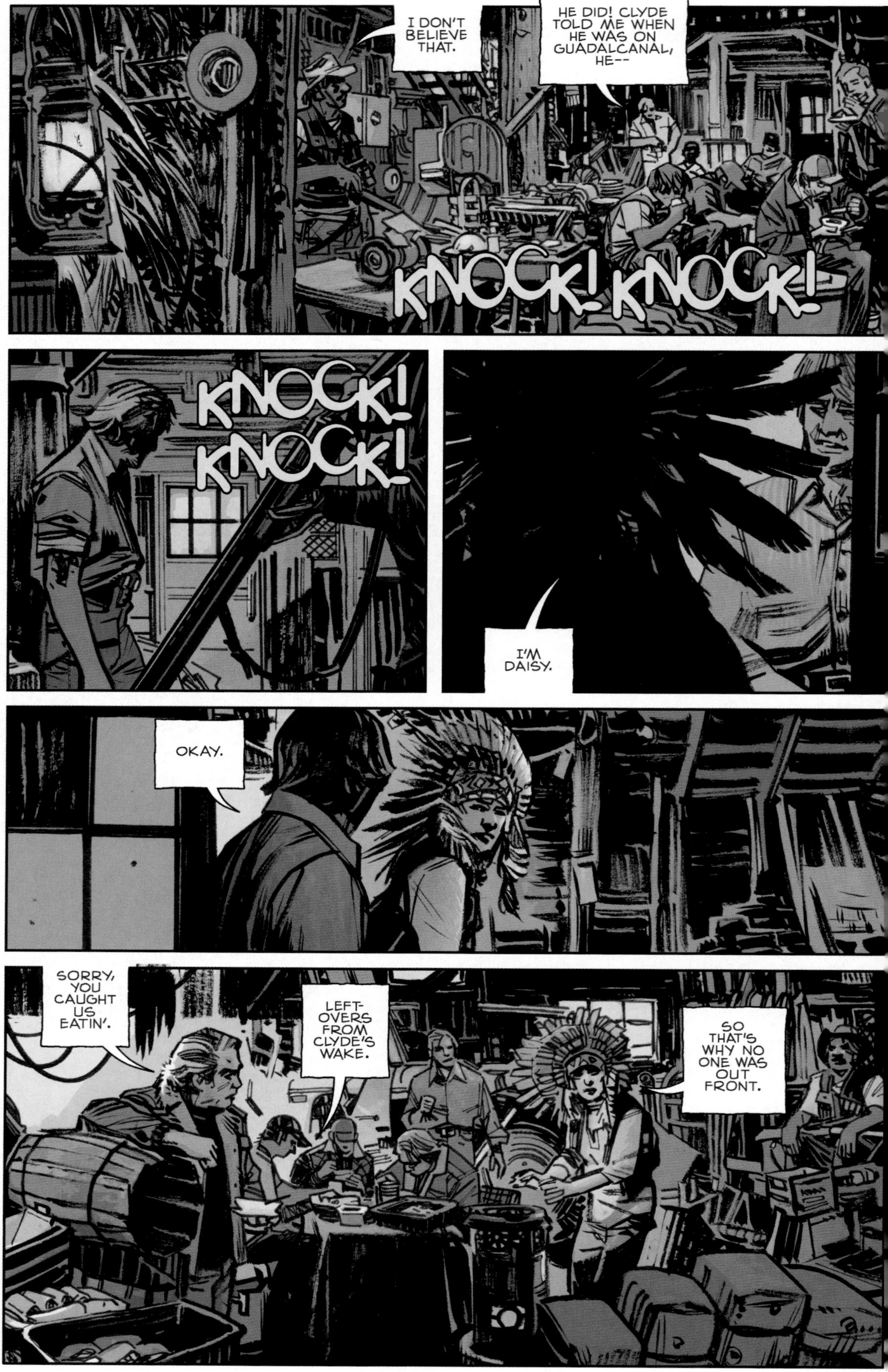
I DON'T BELIEVE THAT.
HE DID! CLYDE TOLD ME WHEN HE WAS ON GUADALCANAL, HE--
KNOCK! KNOCK!
KNOCK! KNOCK!
I'M DAISY.
OKAY.
SORRY, YOU CAUGHT US EATIN'.
LEFT-OVERS FROM CLYDE'S WAKE.
SO THAT'S WHY NO ONE WAS OUT FRONT.

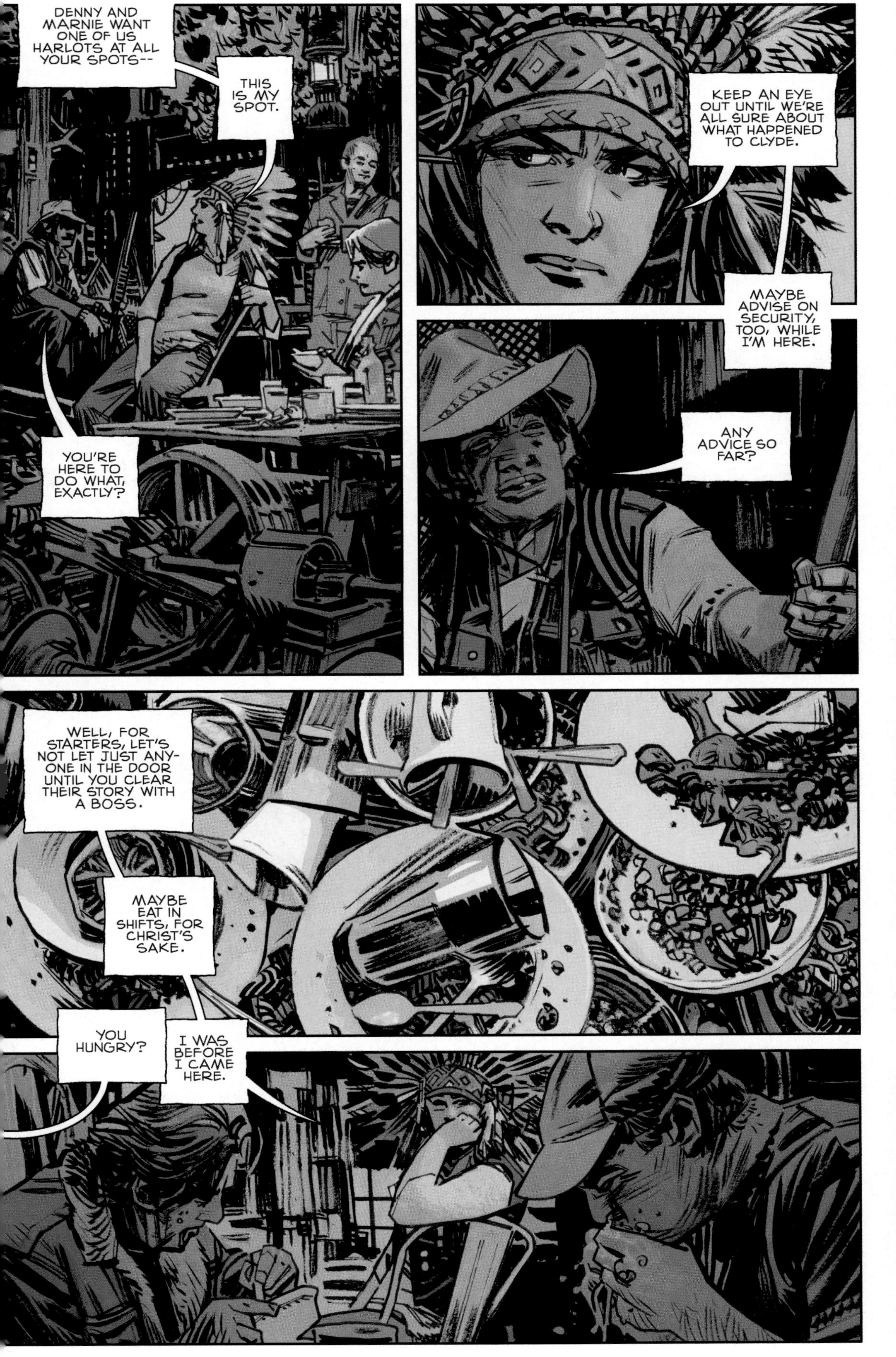
DENNY AND MARNIE WANT ONE OF US HARLOTS AT ALL YOUR SPOTS--
THIS IS MY SPOT.
YOU'RE HERE TO DO WHAT, EXACTLY?
KEEP AN EYE OUT UNTIL WE'RE ALL SURE ABOUT WHAT HAPPENED TO CLYDE.
MAYBE ADVISE ON SECURITY, TOO, WHILE I'M HERE.
ANY ADVICE SO FAR?
WELL, FOR STARTERS, LET'S NOT LET JUST ANY-ONE IN THE DOOR UNTIL YOU CLEAR THEIR STORY WITH A BOSS.
MAYBE EAT IN SHIFTS, FOR CHRIST'S SAKE.
YOU HUNGRY?
I WAS BEFORE I CAME HERE.

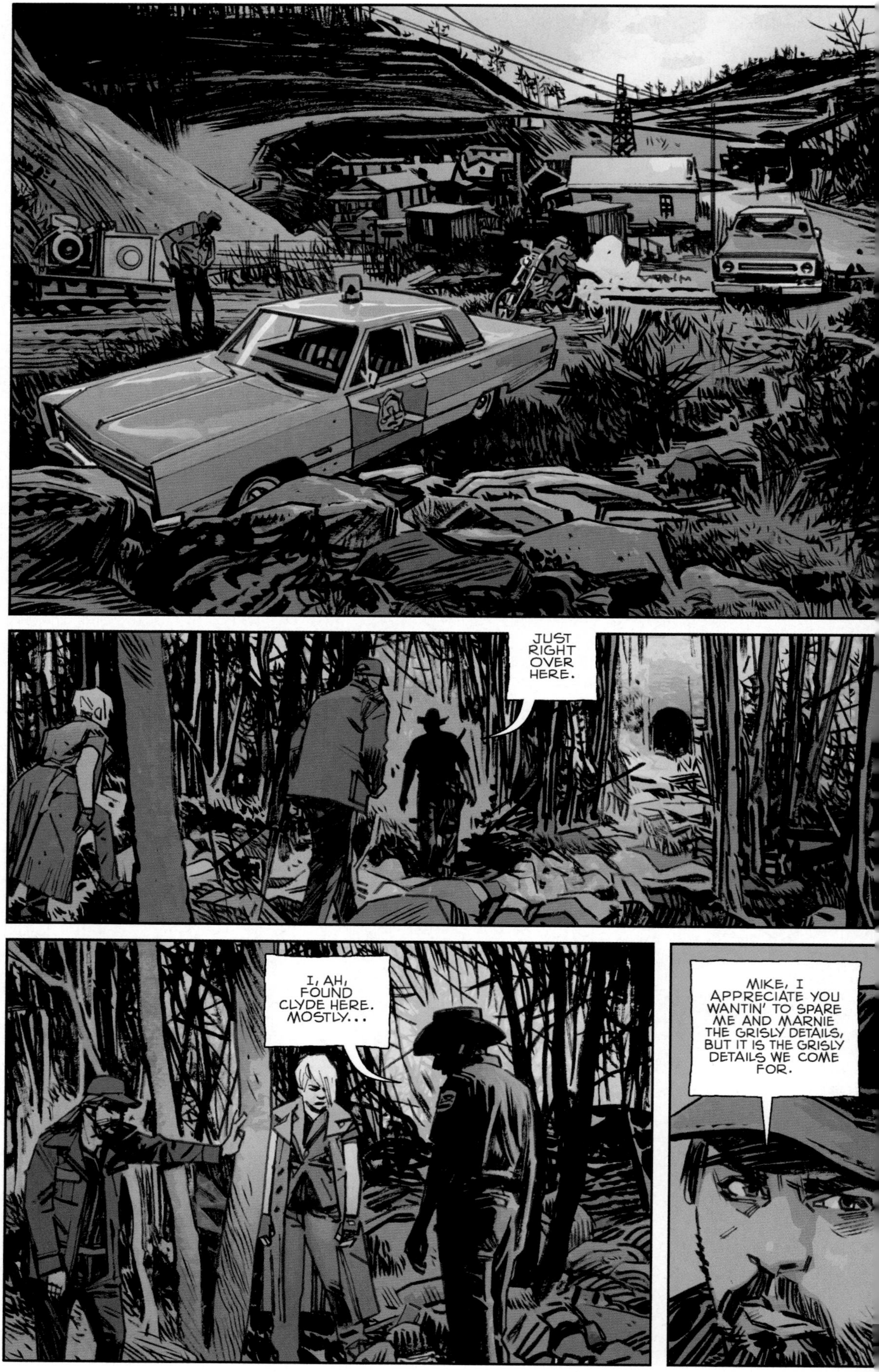
JUST RIGHT OVER HERE.
I, AH, FOUND CLYDE HERE. MOSTLY...
MIKE, I APPRECIATE YOU WANTIN' TO SPARE ME AND MARNIE THE GRISLY DETAILS, BUT IT IS THE GRISLY DETAILS WE COME FOR.

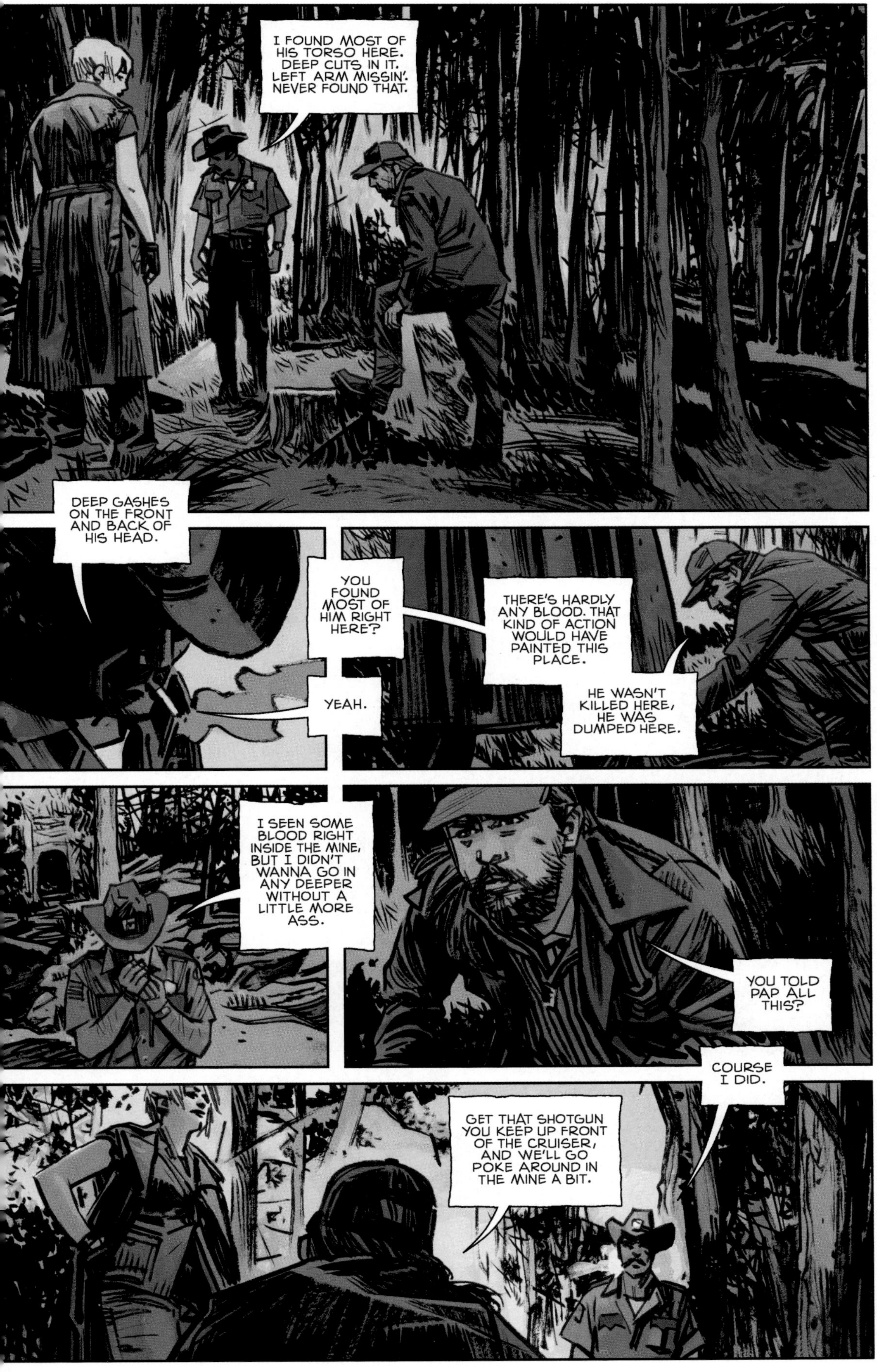
I FOUND MOST OF HIS TORSO HERE. DEEP CUTS IN IT. LEFT ARM MISSIN'. NEVER FOUND THAT.
DEEP GASHES ON THE FRONT AND BACK OF HIS HEAD.
YOU FOUND MOST OF HIM RIGHT HERE?
YEAH.
THERE'S HARDLY ANY BLOOD. THAT KIND OF ACTION WOULD HAVE PAINTED THIS PLACE.
HE WASN'T KILLED HERE, HE WAS DUMPED HERE.
I SEEN SOME BLOOD RIGHT INSIDE THE MINE, BUT I DIDN'T WANNA GO IN ANY DEEPER WITHOUT A LITTLE MORE ASS.
YOU TOLD PAP ALL THIS?
COURSE I DID.
GET THAT SHOTGUN YOU KEEP UP FRONT OF THE CRUISER, AND WE'LL GO POKE AROUND IN THE MINE A BIT.

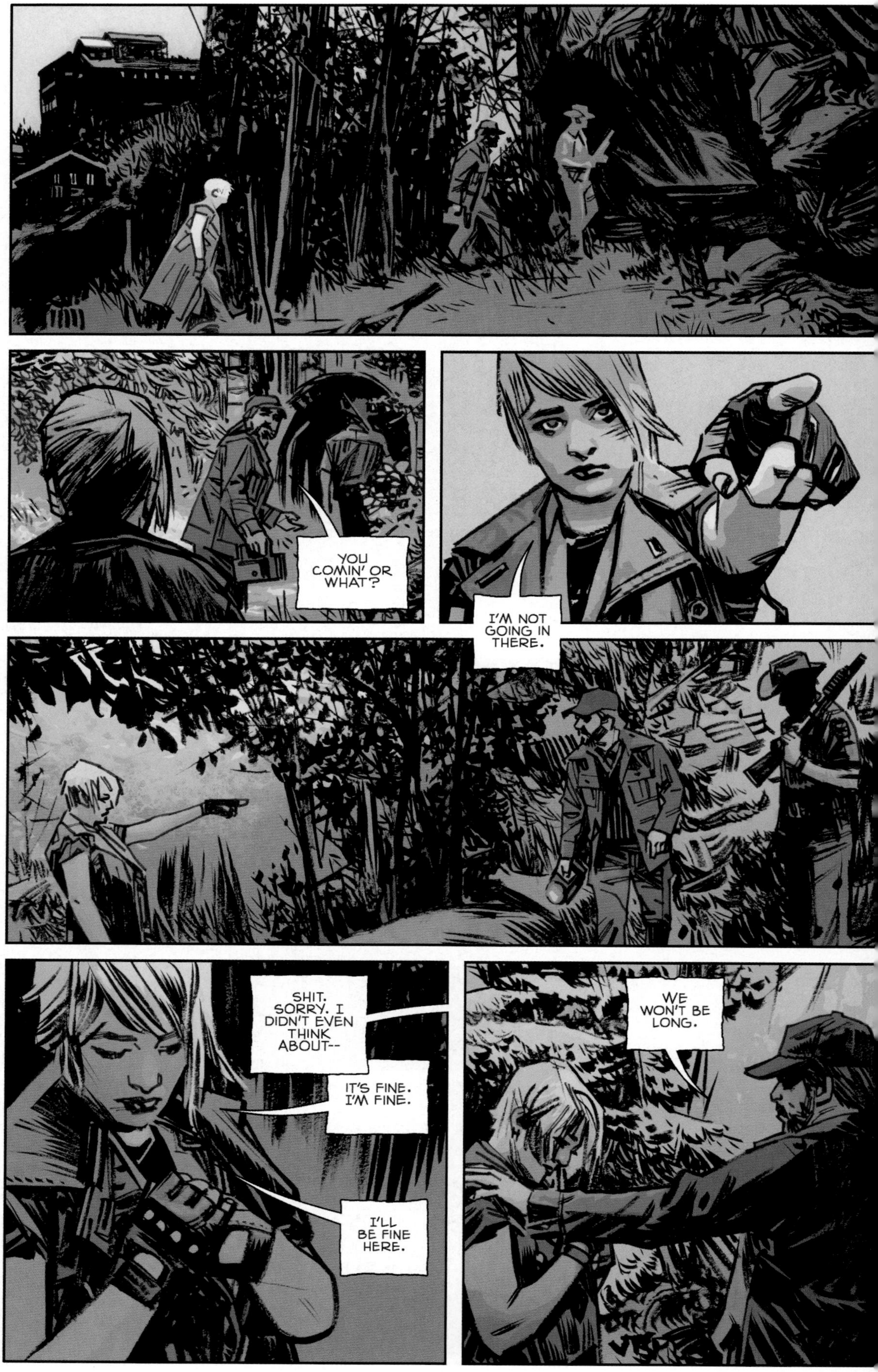
YOU COMIN' OR WHAT?
I'M NOT GOING IN THERE.
SHIT. SORRY. I DIDN'T EVEN THINK ABOUT--
IT'S FINE. I'M FINE.
I'LL BE FINE HERE.
WE WON'T BE LONG.

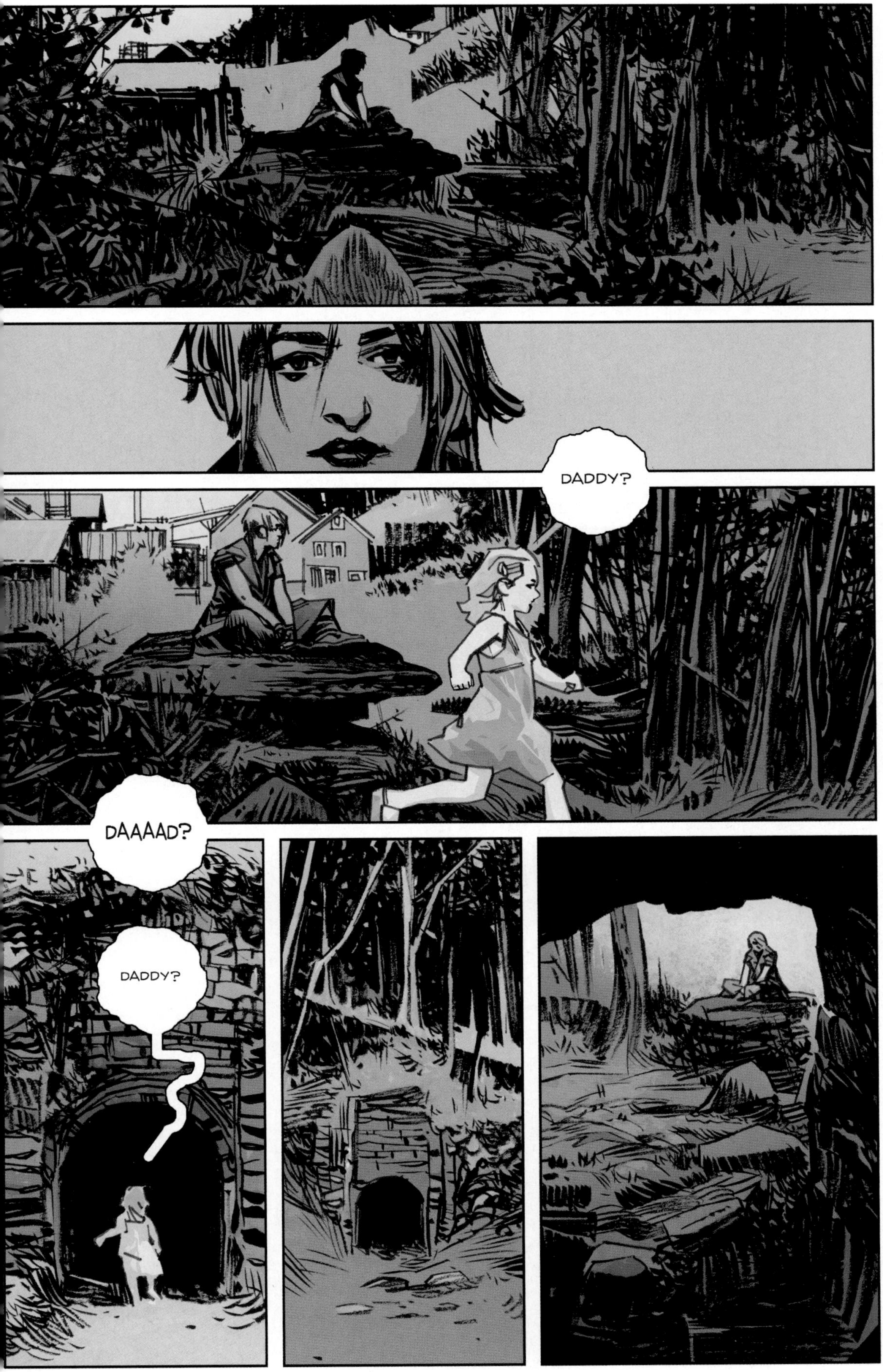
DADDY?
DAAAAD?
DADDY?

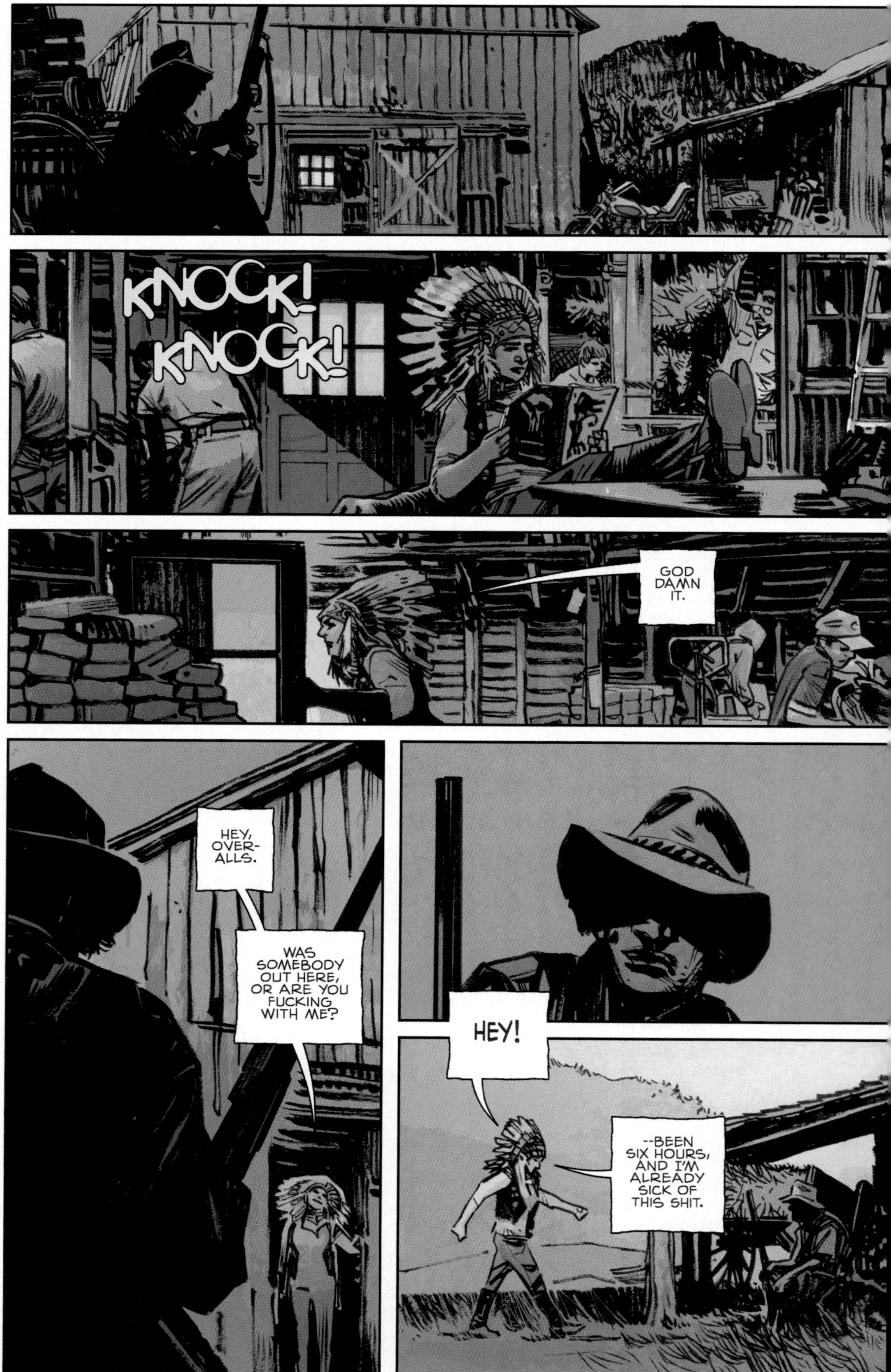
KNOCK! KNOCK!
GOD DAMN IT.
HEY, OVER-ALLS.
WAS SOMEBODY OUT HERE, OR ARE YOU FUCKING WITH ME?
HEY!
--BEEN SIX HOURS, AND I'M ALREADY SICK OF THIS SHIT.

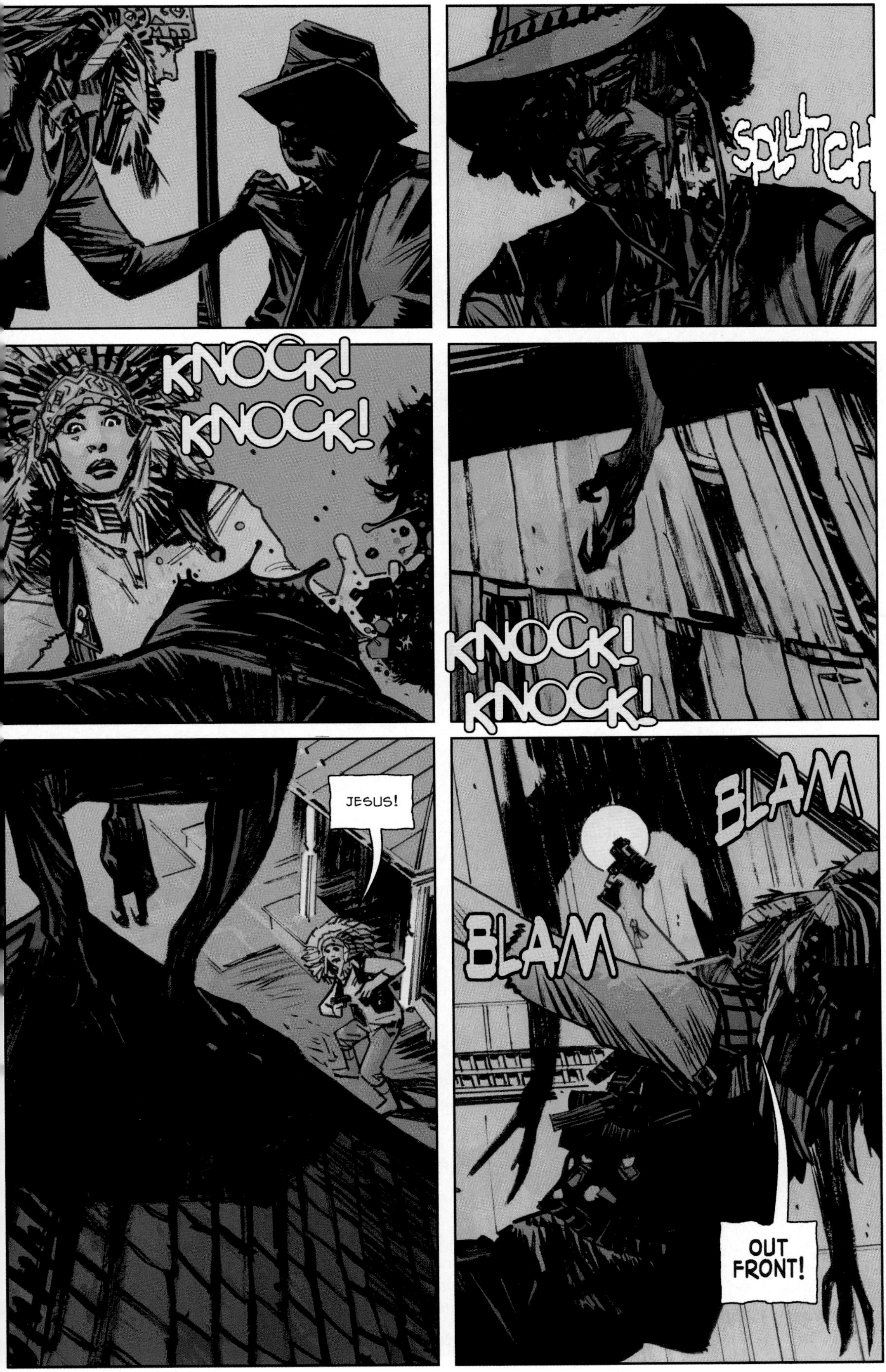
SPLUTCH
KNOCK! KNOCK!
KNOCK! KNOCK!
JESUS!
BLAM
BLAM
OUT FRONT!

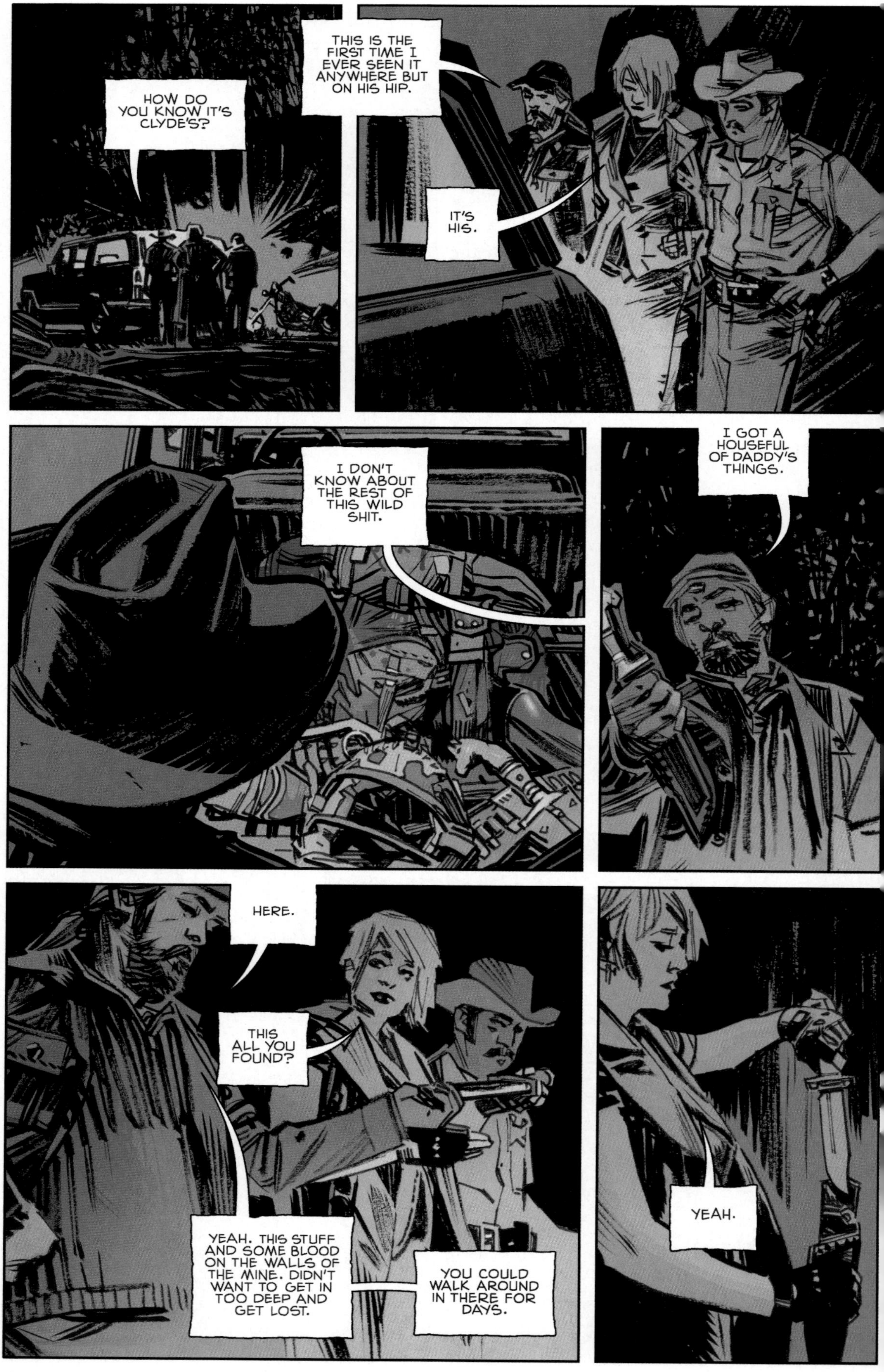
HOW DO YOU KNOW IT'S CLYDE'S?
THIS IS THE FIRST TIME I EVER SEEN IT ANYWHERE BUT ON HIS HIP.
IT'S HIS.
I DON'T KNOW ABOUT THE REST OF THIS WILD SHIT.
I GOT A HOUSEFUL OF DADDY'S THINGS.
HERE.
THIS ALL YOU FOUND?
YEAH. THIS STUFF AND SOME BLOOD ON THE WALLS OF THE MINE. DIDN'T WANT TO GET IN TOO DEEP AND GET LOST.
YOU COULD WALK AROUND IN THERE FOR DAYS.
YEAH.

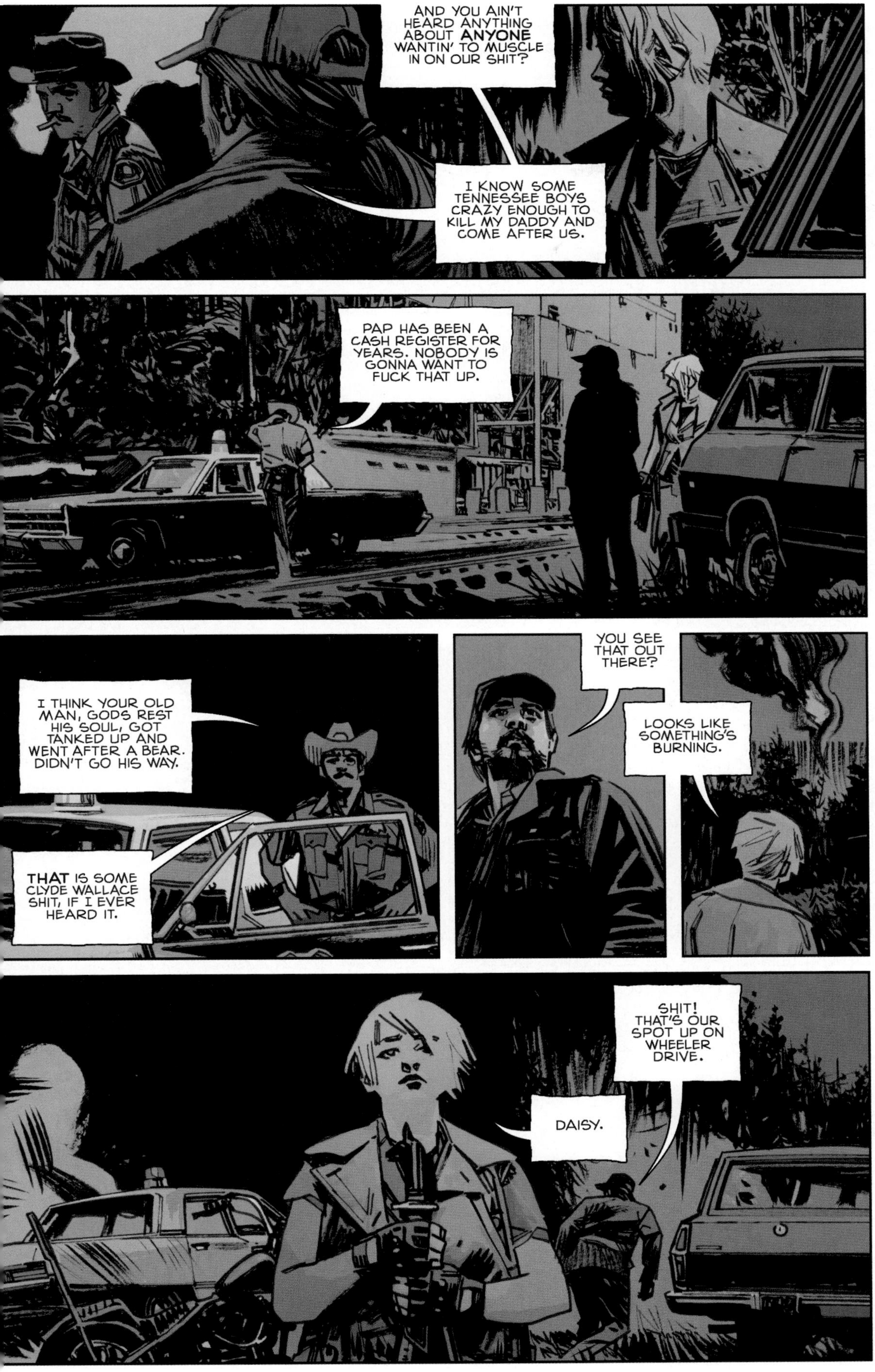
AND YOU AIN'T HEARD ANYTHING ABOUT ANYONE WANTIN' TO MUSCLE IN ON OUR SHIT?
I KNOW SOME TENNESSEE BOYS CRAZY ENOUGH TO KILL MY DADDY AND COME AFTER US.
PAP HAS BEEN A CASH REGISTER FOR YEARS. NOBODY IS GONNA WANT TO FUCK THAT UP.
I THINK YOUR OLD MAN, GODS REST HIS SOUL, GOT TANKED UP AND WENT AFTER A BEAR. DIDN'T GO HIS WAY.
THAT IS SOME CLYDE WALLACE SHIT, IF I EVER HEARD IT.
YOU SEE THAT OUT THERE?
LOOKS LIKE SOMETHING'S BURNING.
SHIT! THAT'S OUR SPOT UP ON WHEELER DRIVE.
DAISY.

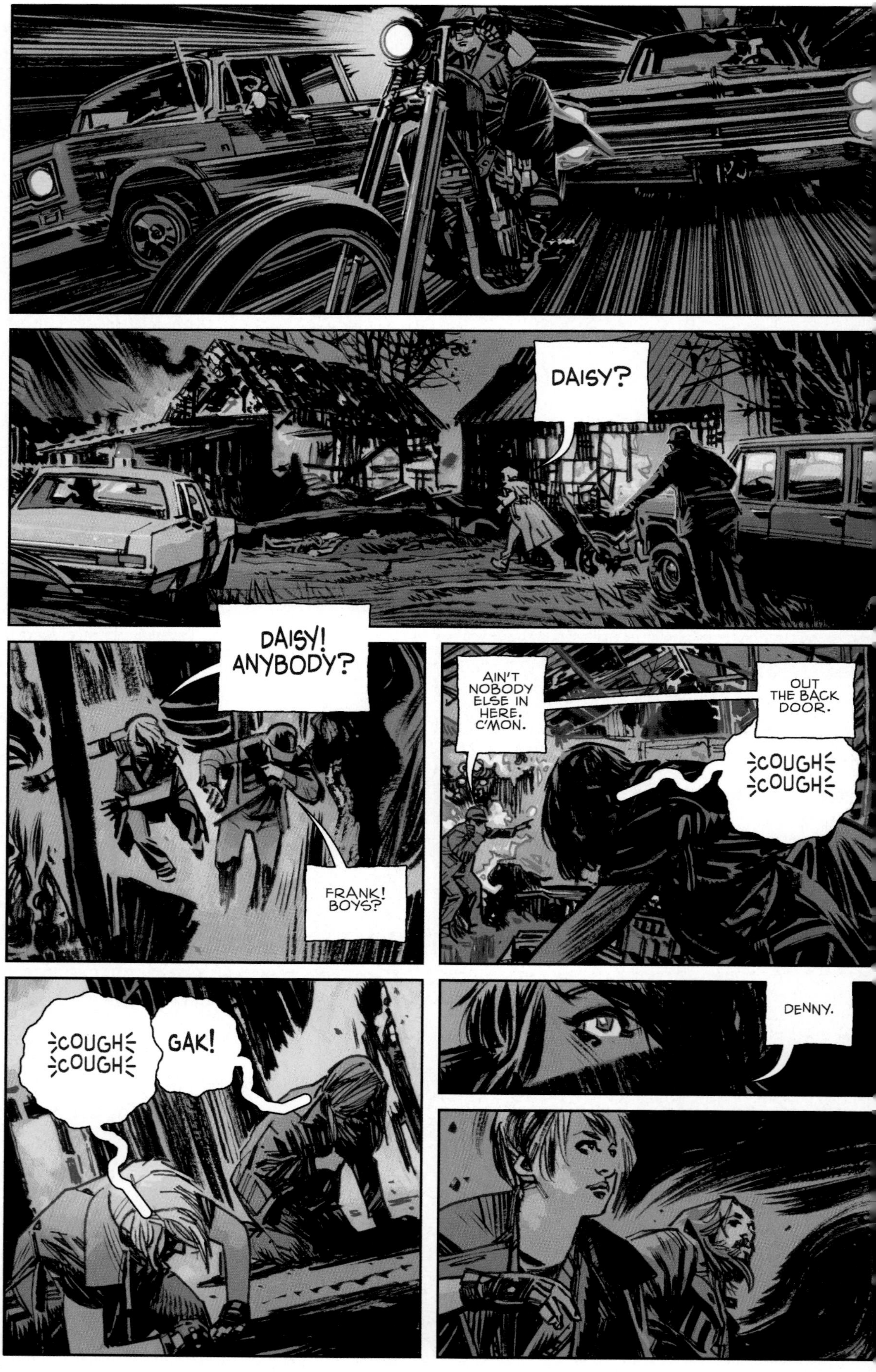
DAISY?
DAISY! ANYBODY?
FRANK! BOYS?
AIN'T NOBODY ELSE IN HERE. C'MON.
OUT THE BACK DOOR.
COUGH COUGH
COUGH COUGH
GAK!
DENNY.

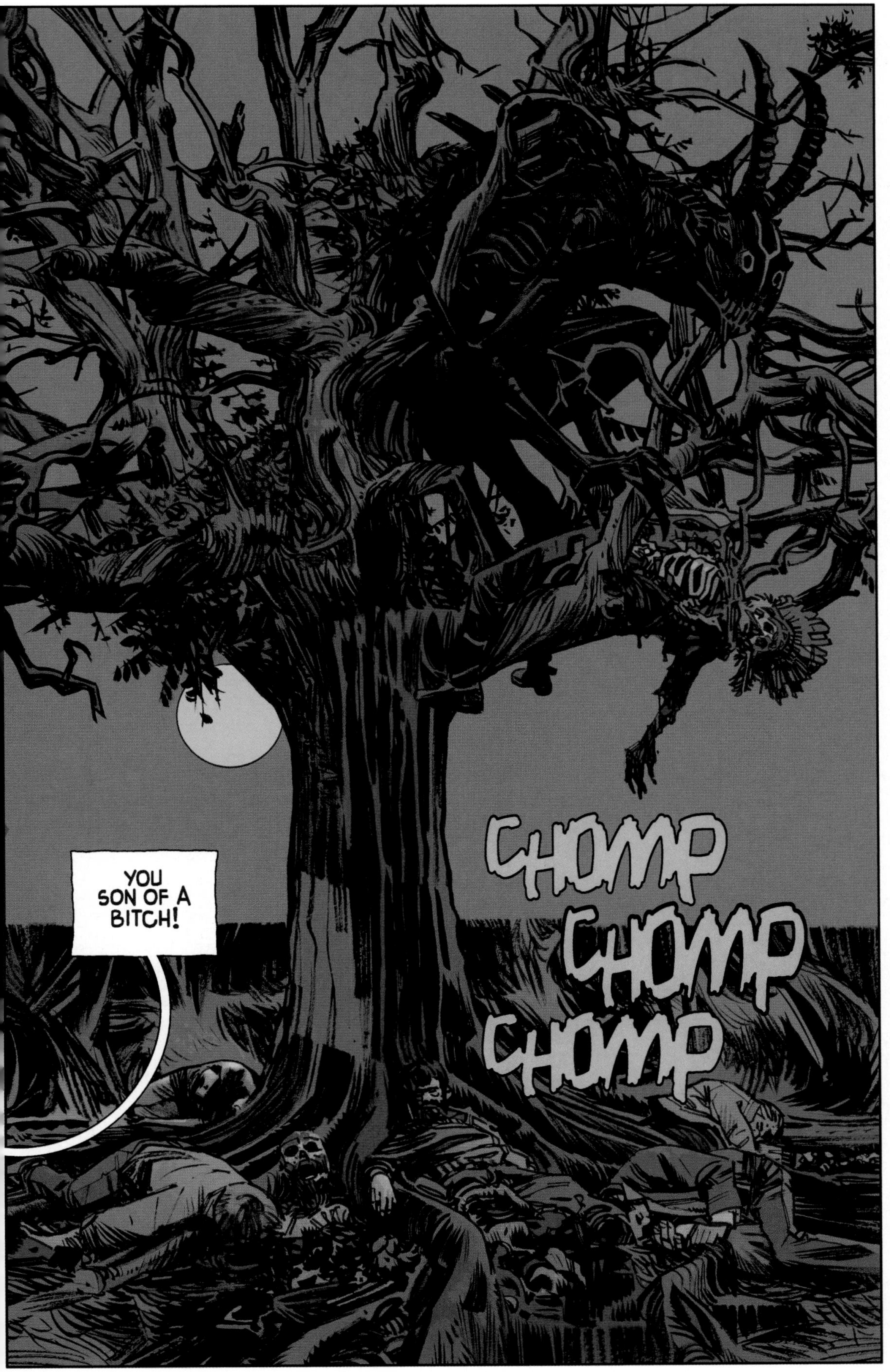
YOU SON OF A BITCH!
CHOMP
CHOMP
CHOMP

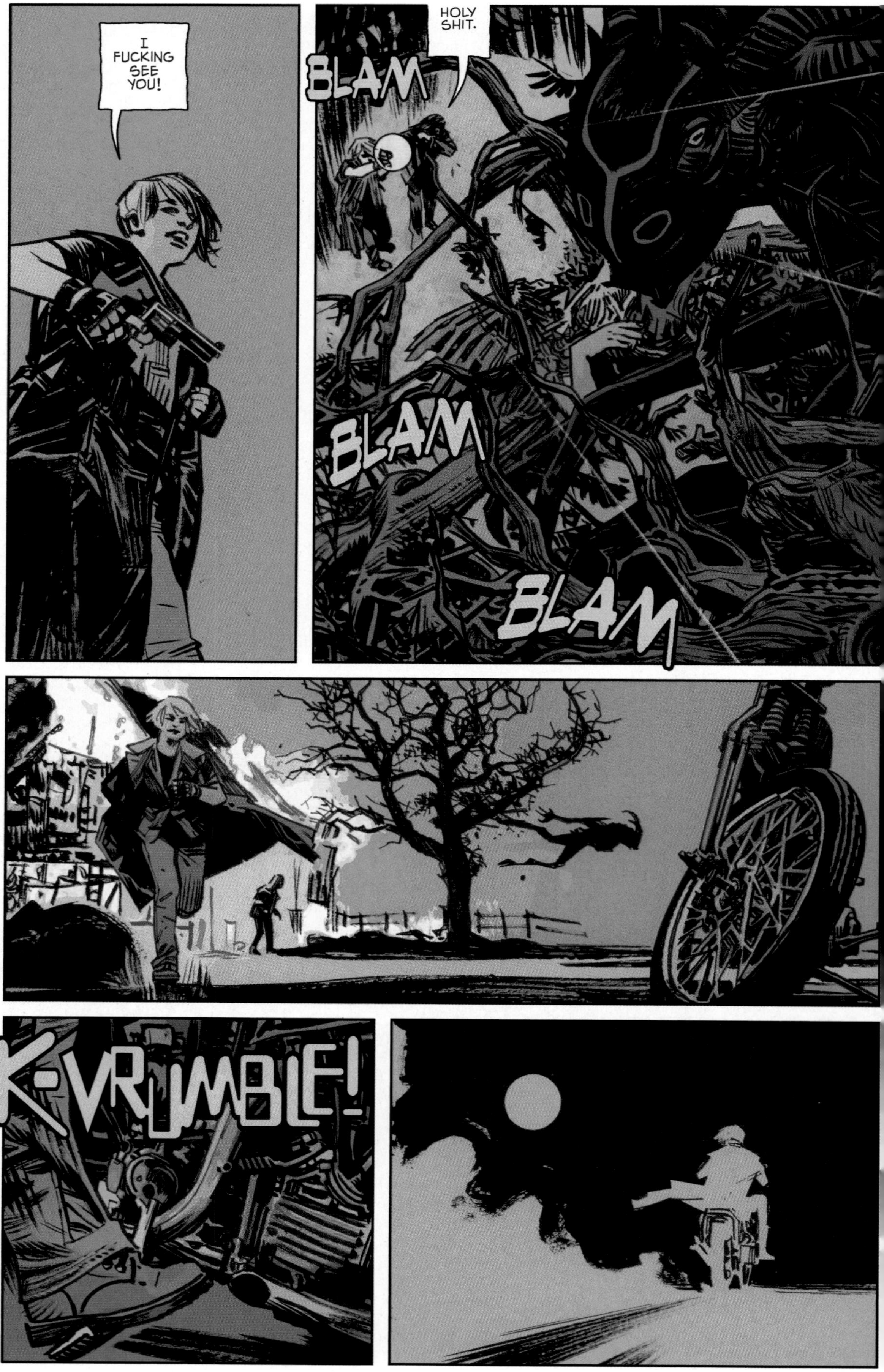
I FUCKING SEE YOU!
HOLY SHIT.
BLAM
BLAM
BLAM
K-VRUMBLE!

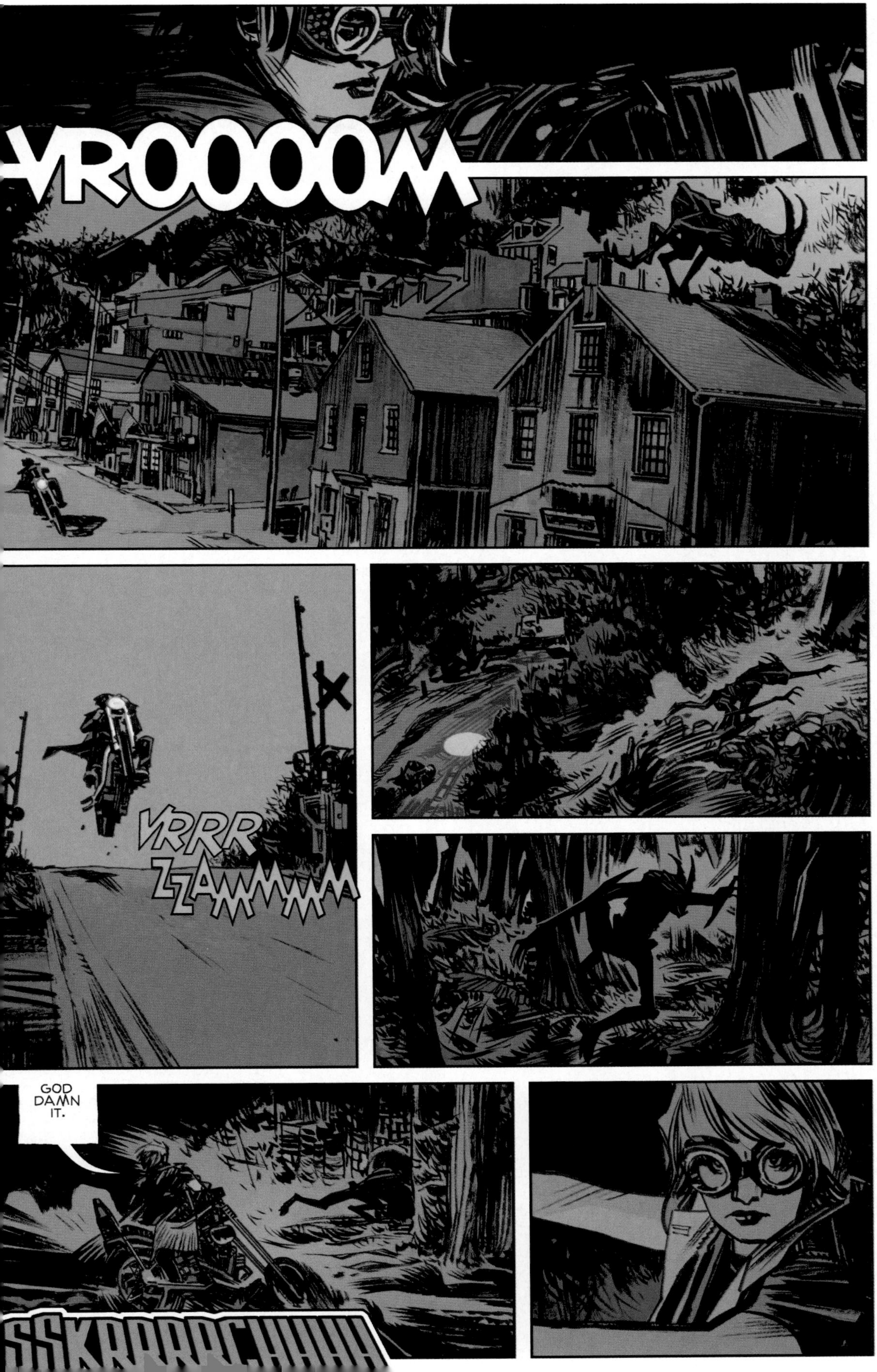
VROOOOM
VRRR ZZAMMMMM
GOD DAMN IT.
SSKRRRRCHHHH

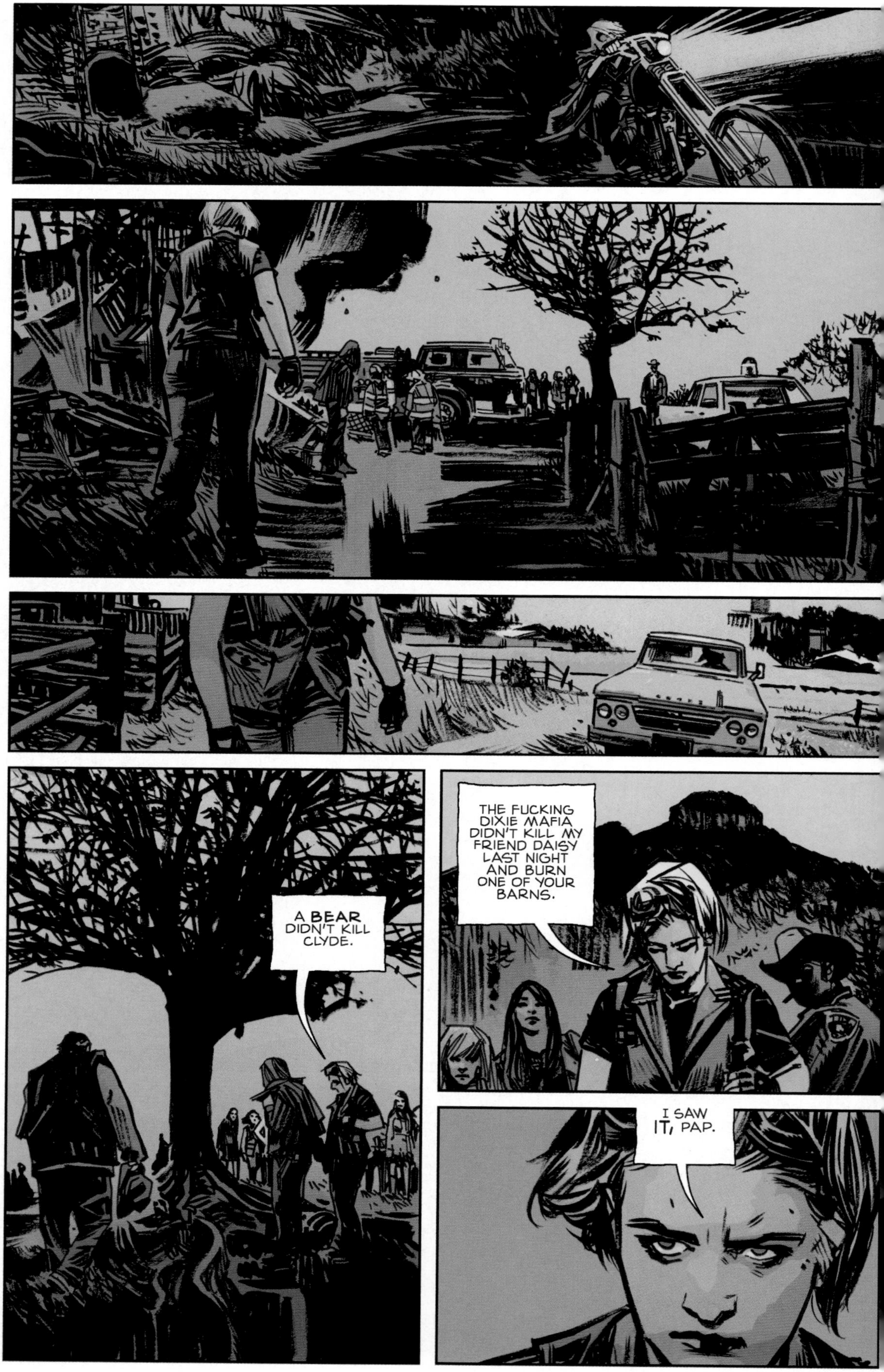
A BEAR DIDN'T KILL CLYDE.
THE FUCKING DIXIE MAFIA DIDN'T KILL MY FRIEND DAISY LAST NIGHT AND BURN ONE OF YOUR BARNS.
I SAW IT, PAP.

MARNIE, WHEN YOU FIRST COME TO LIVE WITH US, YOU WOULDN'T SLEEP AT NIGHT FOR MONTHS, ALMOST A YEAR. WORRIED CLYDE SICK.

"MONSTERS UNDER THE BED."

"MONSTERS IN THE CLOSET."

"MONSTERS COMIN' TO EAT YOU."

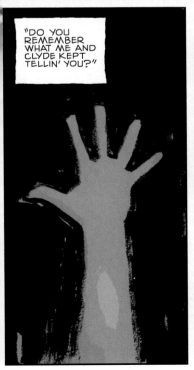
"DO YOU REMEMBER WHAT ME AND CLYDE KEPT TELLIN' YOU?"

"MONSTERS AIN'T REAL."

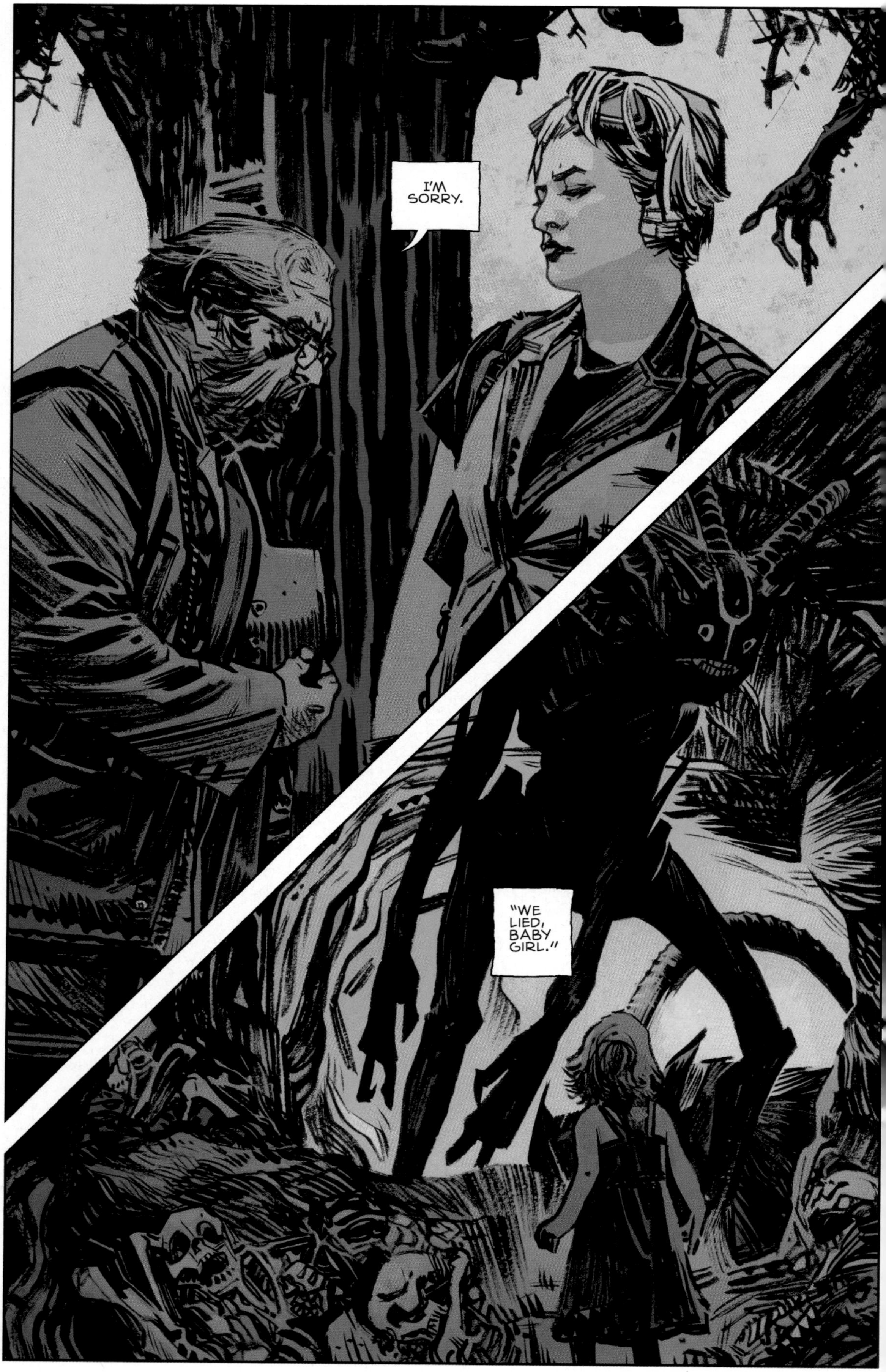
I'M SORRY.
"WE LIED, BABY GIRL."

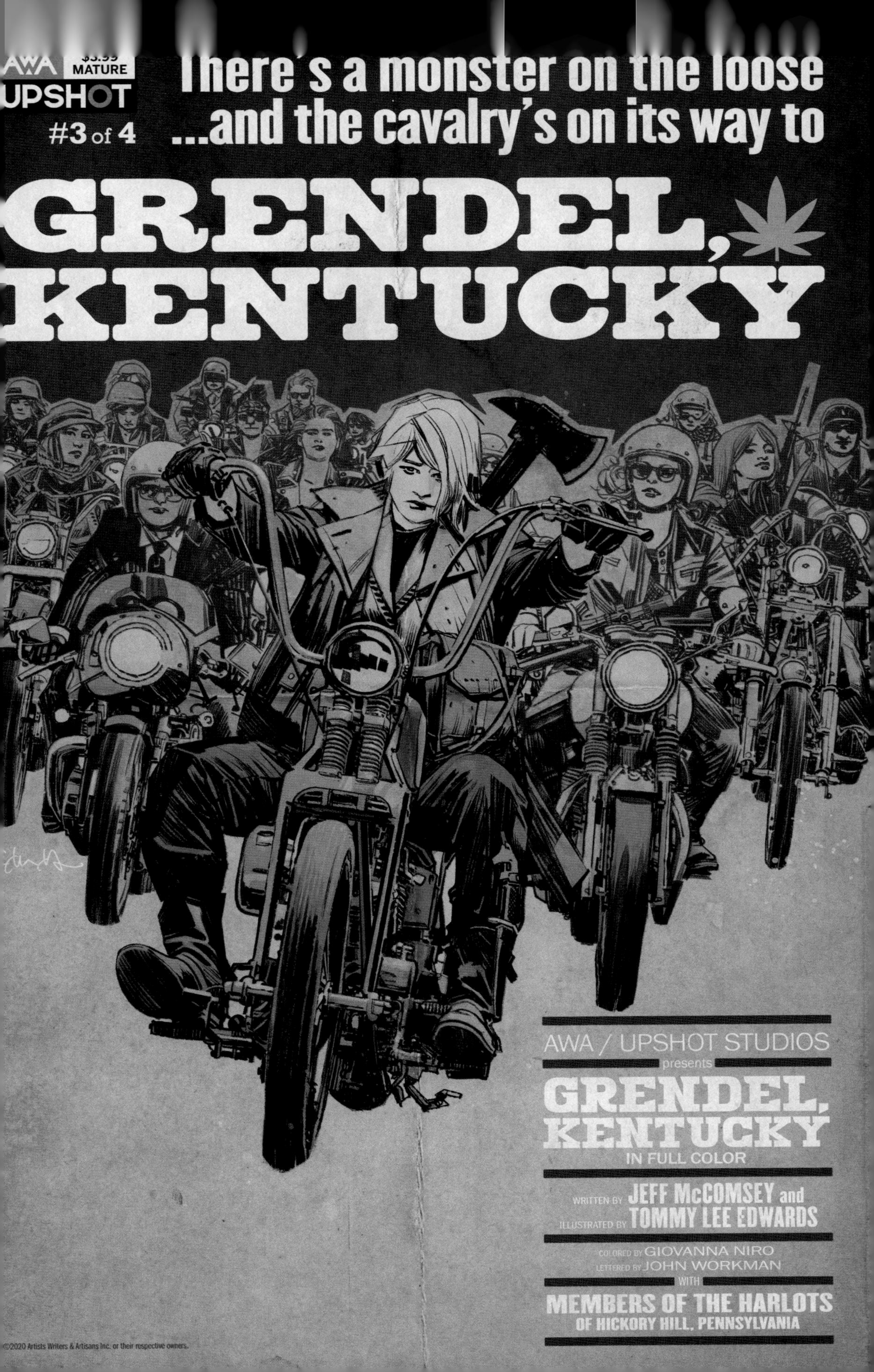
AWA
$3.99
MATURE
UPSHOT
#3 of 4
There's a monster on the loose
...and the cavalry's on its way to
GRENDEL, KENTUCKY
AWA / UPSHOT STUDIOS
presents
GRENDEL, KENTUCKY
IN FULL COLOR
WRITTEN BY JEFF McCOMSEY and TOMMY LEE EDWARDS
ILLUSTRATED BY TOMMY LEE EDWARDS
COLORED BY GIOVANNA NIRO
LETTERED BY JOHN WORKMAN
WITH
MEMBERS OF THE HARLOTS
OF HICKORY HILL, PENNSYLVANIA
©2020 Artists Writers & Artisans Inc. or their respective owners.

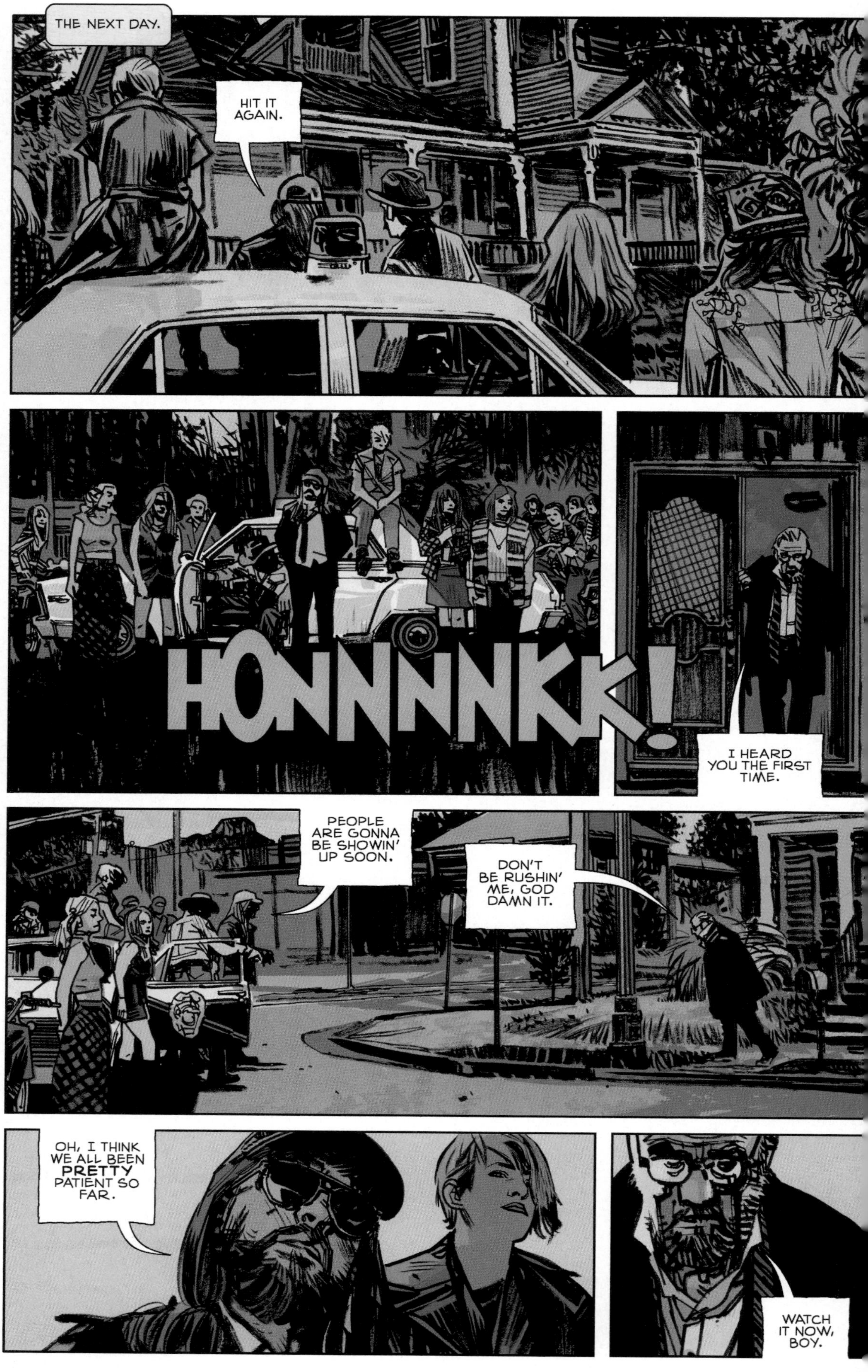
THE NEXT DAY.
HIT IT AGAIN.
HONNNNKK!
I HEARD YOU THE FIRST TIME.
PEOPLE ARE GONNA BE SHOWIN' UP SOON.
DON'T BE RUSHIN' ME, GOD DAMN IT.
OH, I THINK WE ALL BEEN **PRETTY** PATIENT SO FAR.
WATCH IT NOW, BOY.

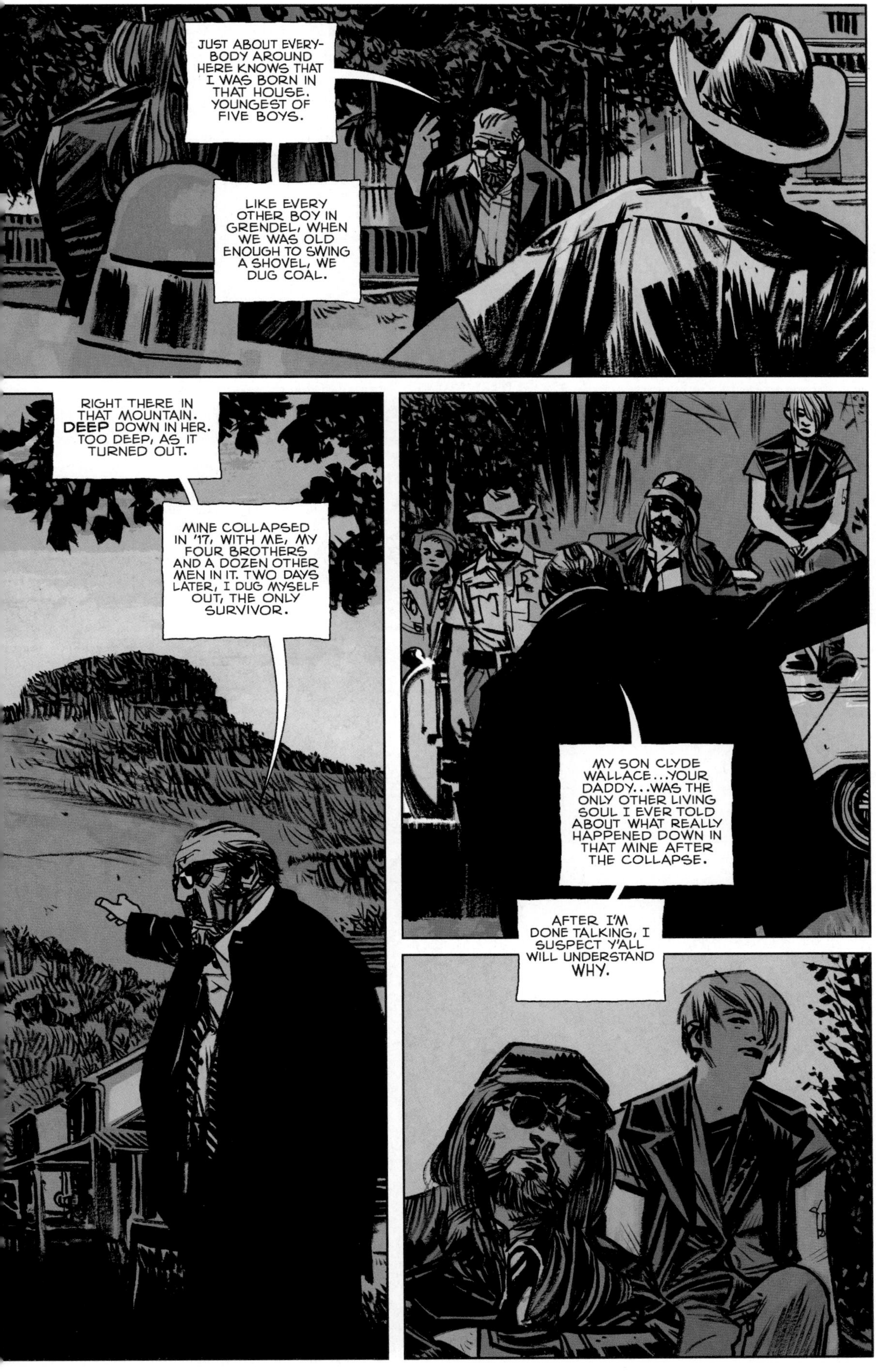
JUST ABOUT EVERY-BODY AROUND HERE KNOWS THAT I WAS BORN IN THAT HOUSE. YOUNGEST OF FIVE BOYS.
LIKE EVERY OTHER BOY IN GRENDEL, WHEN WE WAS OLD ENOUGH TO SWING A SHOVEL, WE DUG COAL.
RIGHT THERE IN THAT MOUNTAIN. DEEP DOWN IN HER. TOO DEEP, AS IT TURNED OUT.
MINE COLLAPSED IN '17, WITH ME, MY FOUR BROTHERS AND A DOZEN OTHER MEN IN IT. TWO DAYS LATER, I DUG MYSELF OUT, THE ONLY SURVIVOR.
MY SON CLYDE WALLACE...YOUR DADDY...WAS THE ONLY OTHER LIVING SOUL I EVER TOLD ABOUT WHAT REALLY HAPPENED DOWN IN THAT MINE AFTER THE COLLAPSE.
AFTER I'M DONE TALKING, I SUSPECT Y'ALL WILL UNDERSTAND WHY.

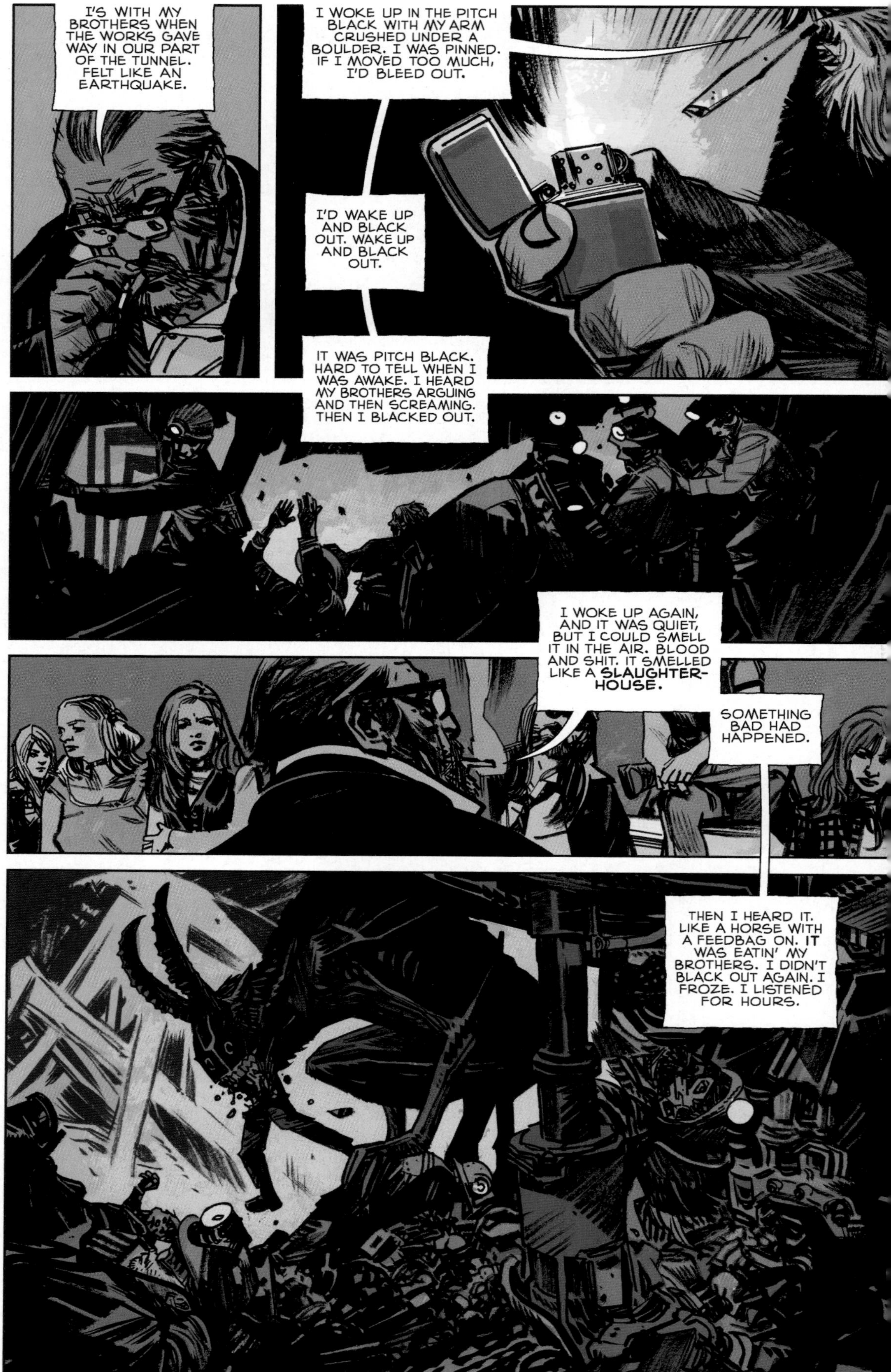
I'S WITH MY BROTHERS WHEN THE WORKS GAVE WAY IN OUR PART OF THE TUNNEL. FELT LIKE AN EARTHQUAKE.
I WOKE UP IN THE PITCH BLACK WITH MY ARM CRUSHED UNDER A BOULDER. I WAS PINNED. IF I MOVED TOO MUCH, I'D BLEED OUT.
I'D WAKE UP AND BLACK OUT. WAKE UP AND BLACK OUT.
IT WAS PITCH BLACK. HARD TO TELL WHEN I WAS AWAKE. I HEARD MY BROTHERS ARGUING AND THEN SCREAMING. THEN I BLACKED OUT.
I WOKE UP AGAIN, AND IT WAS QUIET, BUT I COULD SMELL IT IN THE AIR. BLOOD AND SHIT. IT SMELLED LIKE A **SLAUGHTER-HOUSE.**
SOMETHING BAD HAD HAPPENED.
THEN I HEARD IT. LIKE A HORSE WITH A FEEDBAG ON. **IT** WAS EATIN' MY BROTHERS. I DIDN'T BLACK OUT AGAIN. I FROZE. I LISTENED FOR HOURS.

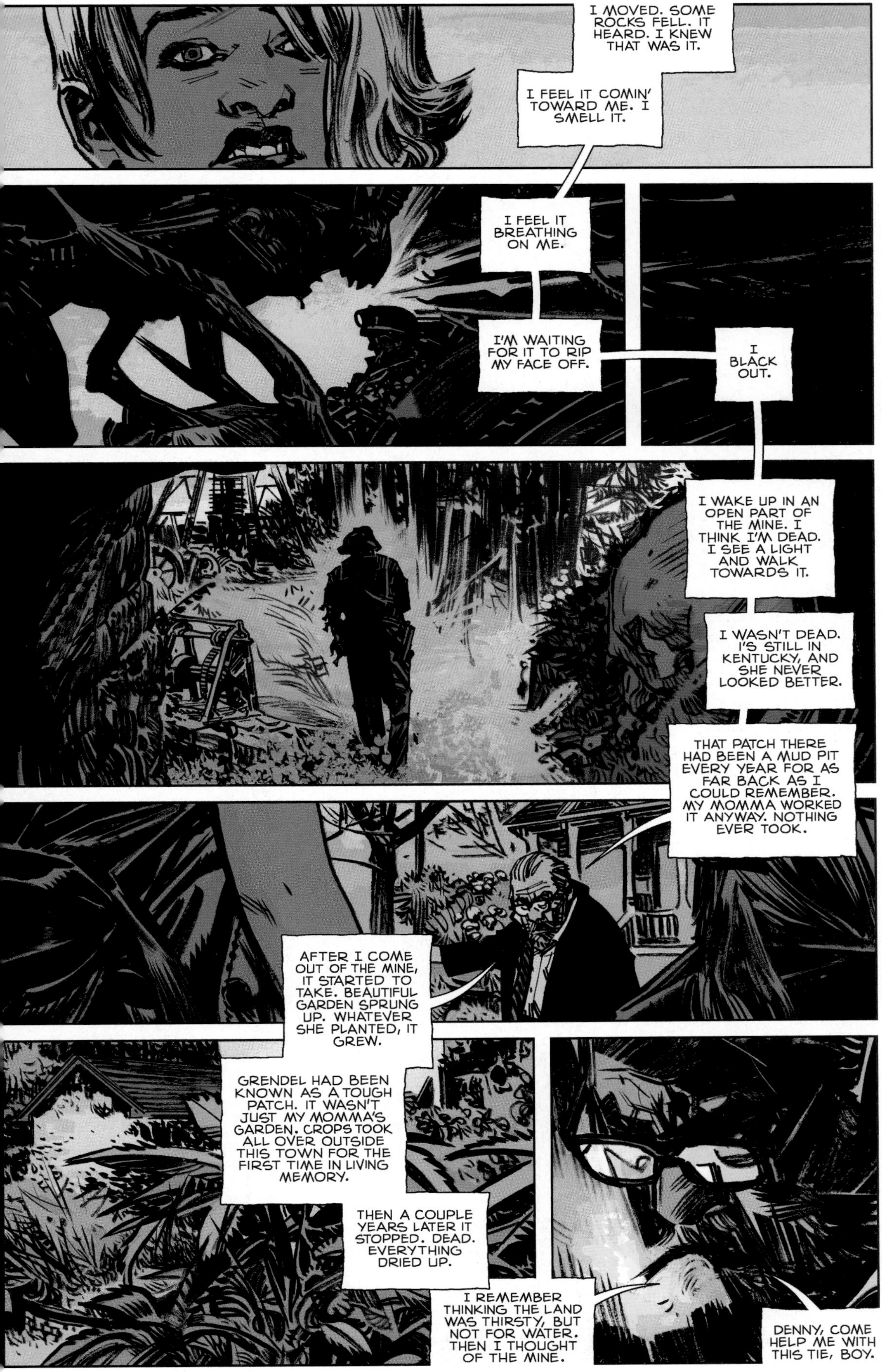
I MOVED. SOME ROCKS FELL. IT HEARD. I KNEW THAT WAS IT.
I FEEL IT COMIN' TOWARD ME. I SMELL IT.
I FEEL IT BREATHING ON ME.
I'M WAITING FOR IT TO RIP MY FACE OFF.
I BLACK OUT.
I WAKE UP IN AN OPEN PART OF THE MINE. I THINK I'M DEAD. I SEE A LIGHT AND WALK TOWARDS IT.
I WASN'T DEAD. I'S STILL IN KENTUCKY, AND SHE NEVER LOOKED BETTER.
THAT PATCH THERE HAD BEEN A MUD PIT EVERY YEAR FOR AS FAR BACK AS I COULD REMEMBER. MY MOMMA WORKED IT ANYWAY. NOTHING EVER TOOK.
AFTER I COME OUT OF THE MINE, IT STARTED TO TAKE. BEAUTIFUL GARDEN SPRUNG UP. WHATEVER SHE PLANTED, IT GREW.
GRENDEL HAD BEEN KNOWN AS A TOUGH PATCH. IT WASN'T JUST MY MOMMA'S GARDEN. CROPS TOOK ALL OVER OUTSIDE THIS TOWN FOR THE FIRST TIME IN LIVING MEMORY.
THEN A COUPLE YEARS LATER IT STOPPED. DEAD. EVERYTHING DRIED UP.
I REMEMBER THINKING THE LAND WAS THIRSTY, BUT NOT FOR WATER. THEN I THOUGHT OF THE MINE.
DENNY, COME HELP ME WITH THIS TIE, BOY.

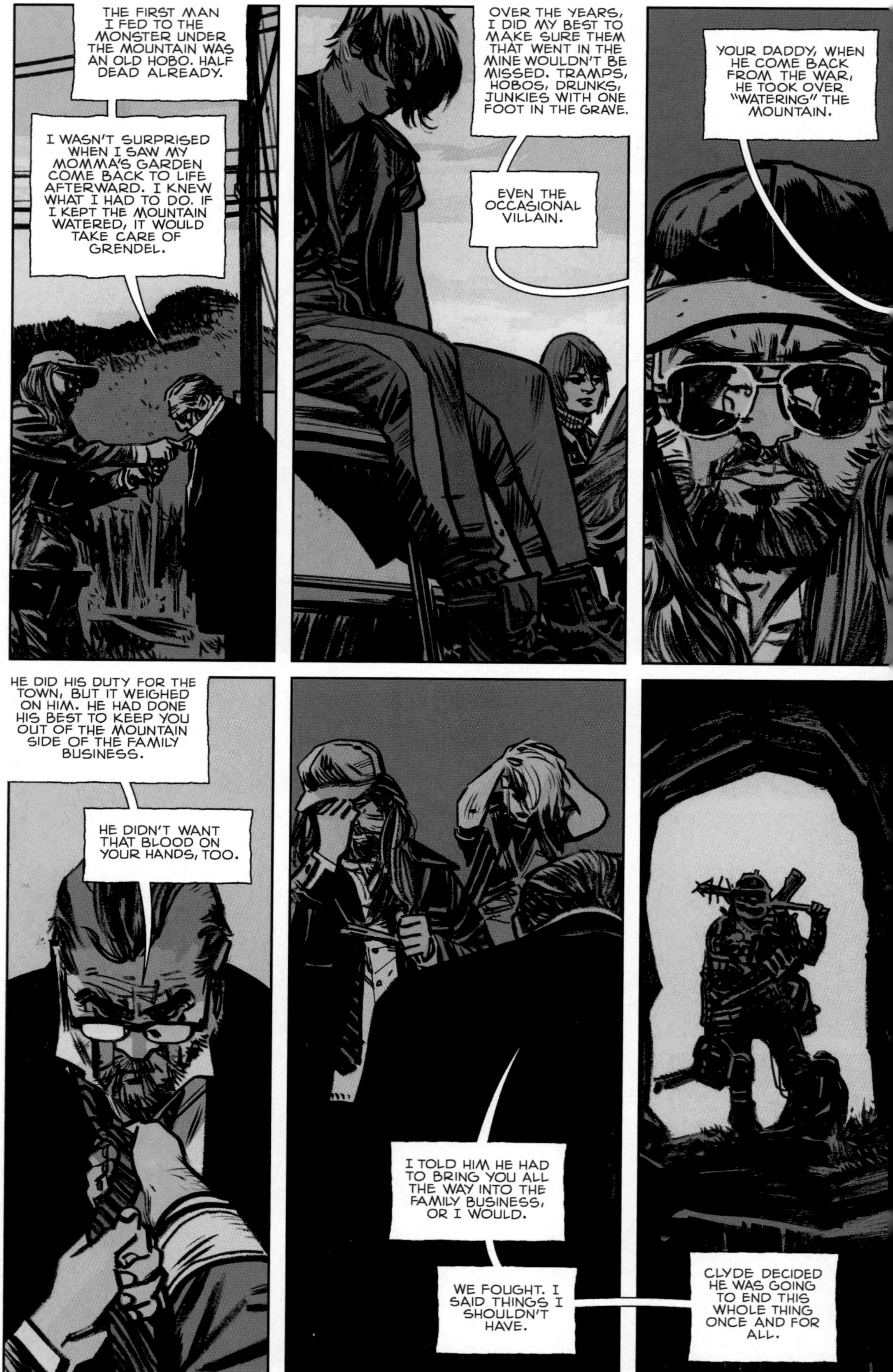
THE FIRST MAN I FED TO THE MONSTER UNDER THE MOUNTAIN WAS AN OLD HOBO. HALF DEAD ALREADY.
I WASN'T SURPRISED WHEN I SAW MY MOMMA'S GARDEN COME BACK TO LIFE AFTERWARD. I KNEW WHAT I HAD TO DO. IF I KEPT THE MOUNTAIN WATERED, IT WOULD TAKE CARE OF GRENDEL.
OVER THE YEARS, I DID MY BEST TO MAKE SURE THEM THAT WENT IN THE MINE WOULDN'T BE MISSED. TRAMPS, HOBOS, DRUNKS, JUNKIES WITH ONE FOOT IN THE GRAVE.
EVEN THE OCCASIONAL VILLAIN.
YOUR DADDY, WHEN HE COME BACK FROM THE WAR, HE TOOK OVER "WATERING" THE MOUNTAIN.
HE DID HIS DUTY FOR THE TOWN, BUT IT WEIGHED ON HIM. HE HAD DONE HIS BEST TO KEEP YOU OUT OF THE MOUNTAIN SIDE OF THE FAMILY BUSINESS.
HE DIDN'T WANT THAT BLOOD ON YOUR HANDS, TOO.
I TOLD HIM HE HAD TO BRING YOU ALL THE WAY INTO THE FAMILY BUSINESS, OR I WOULD.
WE FOUGHT. I SAID THINGS I SHOULDN'T HAVE.
CLYDE DECIDED HE WAS GOING TO END THIS WHOLE THING ONCE AND FOR ALL.

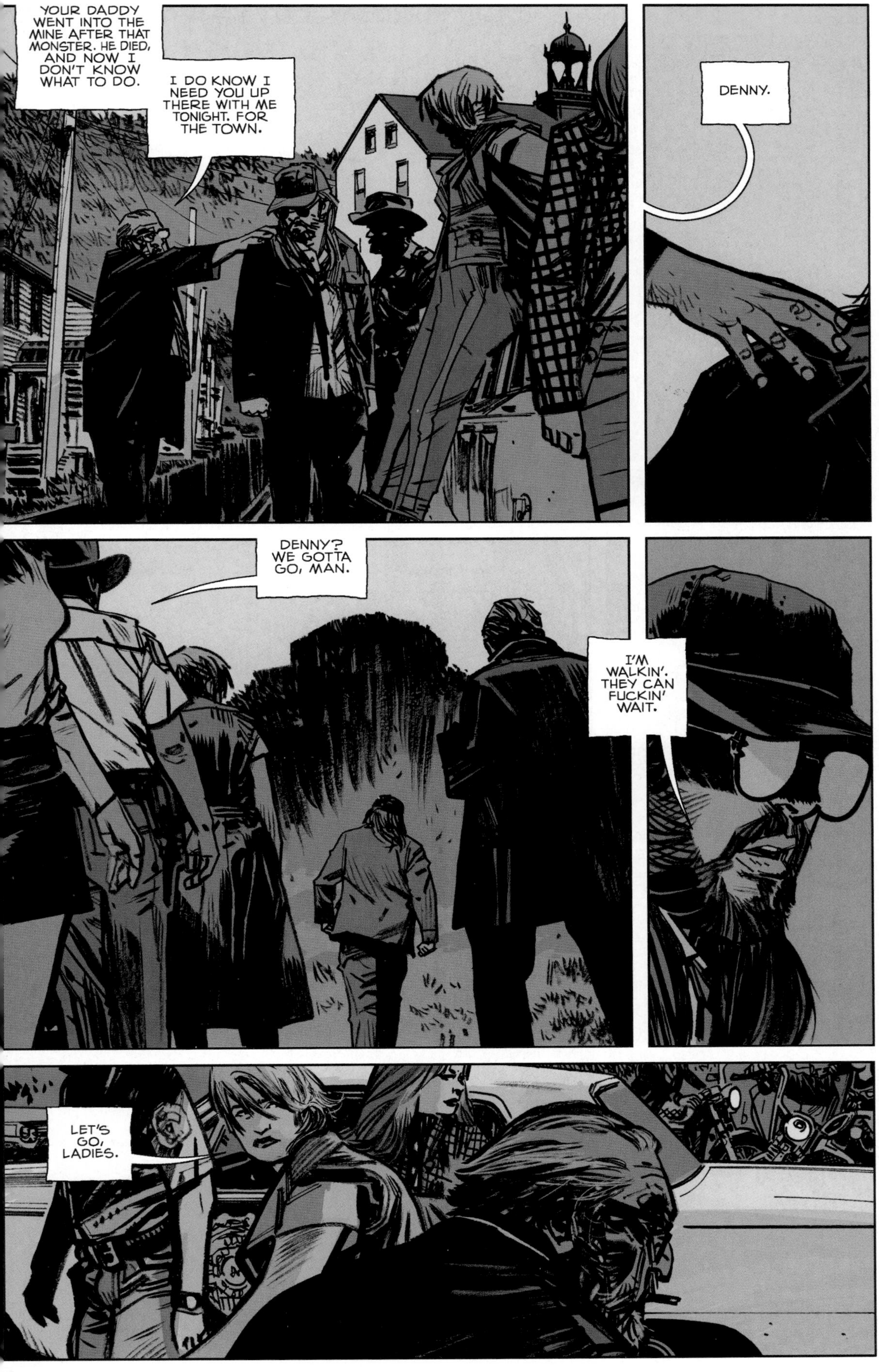
YOUR DADDY WENT INTO THE MINE AFTER THAT MONSTER. HE DIED, AND NOW I DON'T KNOW WHAT TO DO.
I DO KNOW I NEED YOU UP THERE WITH ME TONIGHT. FOR THE TOWN.
DENNY.
DENNY? WE GOTTA GO, MAN.
I'M WALKIN'. THEY CAN FUCKIN' WAIT.
LET'S GO, LADIES.

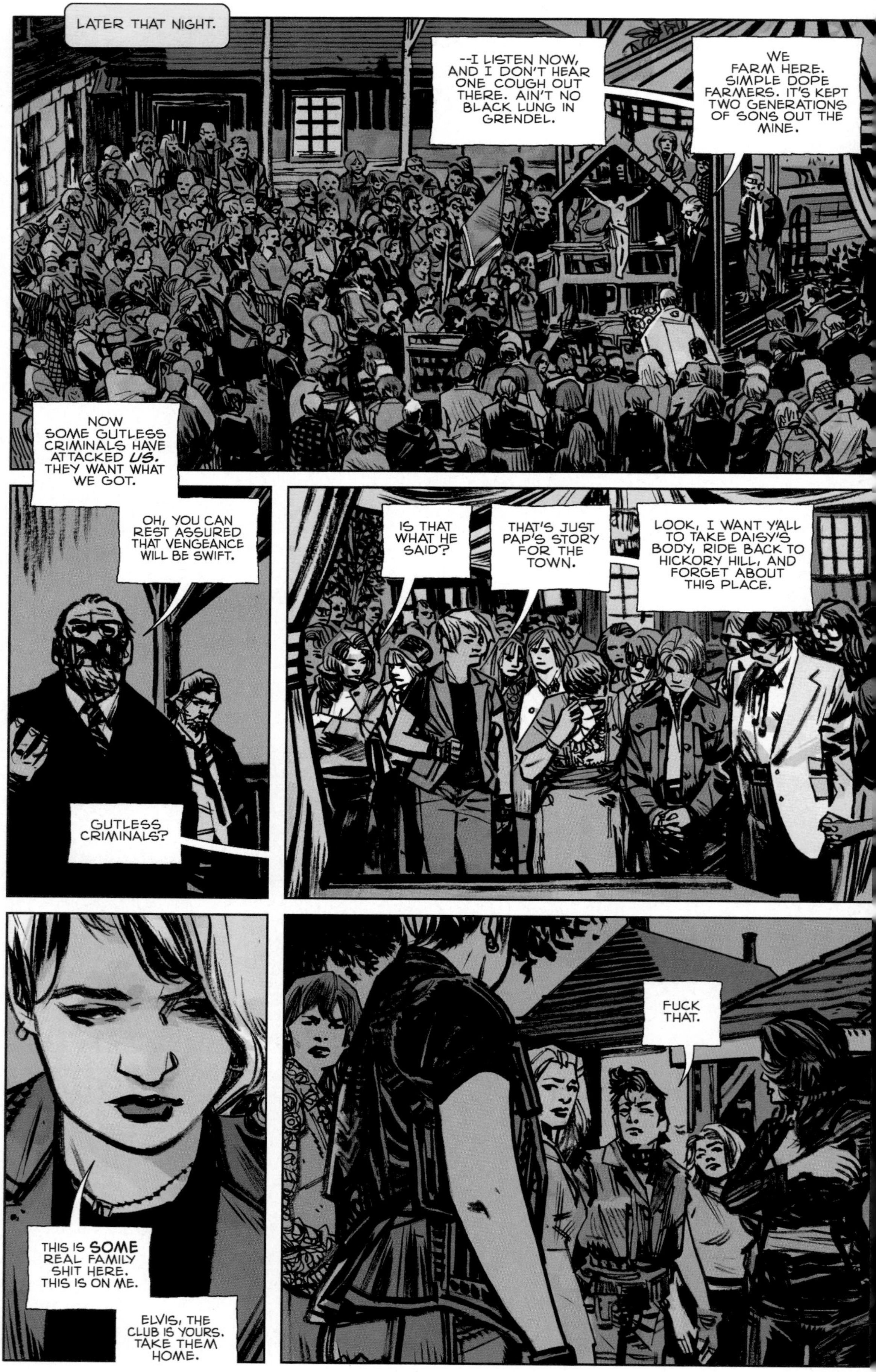
LATER THAT NIGHT.
--I LISTEN NOW, AND I DON'T HEAR ONE COUGH OUT THERE. AIN'T NO BLACK LUNG IN GRENDEL.
WE FARM HERE. SIMPLE DOPE FARMERS. IT'S KEPT TWO GENERATIONS OF SONS OUT THE MINE.
NOW SOME GUTLESS CRIMINALS HAVE ATTACKED *US.* THEY WANT WHAT WE GOT.
OH, YOU CAN REST ASSURED THAT VENGEANCE WILL BE SWIFT.
GUTLESS CRIMINALS?
IS THAT WHAT HE SAID?
THAT'S JUST PAP'S STORY FOR THE TOWN.
LOOK, I WANT Y'ALL TO TAKE DAISY'S BODY, RIDE BACK TO HICKORY HILL, AND FORGET ABOUT THIS PLACE.
THIS IS **SOME** REAL FAMILY SHIT HERE. THIS IS ON ME.
ELVIS, THE CLUB IS YOURS. TAKE THEM HOME.
FUCK THAT.

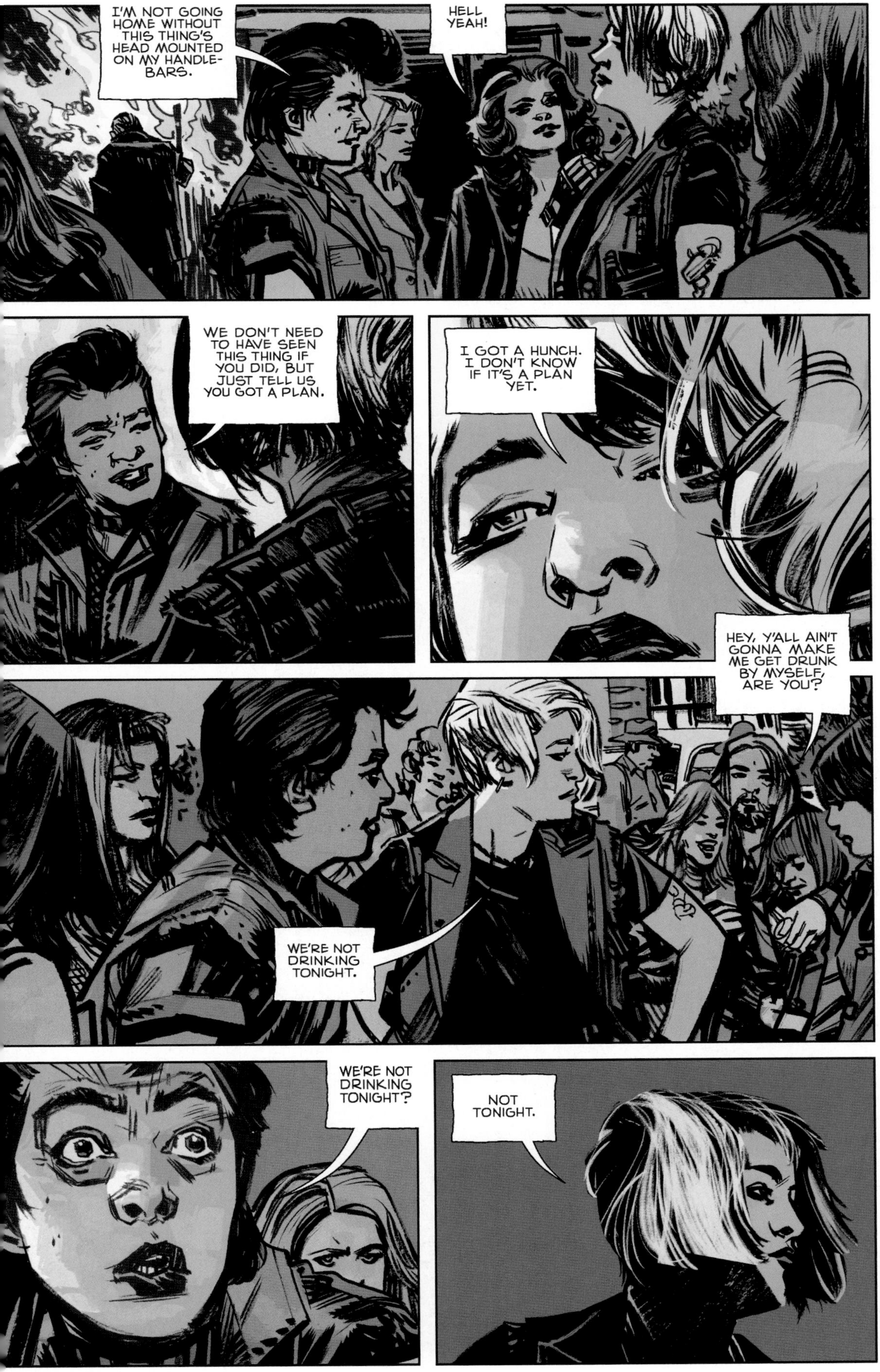
I'M NOT GOING HOME WITHOUT THIS THING'S HEAD MOUNTED ON MY HANDLE-BARS.
HELL YEAH!
WE DON'T NEED TO HAVE SEEN THIS THING IF YOU DID, BUT JUST TELL US YOU GOT A PLAN.
I GOT A HUNCH. I DON'T KNOW IF IT'S A PLAN YET.
HEY, Y'ALL AIN'T GONNA MAKE ME GET DRUNK BY MYSELF, ARE YOU?
WE'RE NOT DRINKING TONIGHT.
WE'RE NOT DRINKING TONIGHT?
NOT TONIGHT.

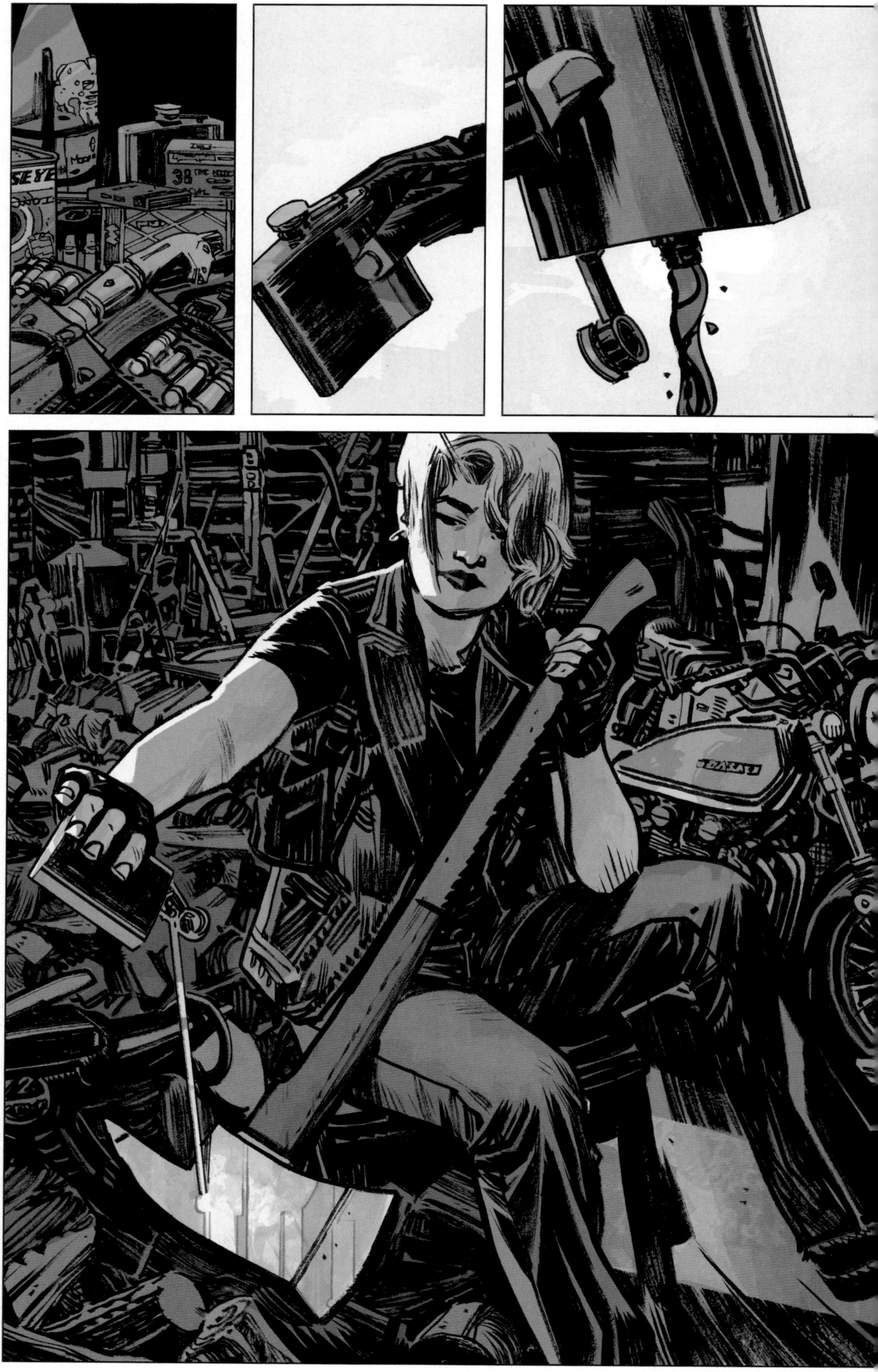

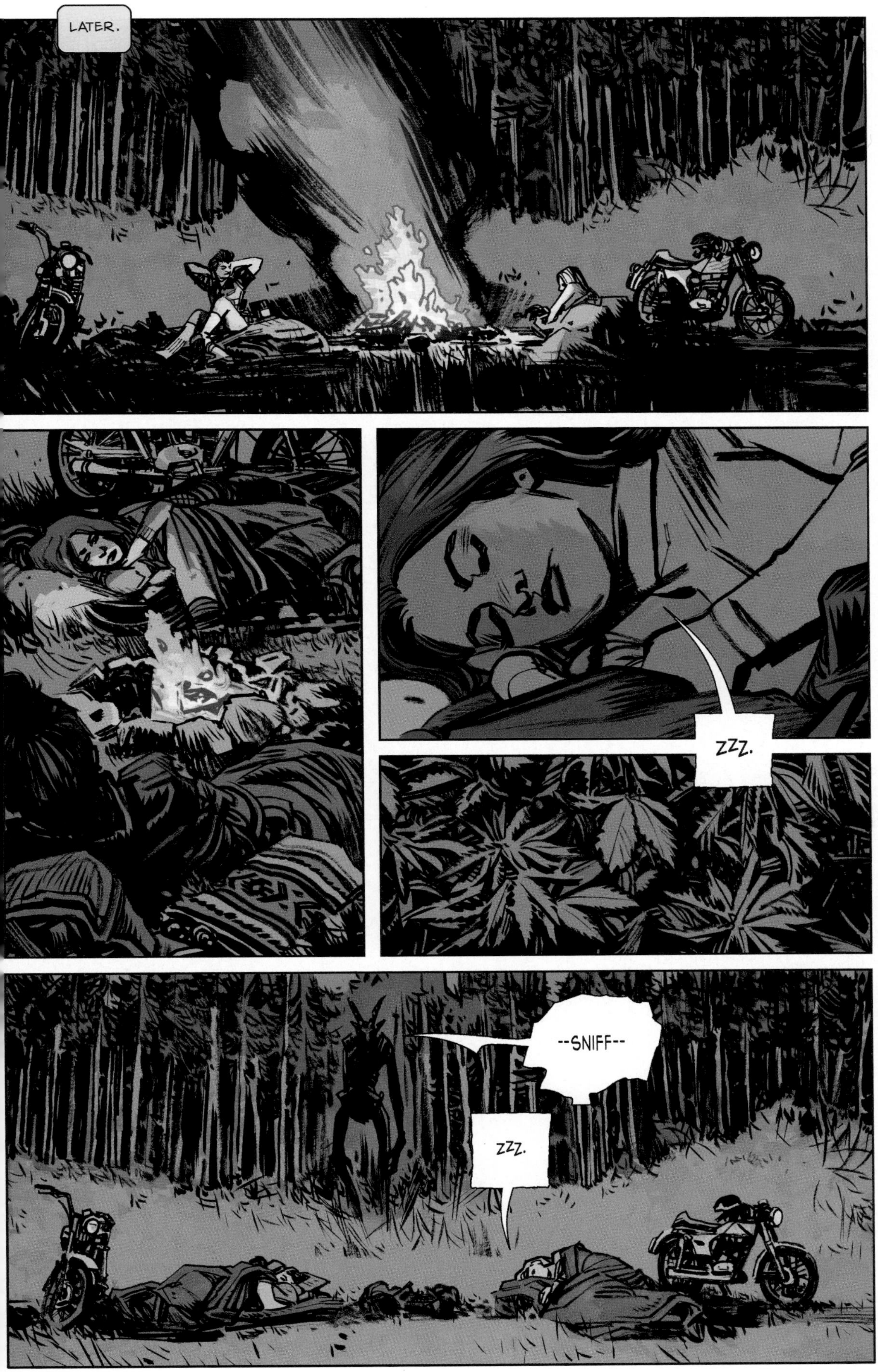
LATER.
ZZZ.
--SNIFF--
ZZZ.

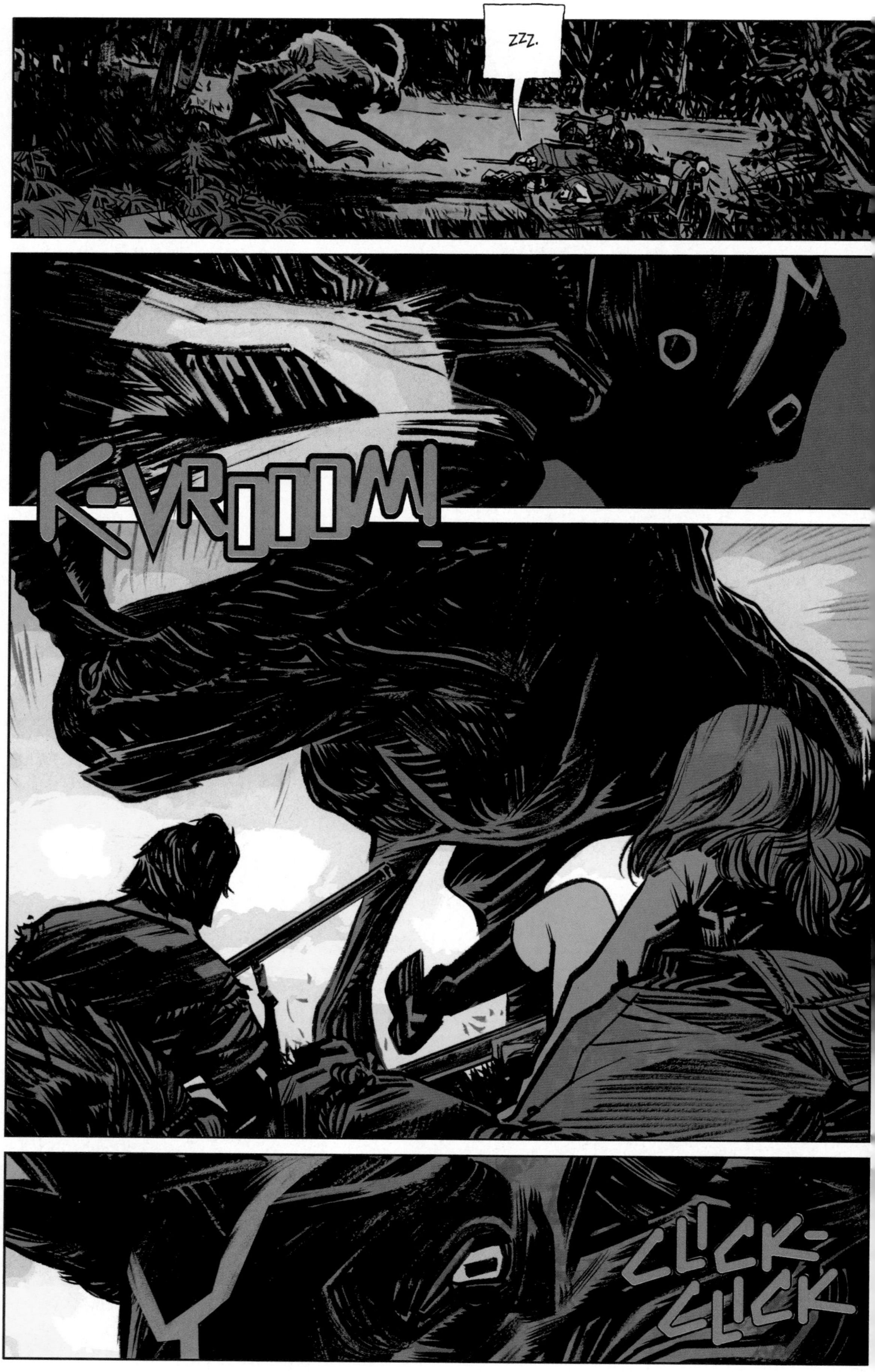
ZZZ.
K-VROOOM!
CLICK-CLICK

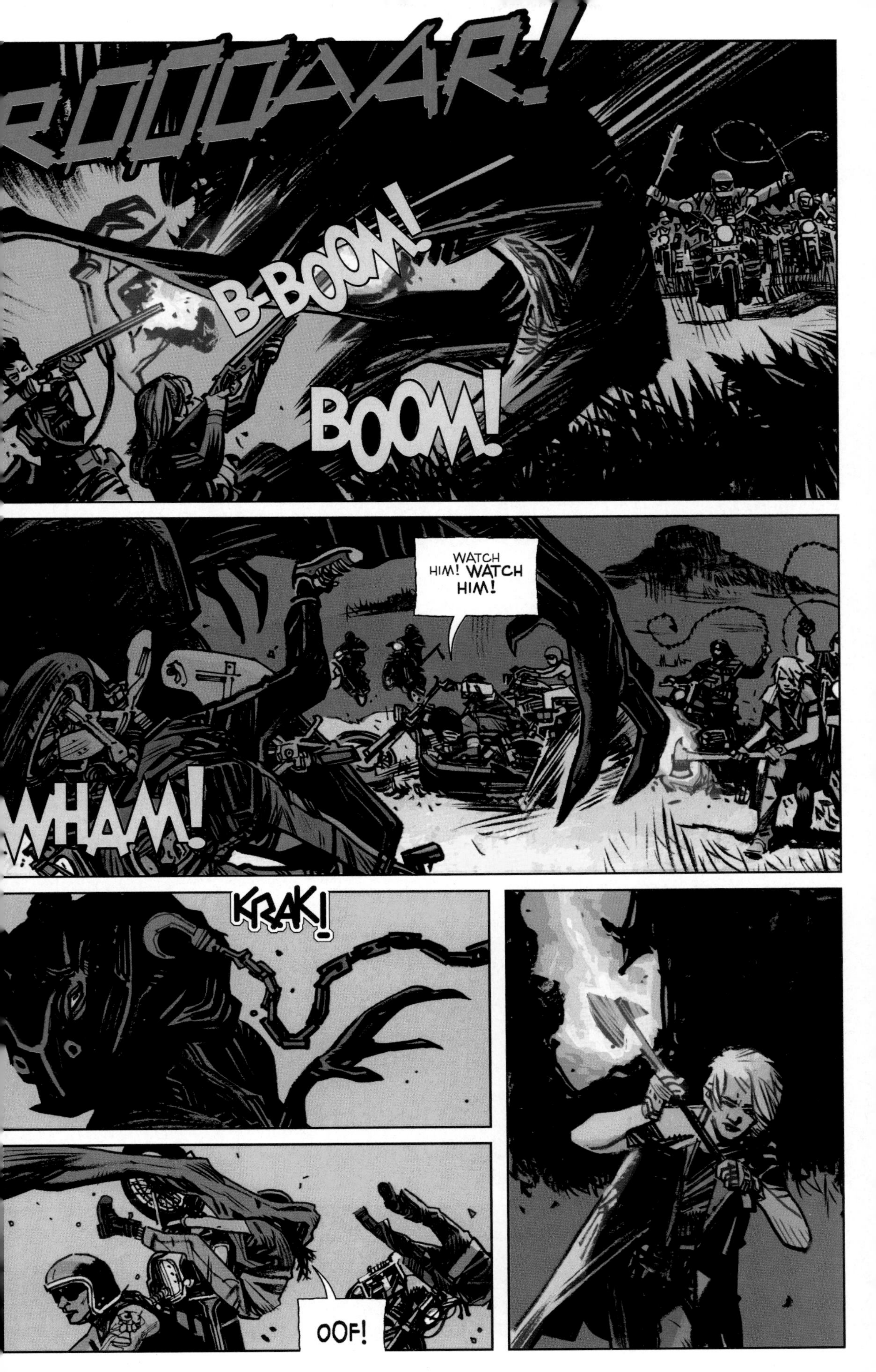
ROOOAAR!
B-BOOM!
BOOM!
WATCH HIM! WATCH HIM!
WHAM!
KRAK!
OOF!

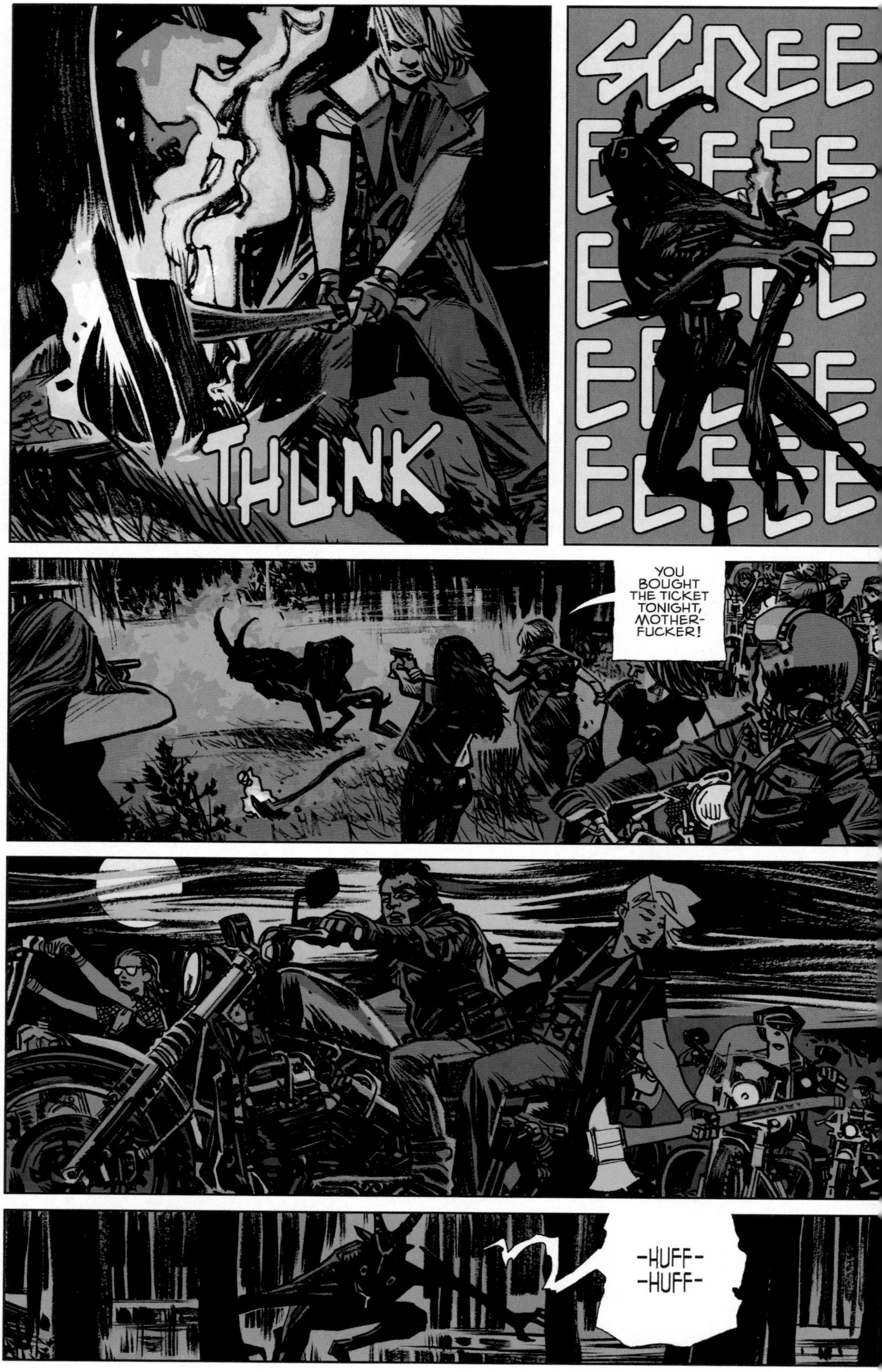
THUNK
SCREEEEEEEEEEEEEEEEEEEEEEEEE
YOU BOUGHT THE TICKET TONIGHT, MOTHER-FUCKER!
-HUFF-
-HUFF-

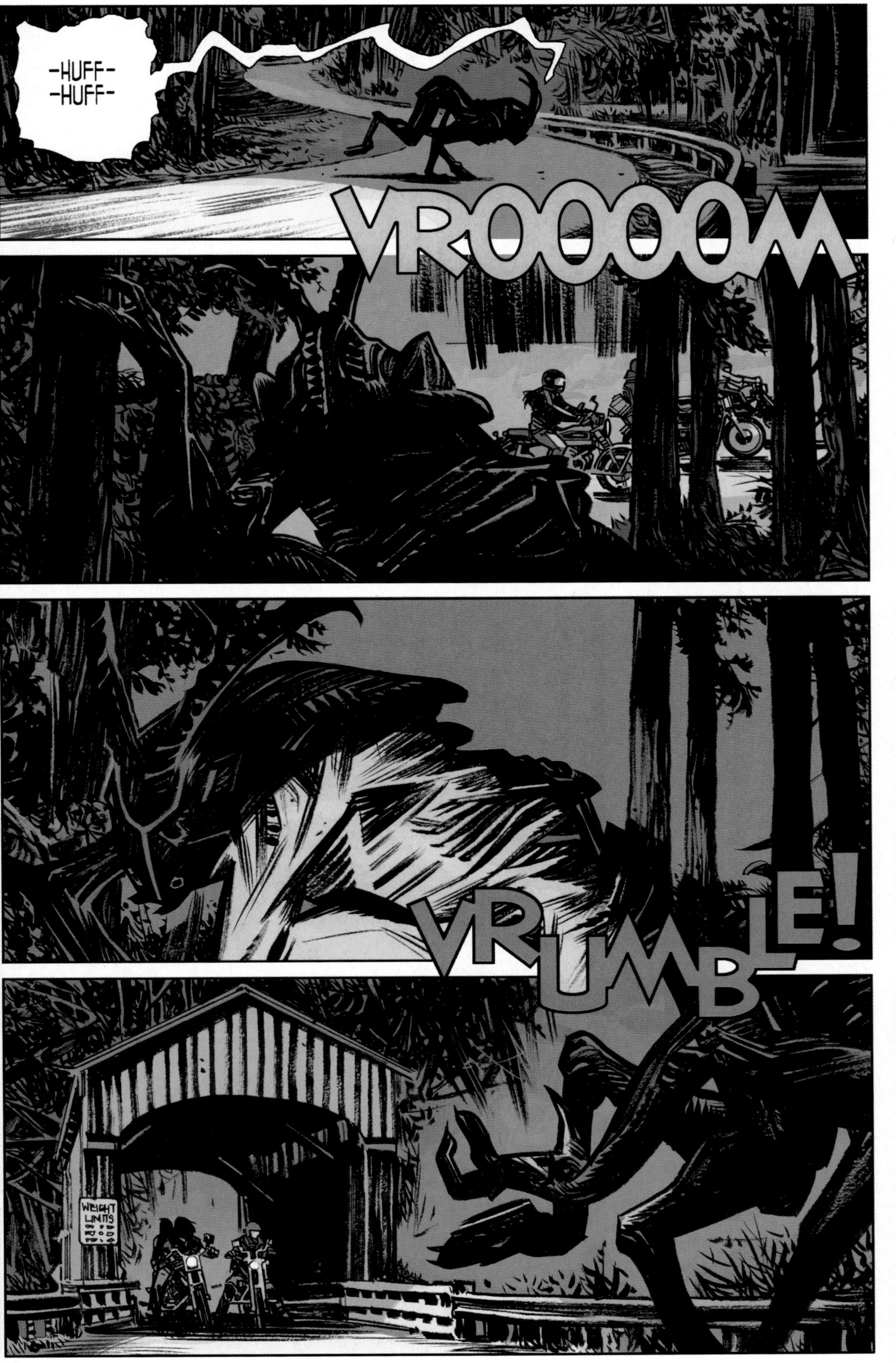
-HUFF-
-HUFF-
VROOOOM
VRUMBLE!
WEIGHT LIMITS

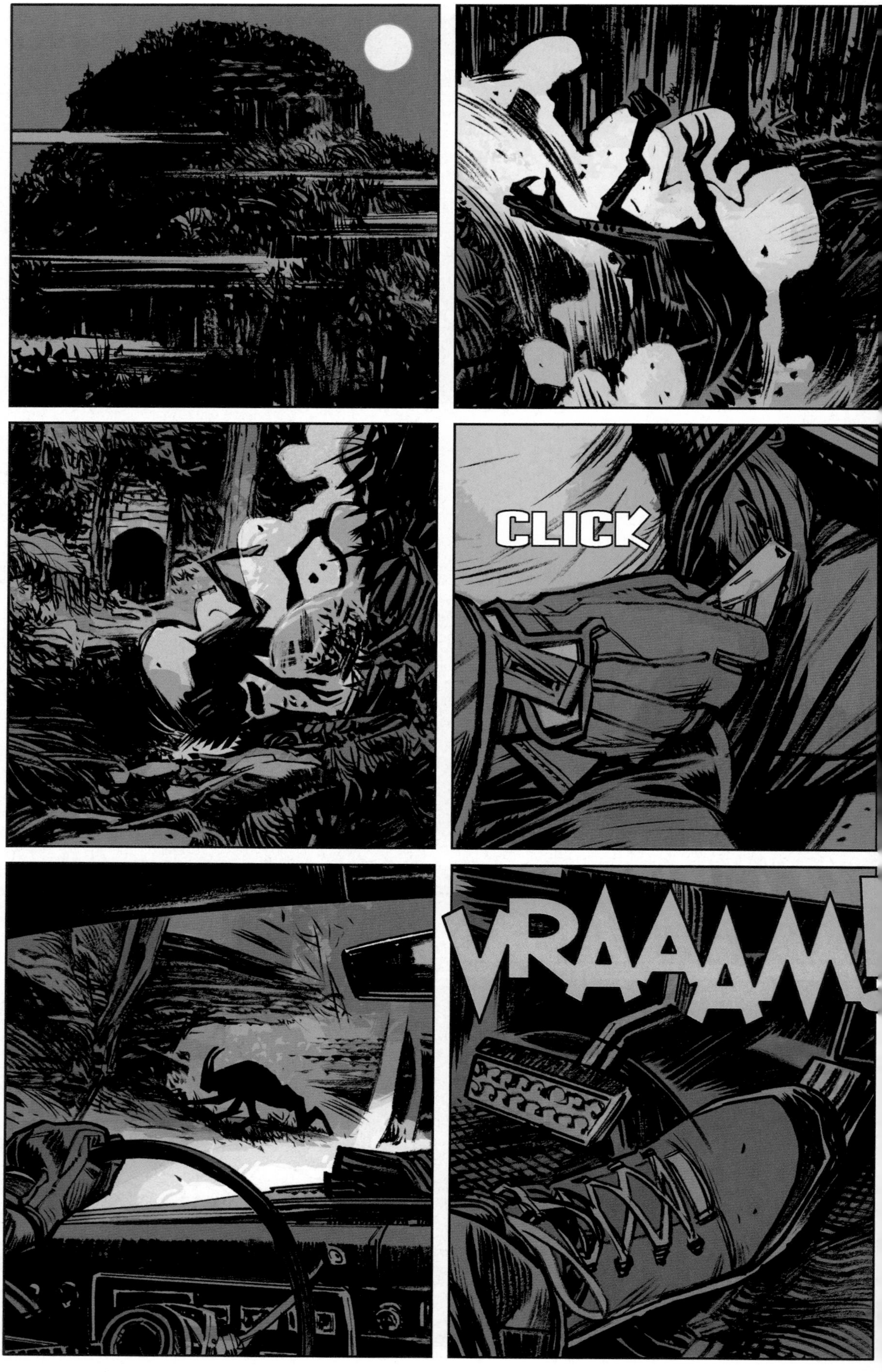
CLICK
VRAAAM

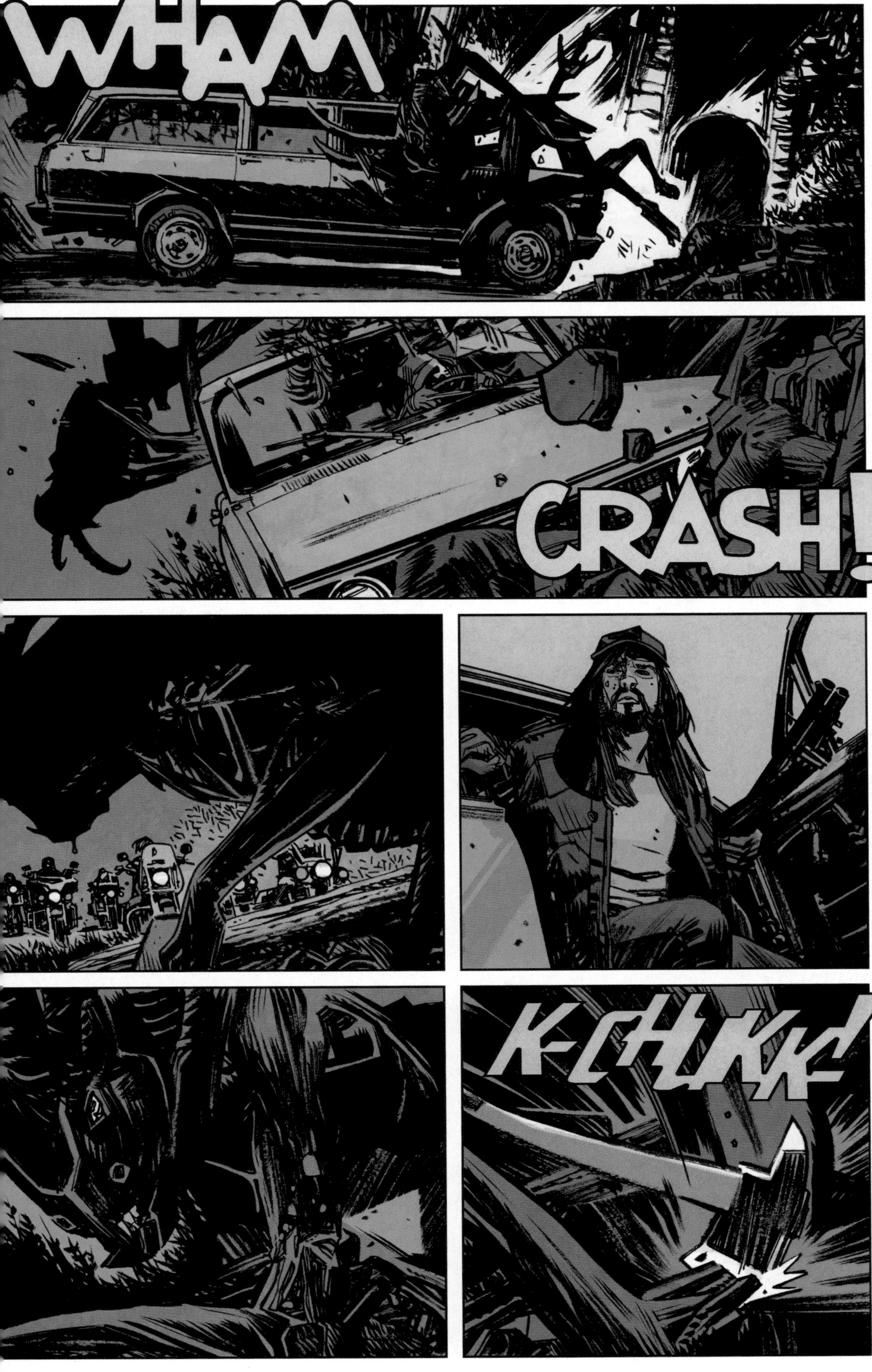
WHAM
CRASH!
K-CHUKK!

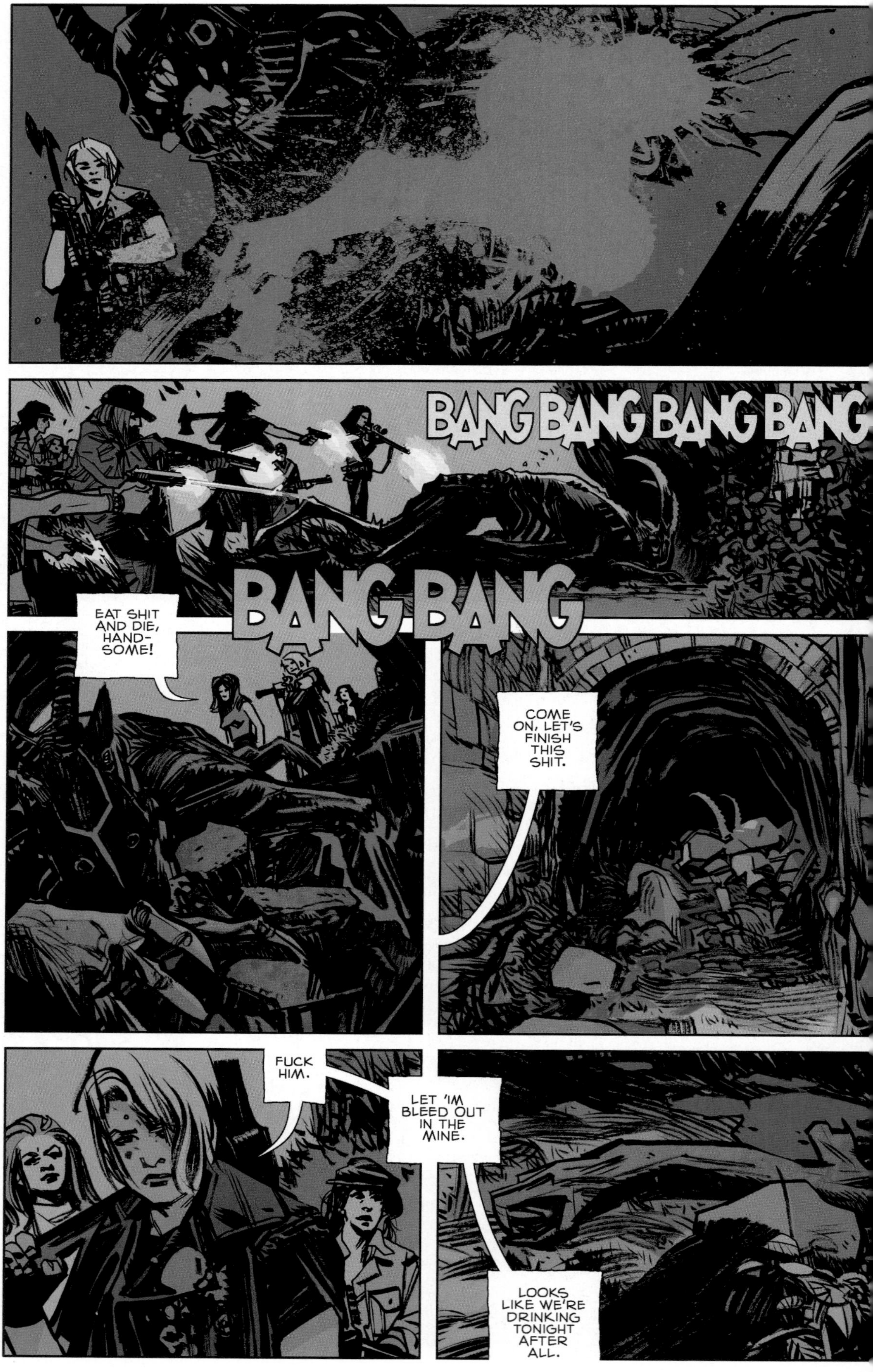

BANG BANG BANG BANG
BANG BANG
EAT SHIT AND DIE, HAND-SOME!
COME ON, LET'S FINISH THIS SHIT.
FUCK HIM.
LET 'IM BLEED OUT IN THE MINE.
LOOKS LIKE WE'RE DRINKING TONIGHT AFTER ALL.

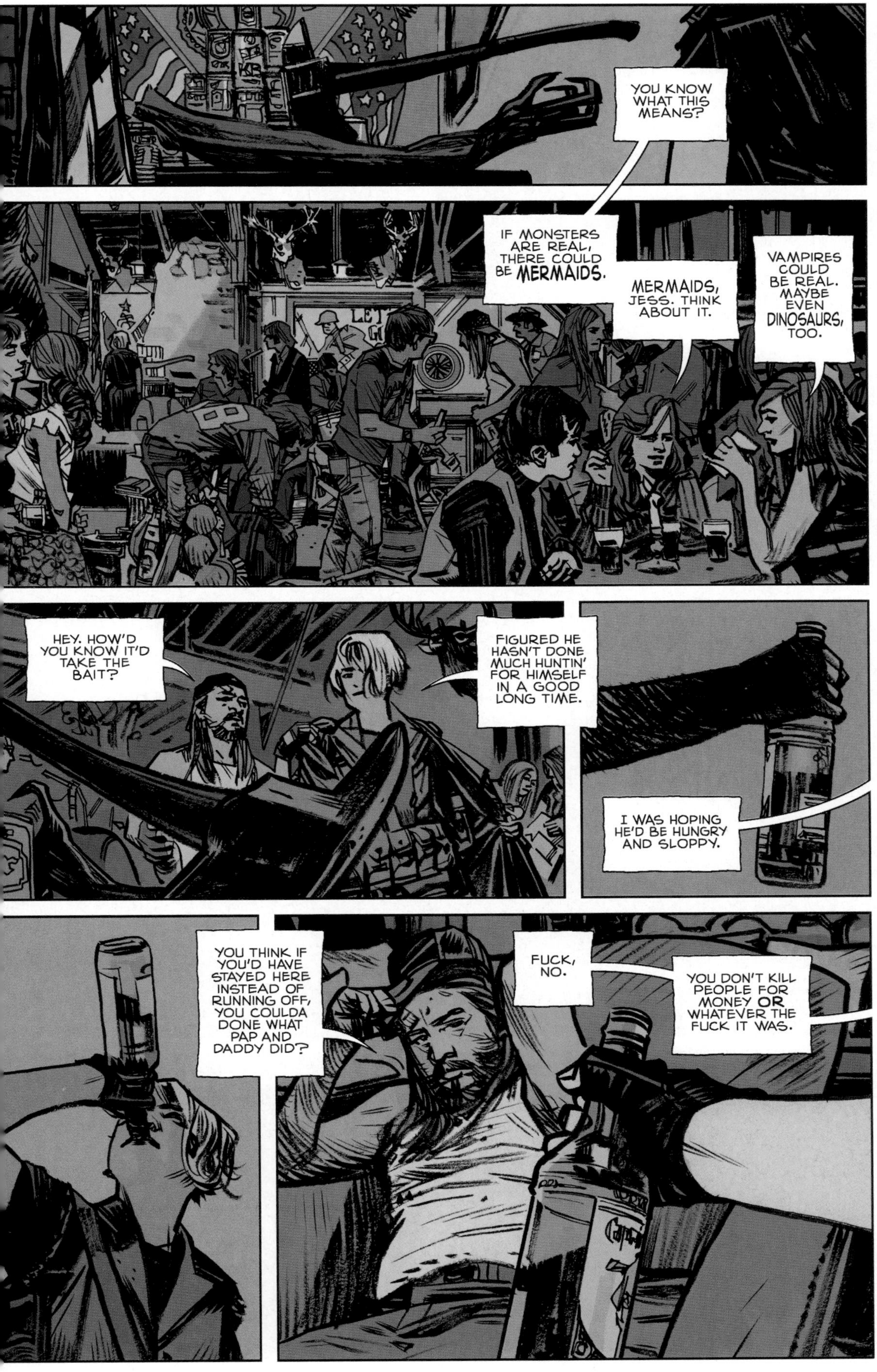
YOU KNOW WHAT THIS MEANS?
IF MONSTERS ARE REAL, THERE COULD BE MERMAIDS.
MERMAIDS, JESS. THINK ABOUT IT.
VAMPIRES COULD BE REAL. MAYBE EVEN DINOSAURS, TOO.
HEY. HOW'D YOU KNOW IT'D TAKE THE BAIT?
FIGURED HE HASN'T DONE MUCH HUNTIN' FOR HIMSELF IN A GOOD LONG TIME.
I WAS HOPING HE'D BE HUNGRY AND SLOPPY.
YOU THINK IF YOU'D HAVE STAYED HERE INSTEAD OF RUNNING OFF, YOU COULDA DONE WHAT PAP AND DADDY DID?
FUCK, NO.
YOU DON'T KILL PEOPLE FOR MONEY OR WHATEVER THE FUCK IT WAS.

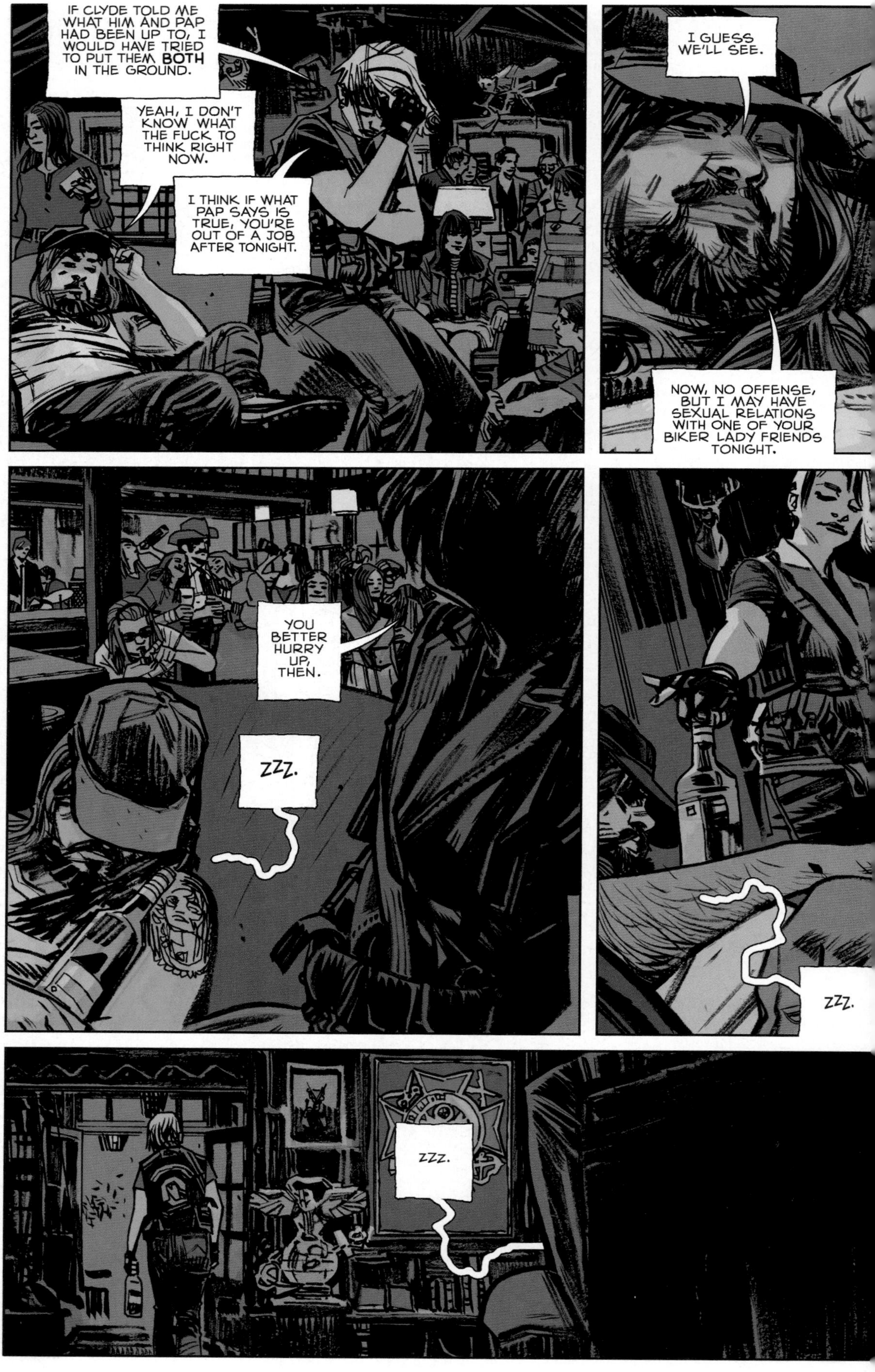
IF CLYDE TOLD ME WHAT HIM AND PAP HAD BEEN UP TO, I WOULD HAVE TRIED TO PUT THEM **BOTH** IN THE GROUND.
YEAH, I DON'T KNOW WHAT THE FUCK TO THINK RIGHT NOW.
I THINK IF WHAT PAP SAYS IS TRUE, YOU'RE OUT OF A JOB AFTER TONIGHT.
I GUESS WE'LL SEE.
NOW, NO OFFENSE, BUT I MAY HAVE SEXUAL RELATIONS WITH ONE OF YOUR BIKER LADY FRIENDS TONIGHT.
YOU BETTER HURRY UP, THEN.
ZZZ.
ZZZ.
ZZZ.

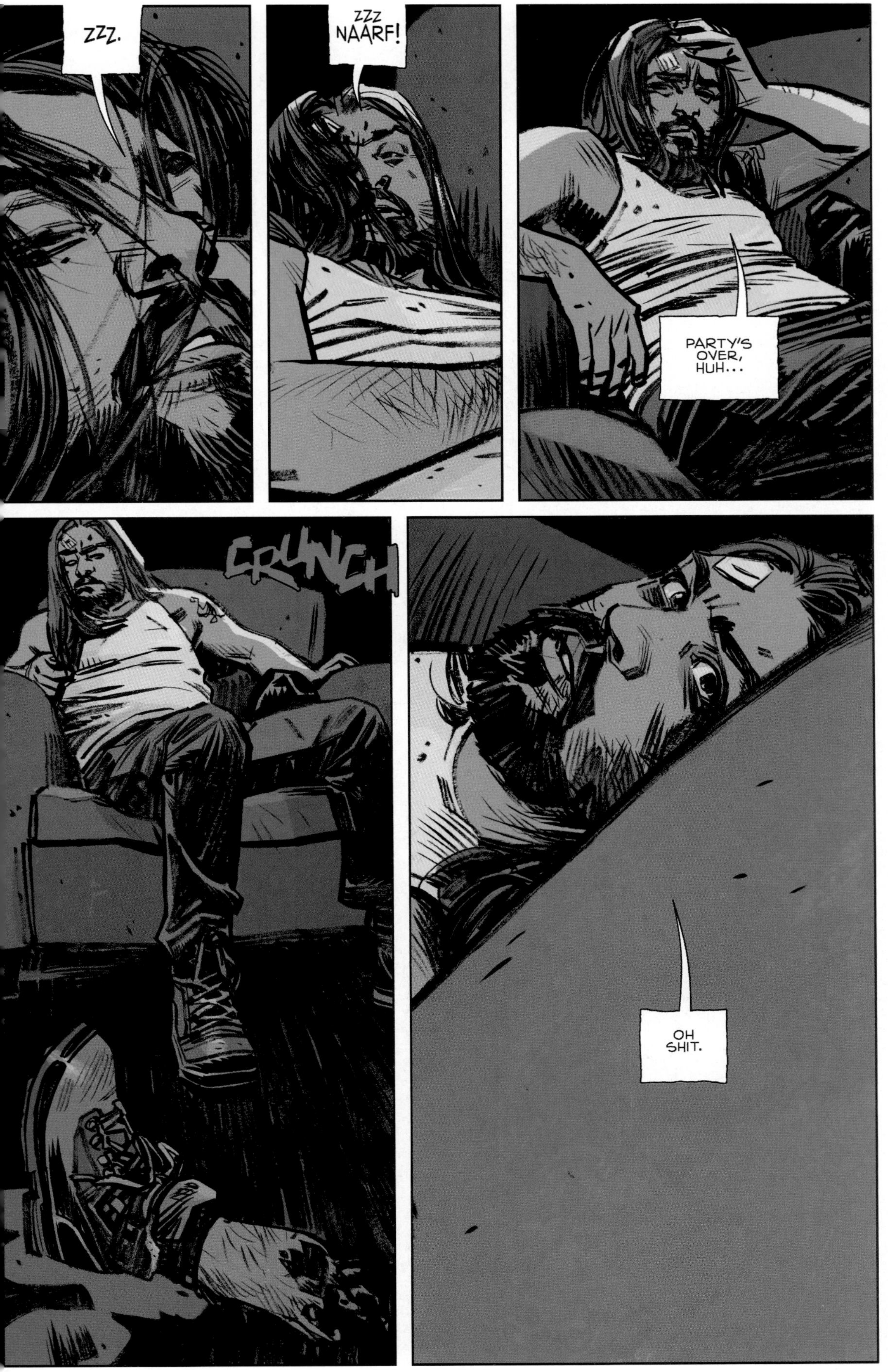
ZZZ.
ZZZ NAARF!
PARTY'S OVER, HUH...
CRUNCH
OH SHIT.

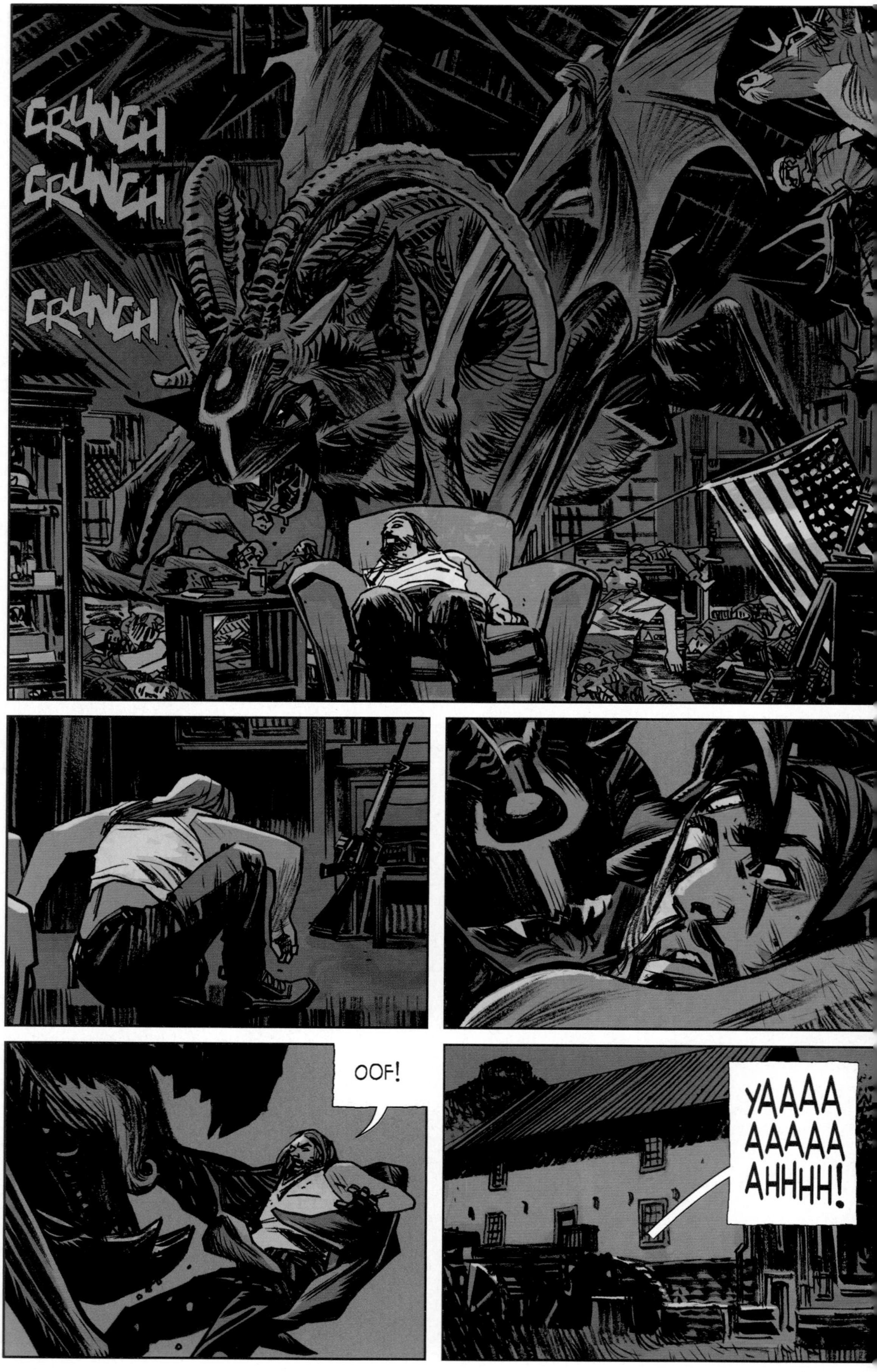
CRUNCH
CRUNCH
CRUNCH
OOF!
YAAAA AAAAA AHHHH!

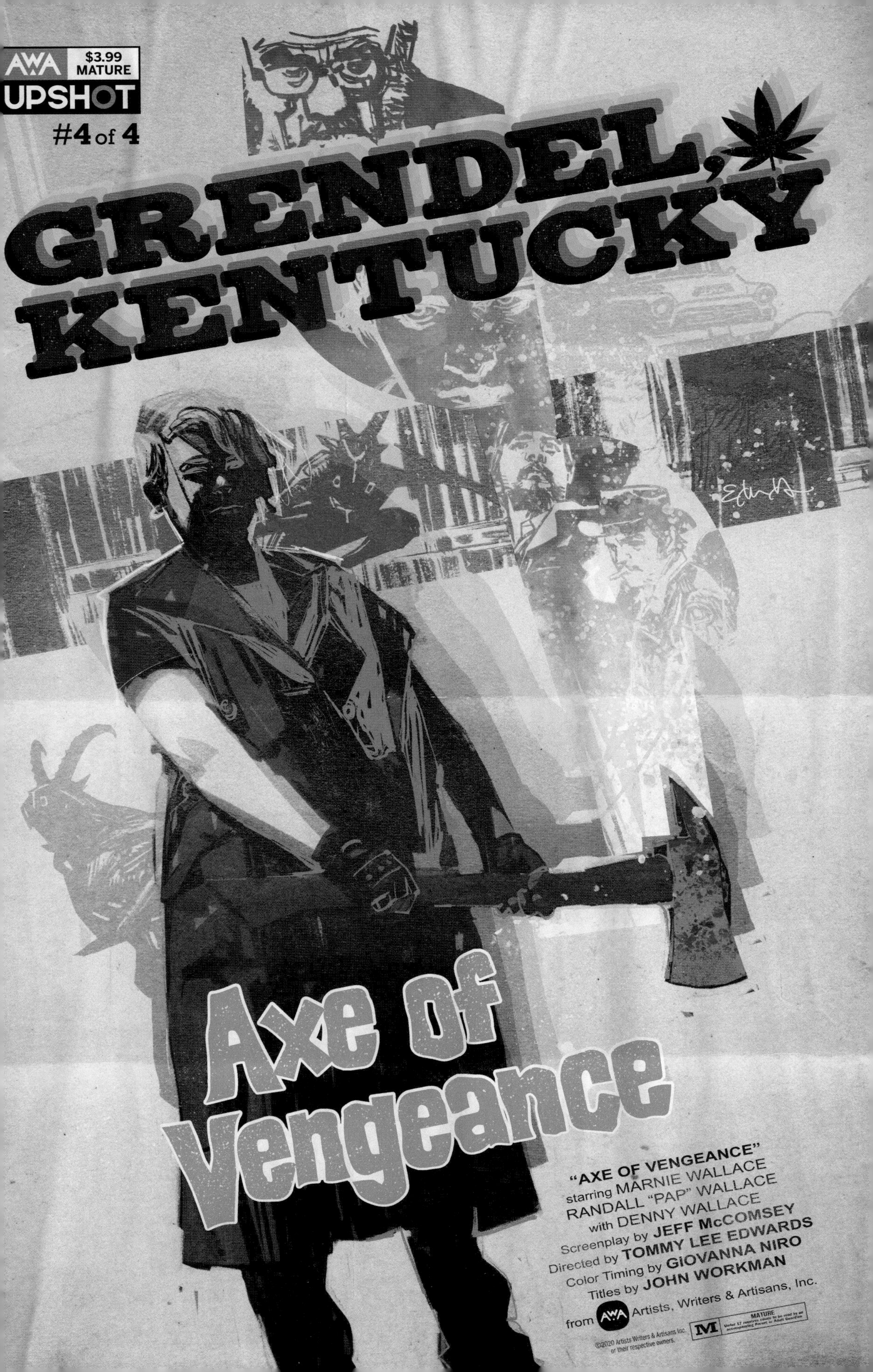
AWA
$3.99
MATURE
UPSHOT
#4 of 4
GRENDEL, KENTUCKY
Axe of Vengeance
"AXE OF VENGEANCE"
starring MARNIE WALLACE
RANDALL "PAP" WALLACE
with DENNY WALLACE
Screenplay by JEFF McCOMSEY
Directed by TOMMY LEE EDWARDS
Color Timing by GIOVANNA NIRO
Titles by JOHN WORKMAN
from AWA Artists, Writers & Artisans, Inc.
M MATURE
Under 17 requires comic to be read by an accompanying Parent or Adult Guardian
©2020 Artists Writers & Artisans Inc. or their respective owners.

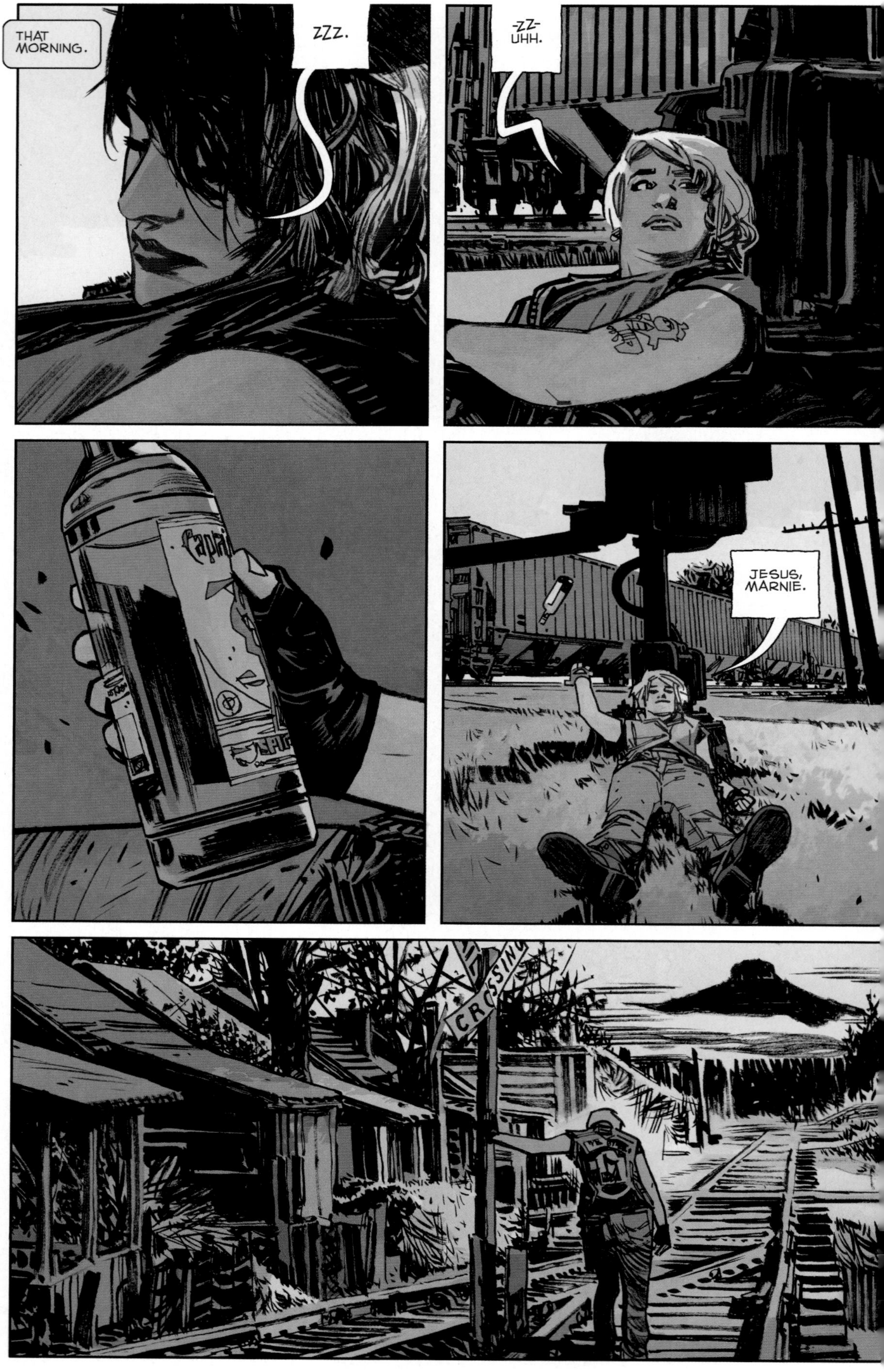
THAT MORNING.
ZZZ.
-ZZ-
UHH.
JESUS, MARNIE.
CROSSING

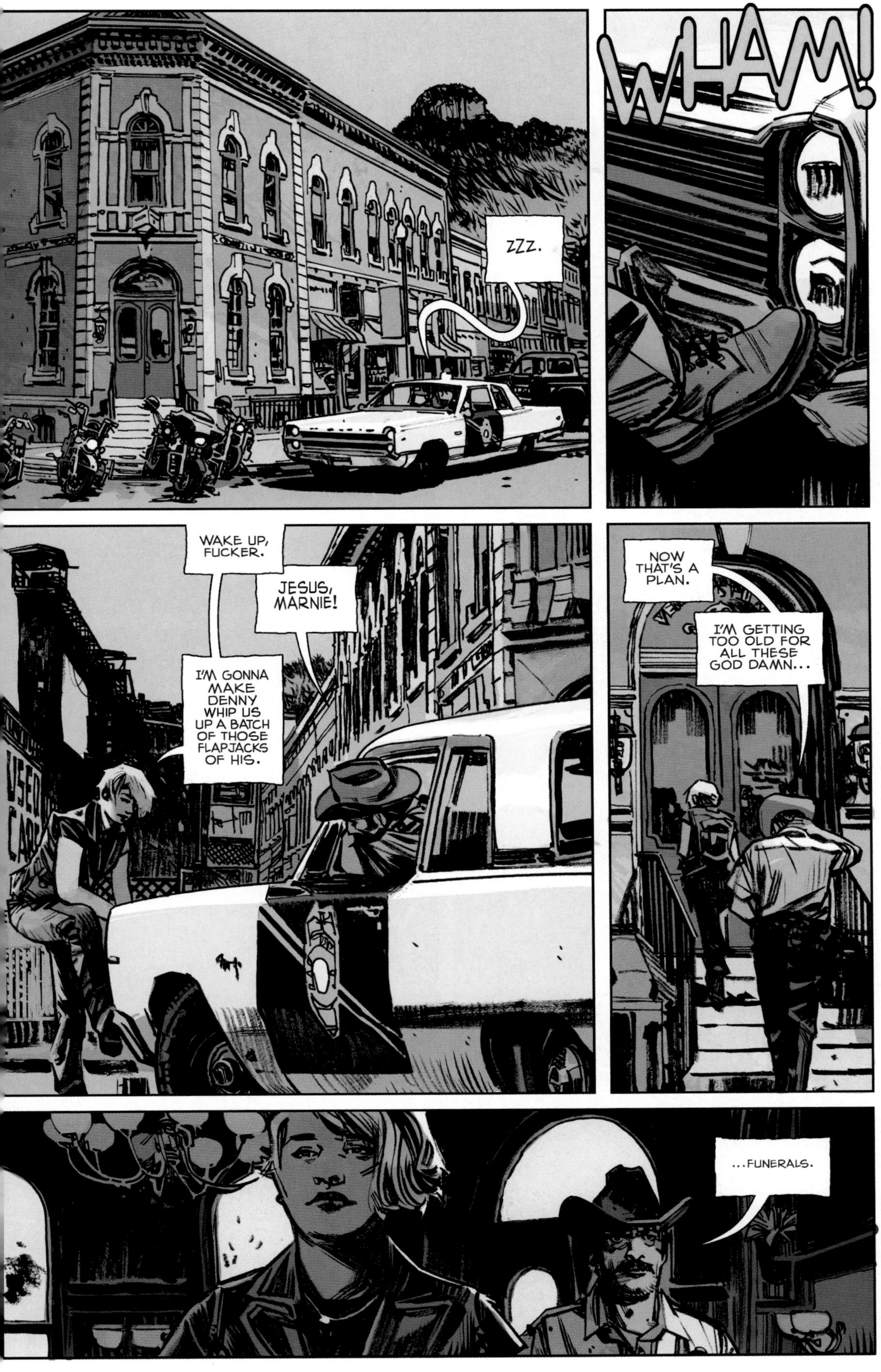
ZZZ.
WHAM!
WAKE UP, FUCKER.
JESUS, MARNIE!
I'M GONNA MAKE DENNY WHIP US UP A BATCH OF THOSE FLAPJACKS OF HIS.
NOW THAT'S A PLAN.
I'M GETTING TOO OLD FOR ALL THESE GOD DAMN...
...FUNERALS.

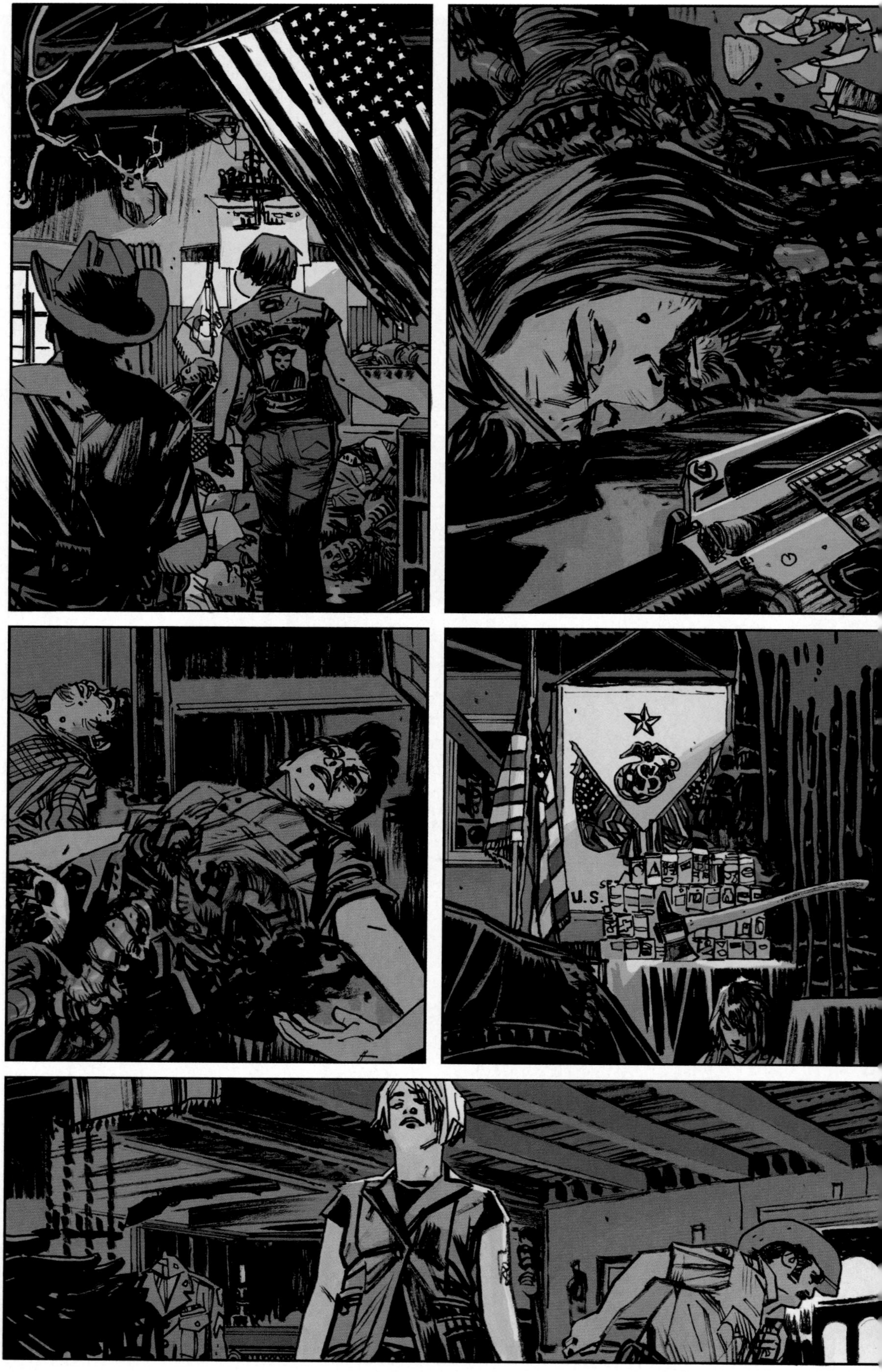
U.S.

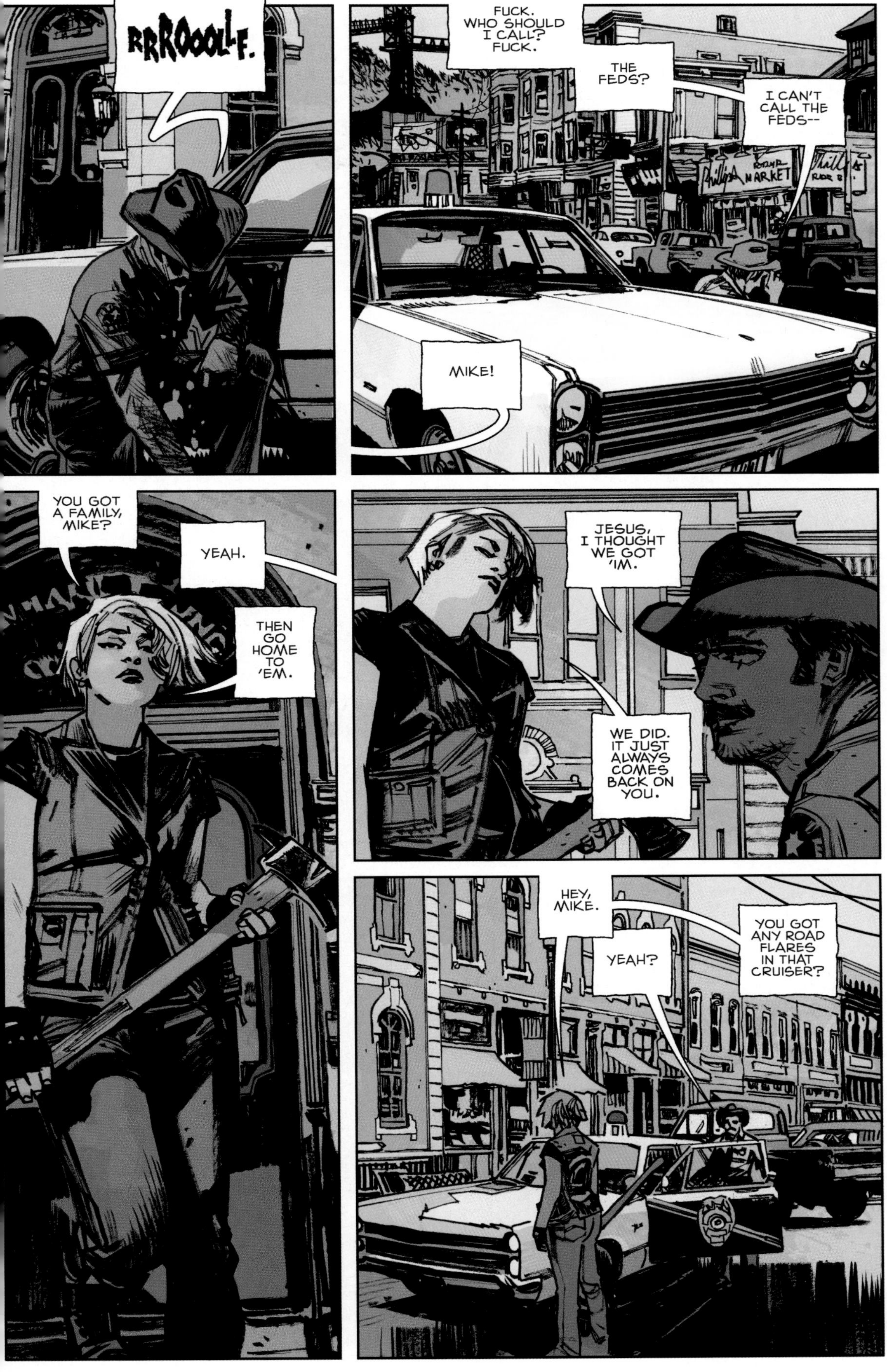
RRROOOLLF.
FUCK. WHO SHOULD I CALL? FUCK.
THE FEDS?
I CAN'T CALL THE FEDS--
MIKE!
YOU GOT A FAMILY, MIKE?
YEAH.
THEN GO HOME TO 'EM.
JESUS, I THOUGHT WE GOT 'IM.
WE DID. IT JUST ALWAYS COMES BACK ON YOU.
HEY, MIKE.
YEAH?
YOU GOT ANY ROAD FLARES IN THAT CRUISER?

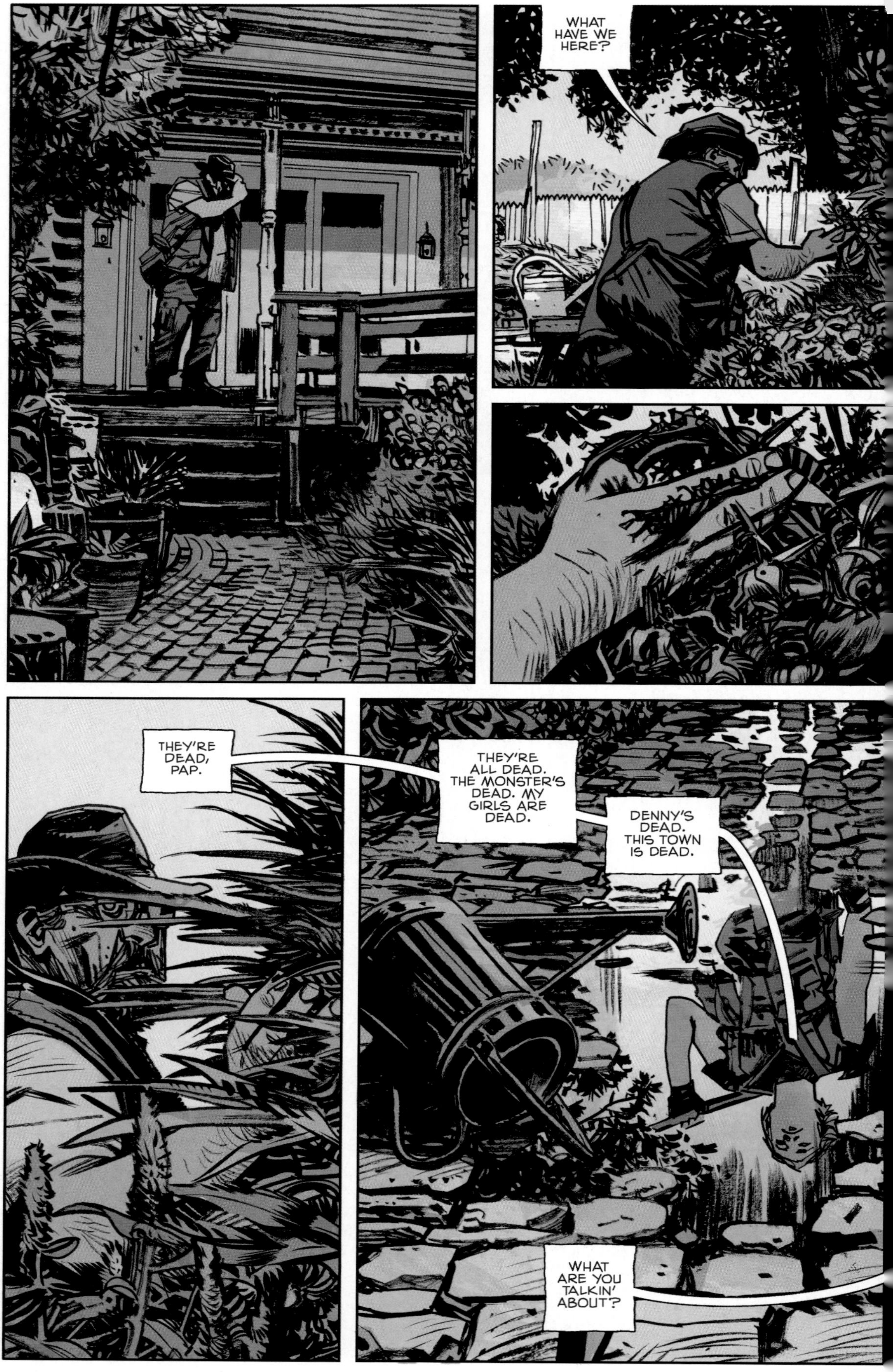
WHAT HAVE WE HERE?
THEY'RE DEAD, PAP.
THEY'RE ALL DEAD. THE MONSTER'S DEAD. MY GIRLS ARE DEAD.
DENNY'S DEAD. THIS TOWN IS DEAD.
WHAT ARE YOU TALKIN' ABOUT?

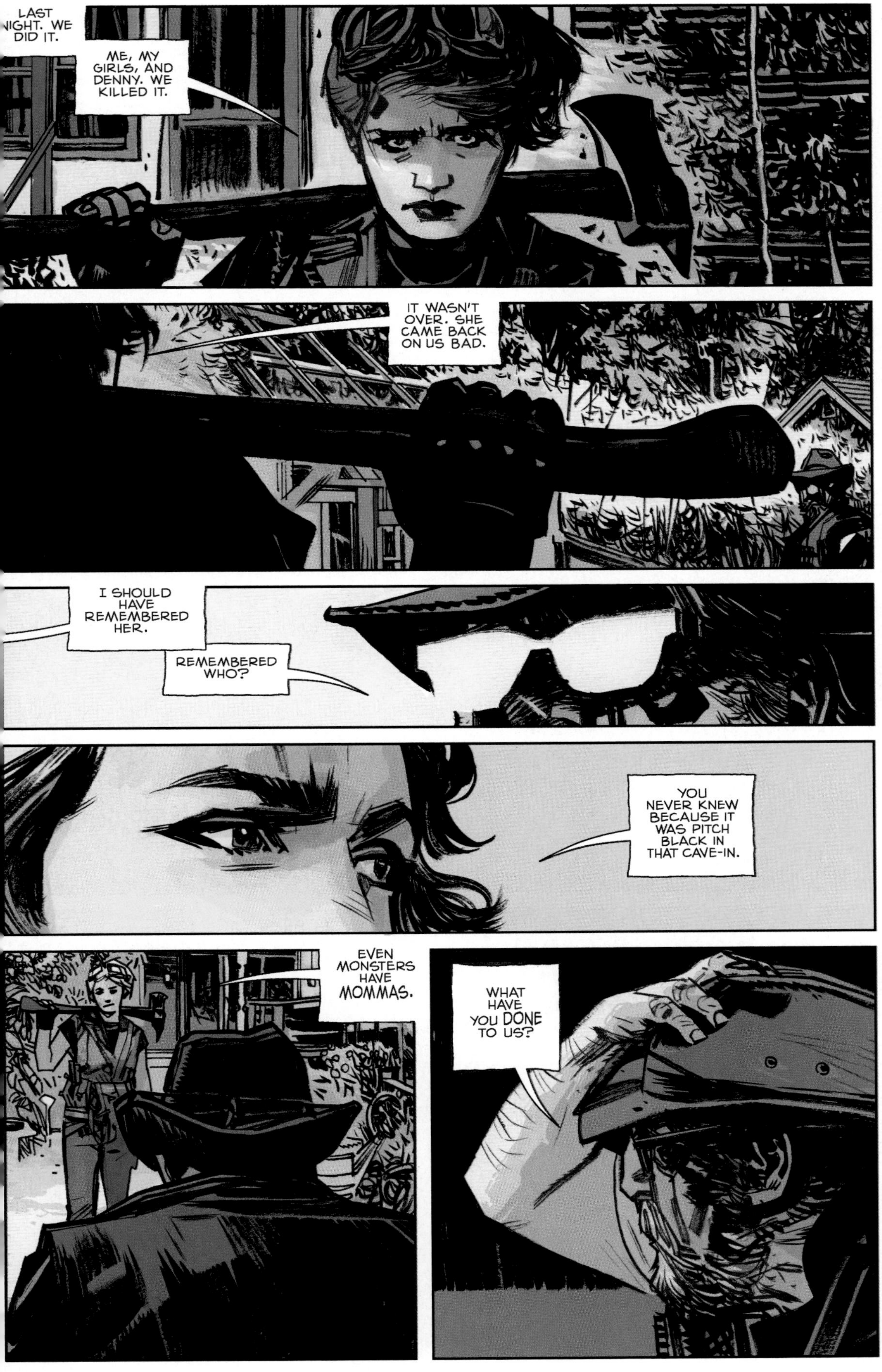
LAST NIGHT. WE DID IT.
ME, MY GIRLS, AND DENNY. WE KILLED IT.
IT WASN'T OVER. SHE CAME BACK ON US BAD.
I SHOULD HAVE REMEMBERED HER.
REMEMBERED WHO?
YOU NEVER KNEW BECAUSE IT WAS PITCH BLACK IN THAT CAVE-IN.
EVEN MONSTERS HAVE MOMMAS.
WHAT HAVE YOU DONE TO US?

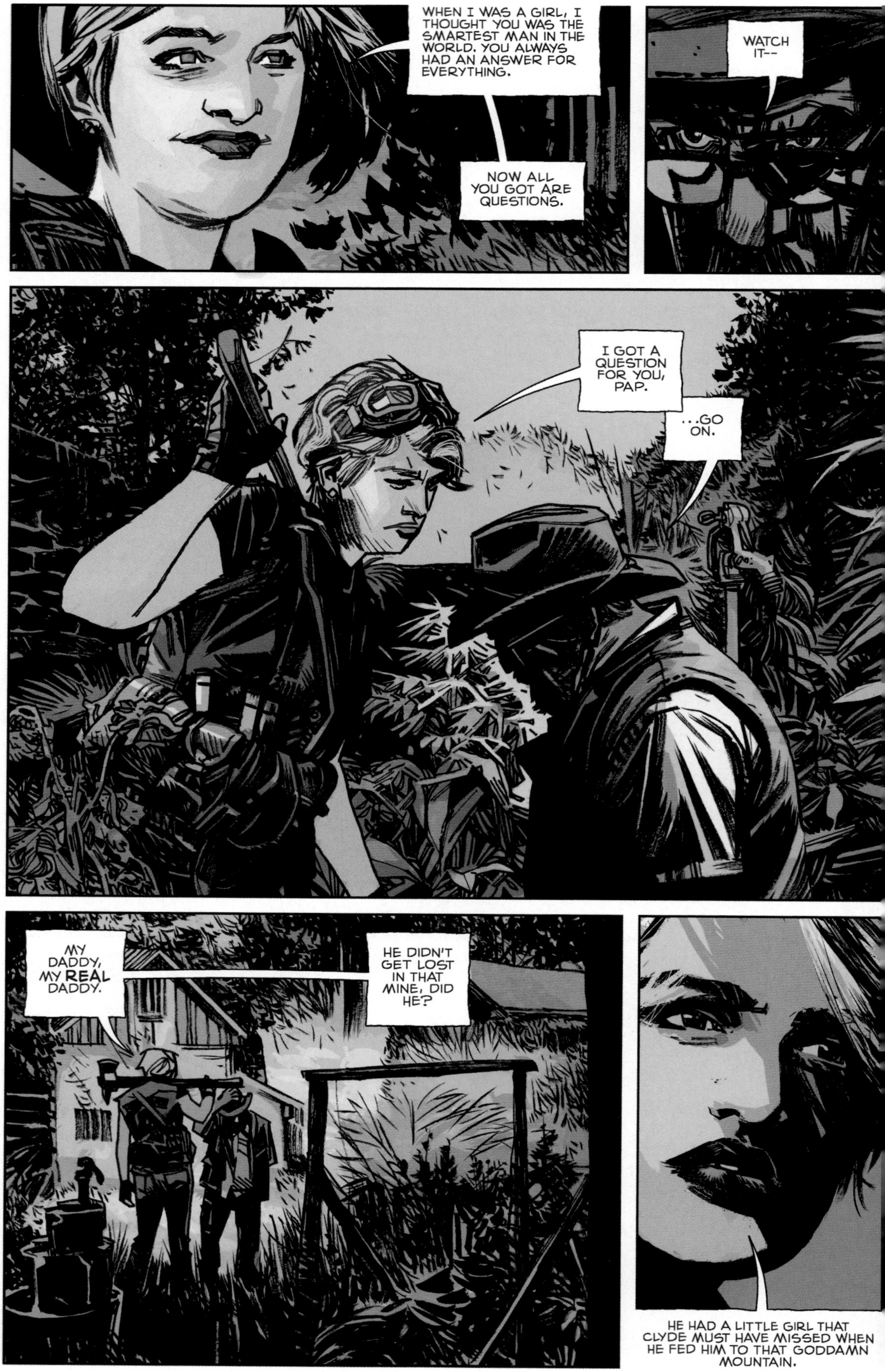

WHEN I WAS A GIRL, I THOUGHT YOU WAS THE SMARTEST MAN IN THE WORLD. YOU ALWAYS HAD AN ANSWER FOR EVERYTHING.
NOW ALL YOU GOT ARE QUESTIONS.
WATCH IT--
I GOT A QUESTION FOR YOU, PAP.
...GO ON.
MY DADDY, MY **REAL** DADDY.
HE DIDN'T GET LOST IN THAT MINE, DID HE?
HE HAD A LITTLE GIRL THAT CLYDE MUST HAVE MISSED WHEN HE FED HIM TO THAT GODDAMN MOUNTAIN.

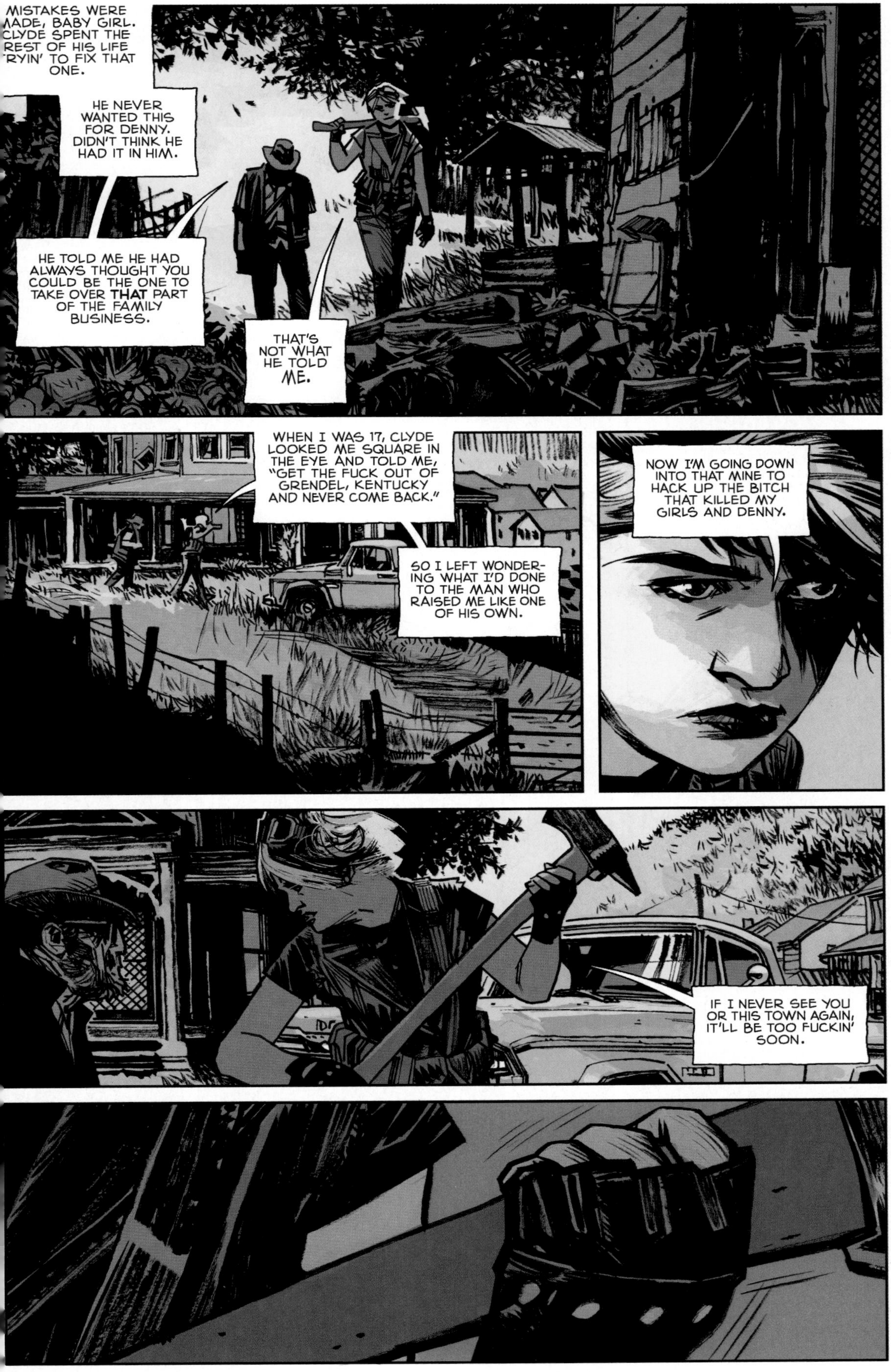

MISTAKES WERE MADE, BABY GIRL. CLYDE SPENT THE REST OF HIS LIFE TRYIN' TO FIX THAT ONE.
HE NEVER WANTED THIS FOR DENNY. DIDN'T THINK HE HAD IT IN HIM.
HE TOLD ME HE HAD ALWAYS THOUGHT YOU COULD BE THE ONE TO TAKE OVER **THAT** PART OF THE FAMILY BUSINESS.
THAT'S NOT WHAT HE TOLD ME.
WHEN I WAS 17, CLYDE LOOKED ME SQUARE IN THE EYE AND TOLD ME, "GET THE FUCK OUT OF GRENDEL, KENTUCKY AND NEVER COME BACK."
SO I LEFT WONDERING WHAT I'D DONE TO THE MAN WHO RAISED ME LIKE ONE OF HIS OWN.
NOW I'M GOING DOWN INTO THAT MINE TO HACK UP THE BITCH THAT KILLED MY GIRLS AND DENNY.
IF I NEVER SEE YOU OR THIS TOWN AGAIN, IT'LL BE TOO FUCKIN' SOON.

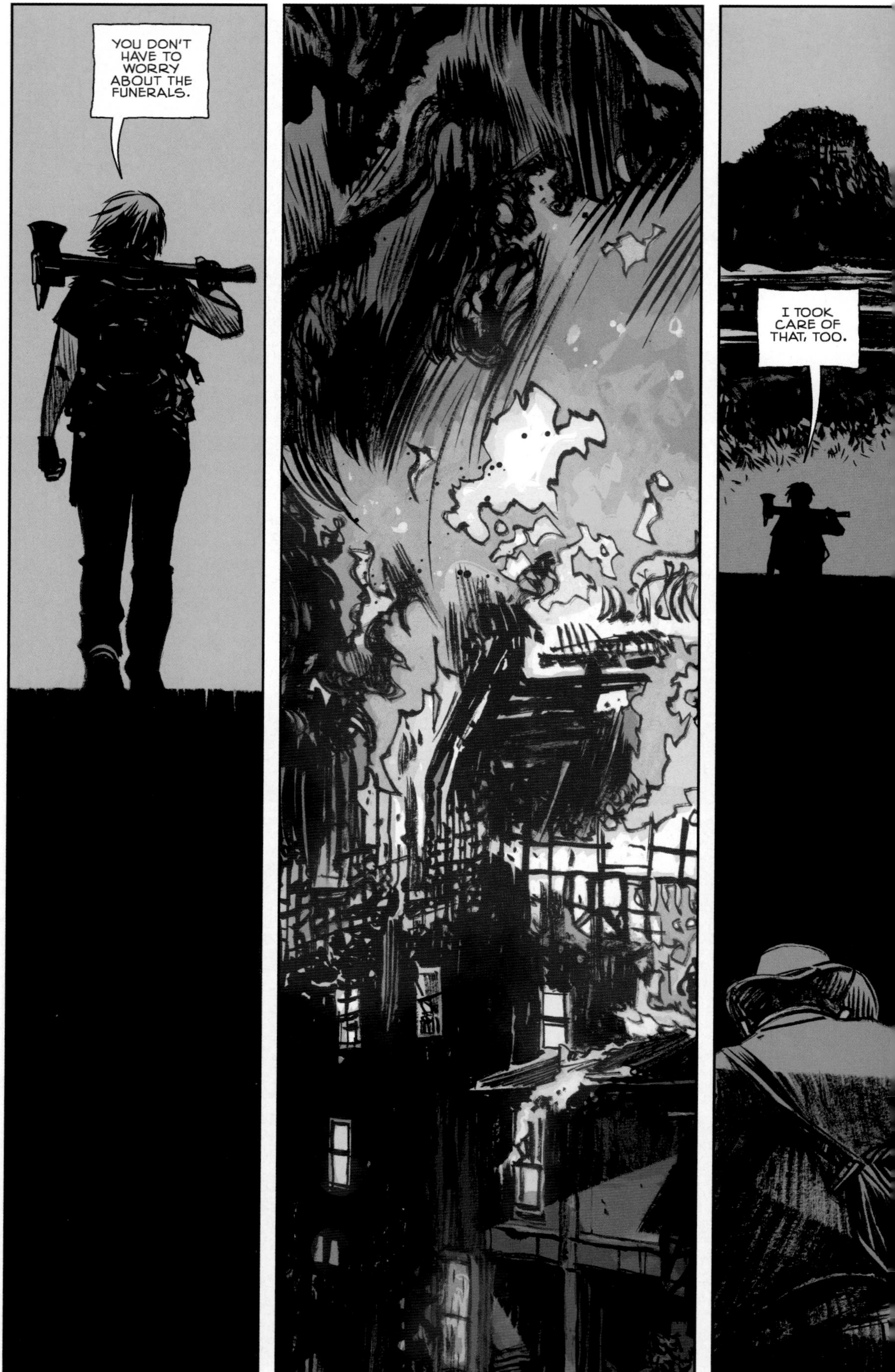
YOU DON'T HAVE TO WORRY ABOUT THE FUNERALS.
I TOOK CARE OF THAT, TOO.

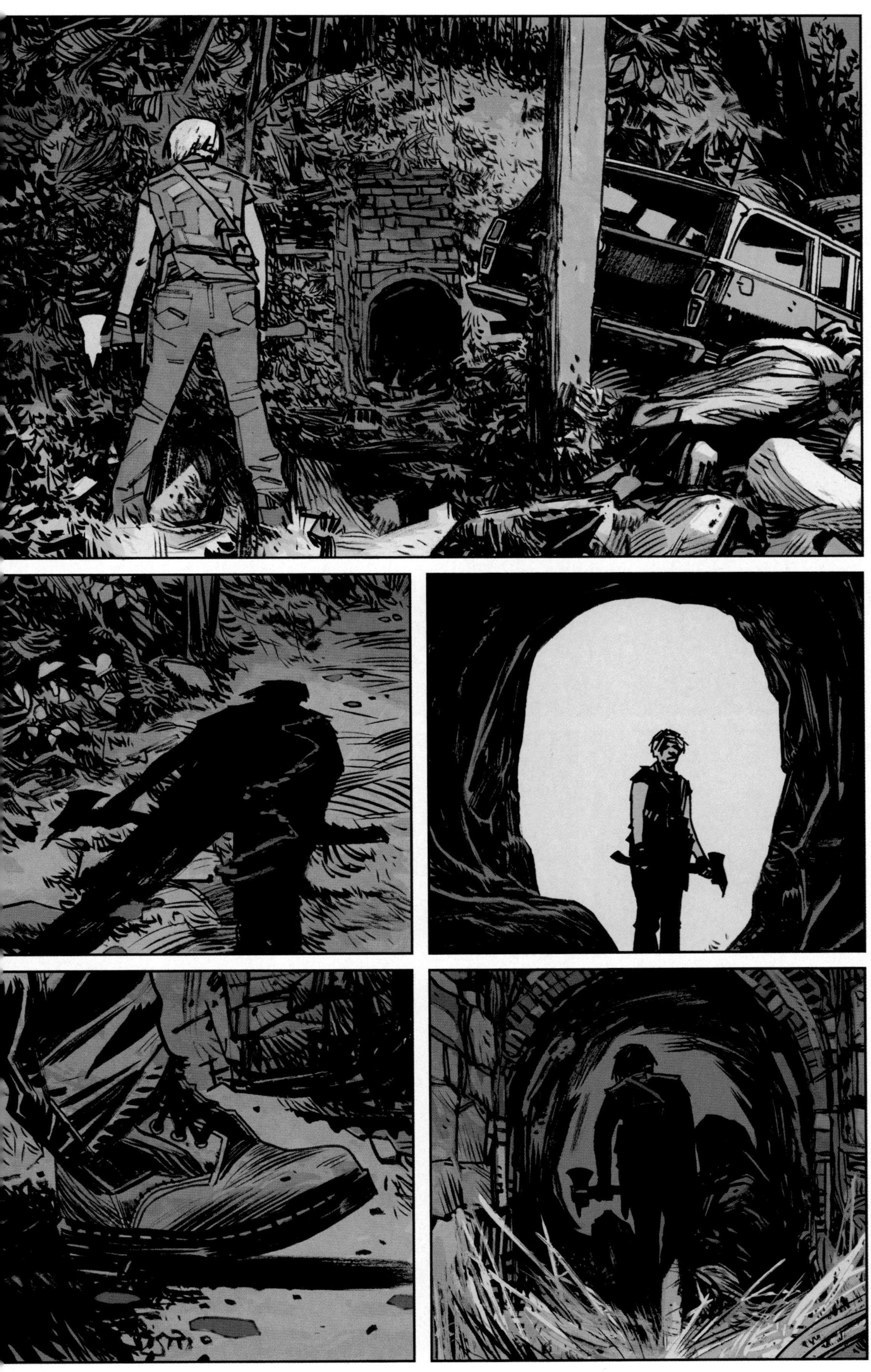

SCHRIIIIPPP!

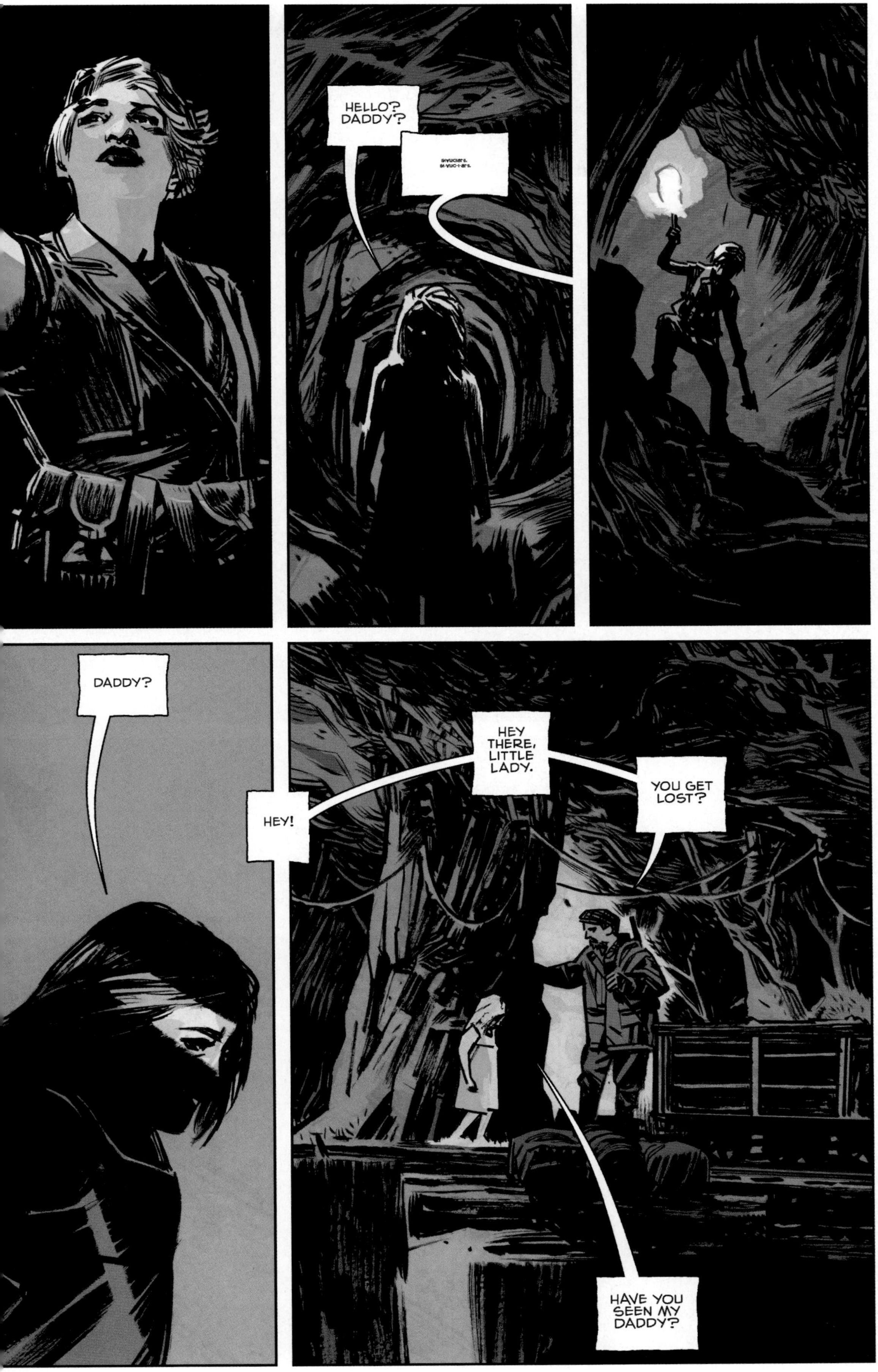
HELLO? DADDY?
DADDY?
HEY!
HEY THERE, LITTLE LADY.
YOU GET LOST?
HAVE YOU SEEN MY DADDY?

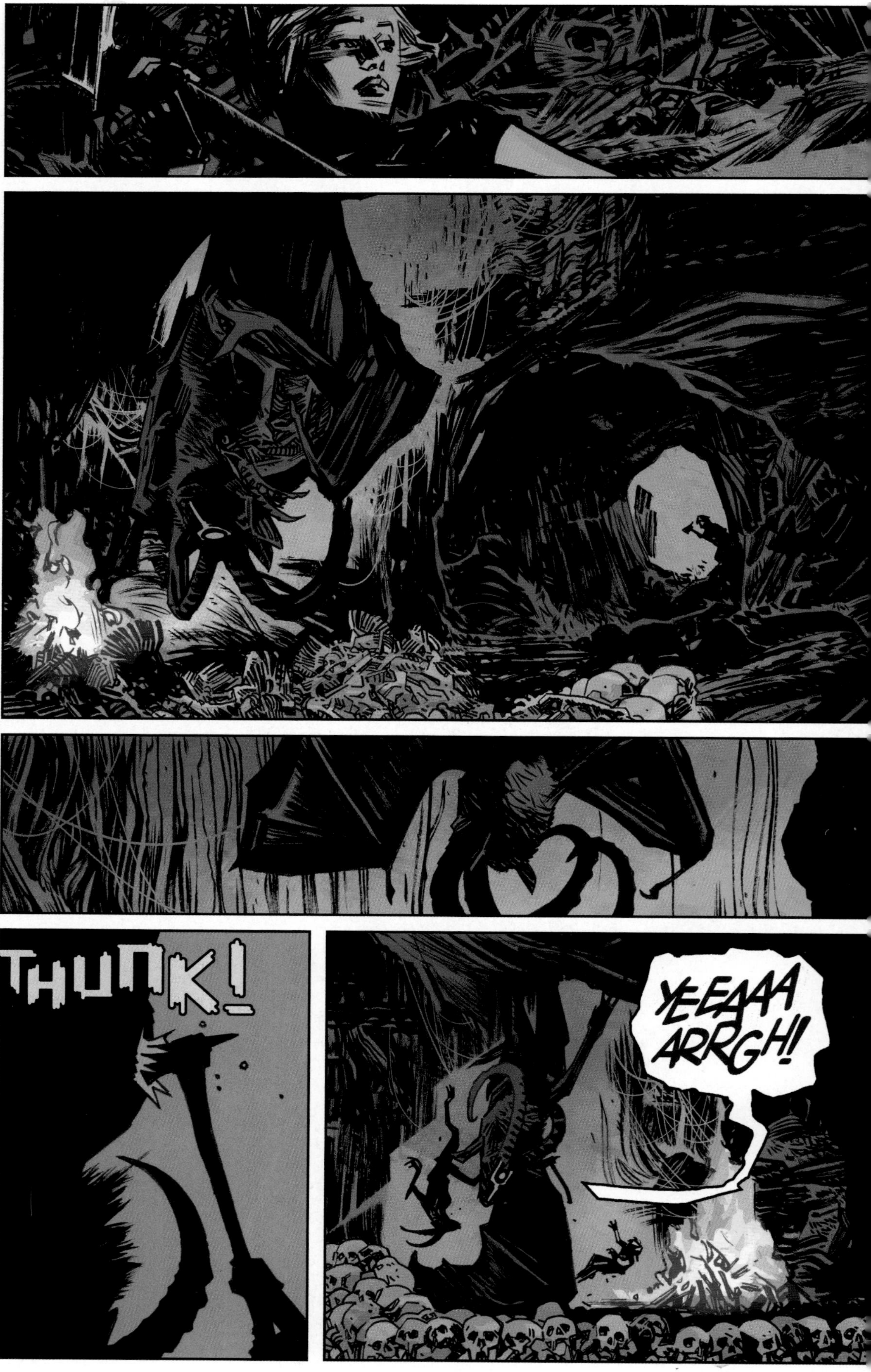
THUNK!
YEEAAA ARRGH!

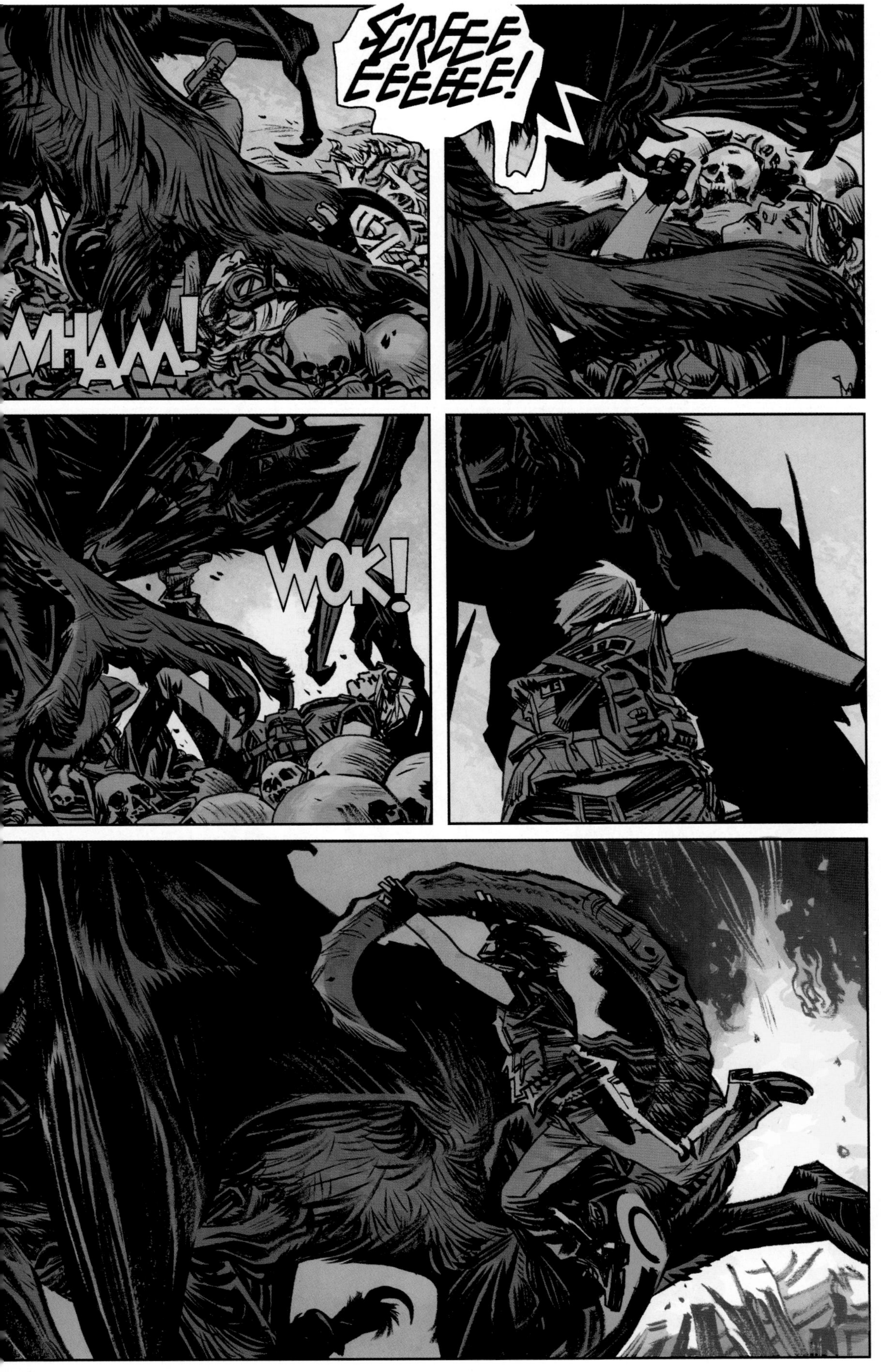
SCREEEE EEEEEEE!
WHAM!
WOK!

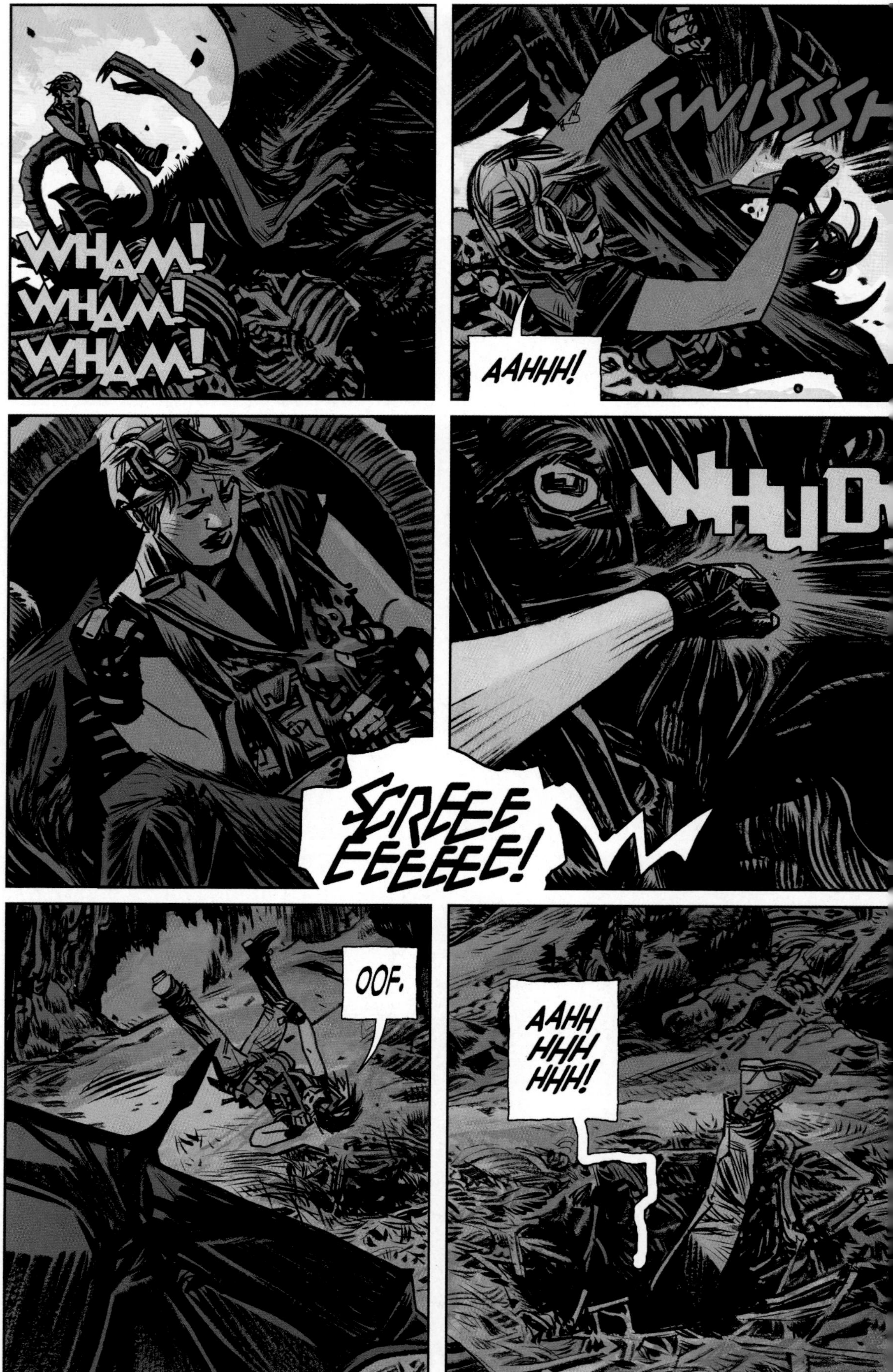
WHAM!
WHAM!
WHAM!
SWISSSH
AAHHH!
WHUD
SCREEE
EEEEEEE!
OOF.
AAHH
HHH
HHH!

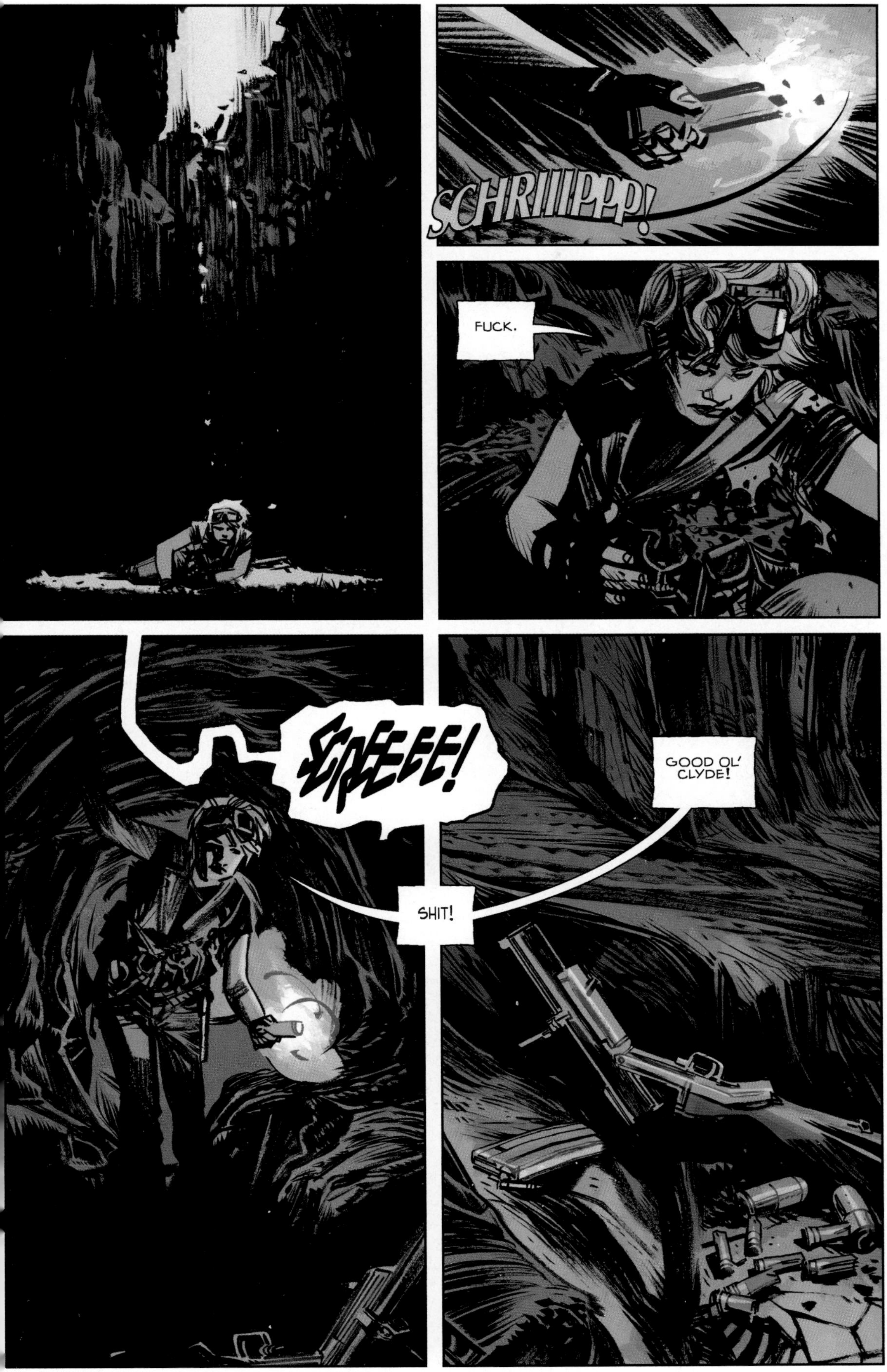

SCHRIIIPPP!
FUCK.
SCREEEE!
GOOD OL' CLYDE!
SHIT!

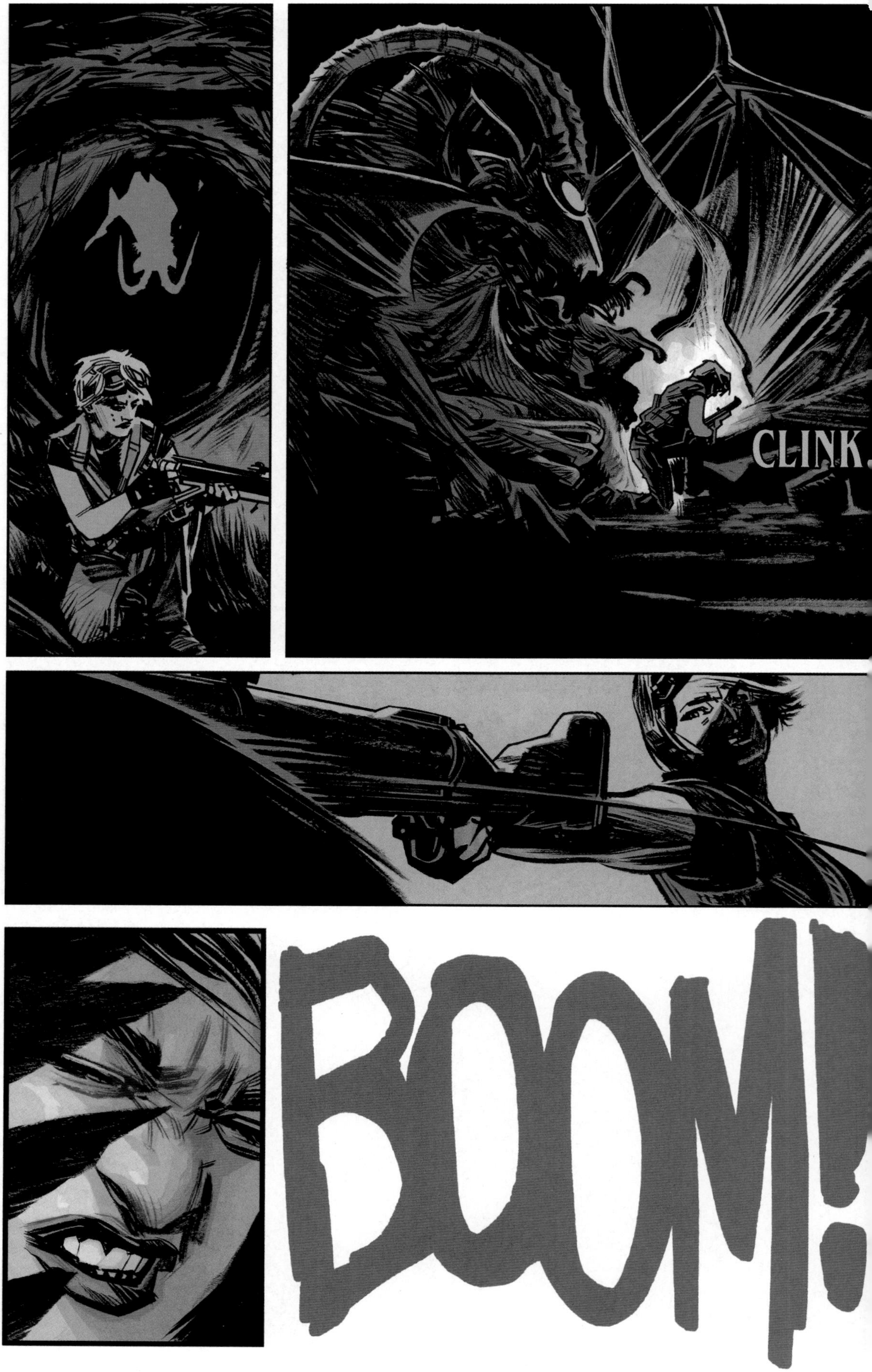
CLINK.
BOOM!

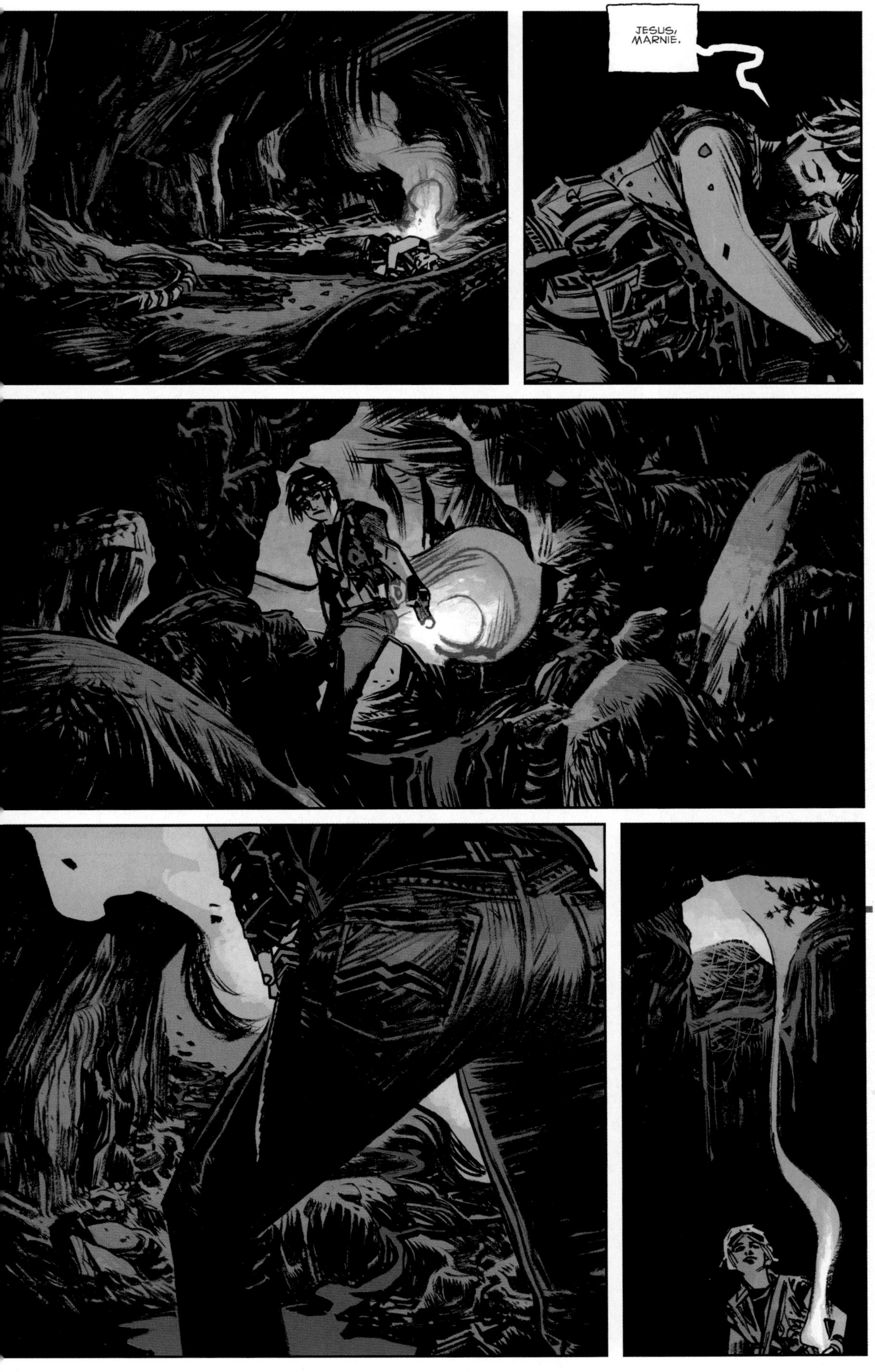
JESUS, MARNIE.

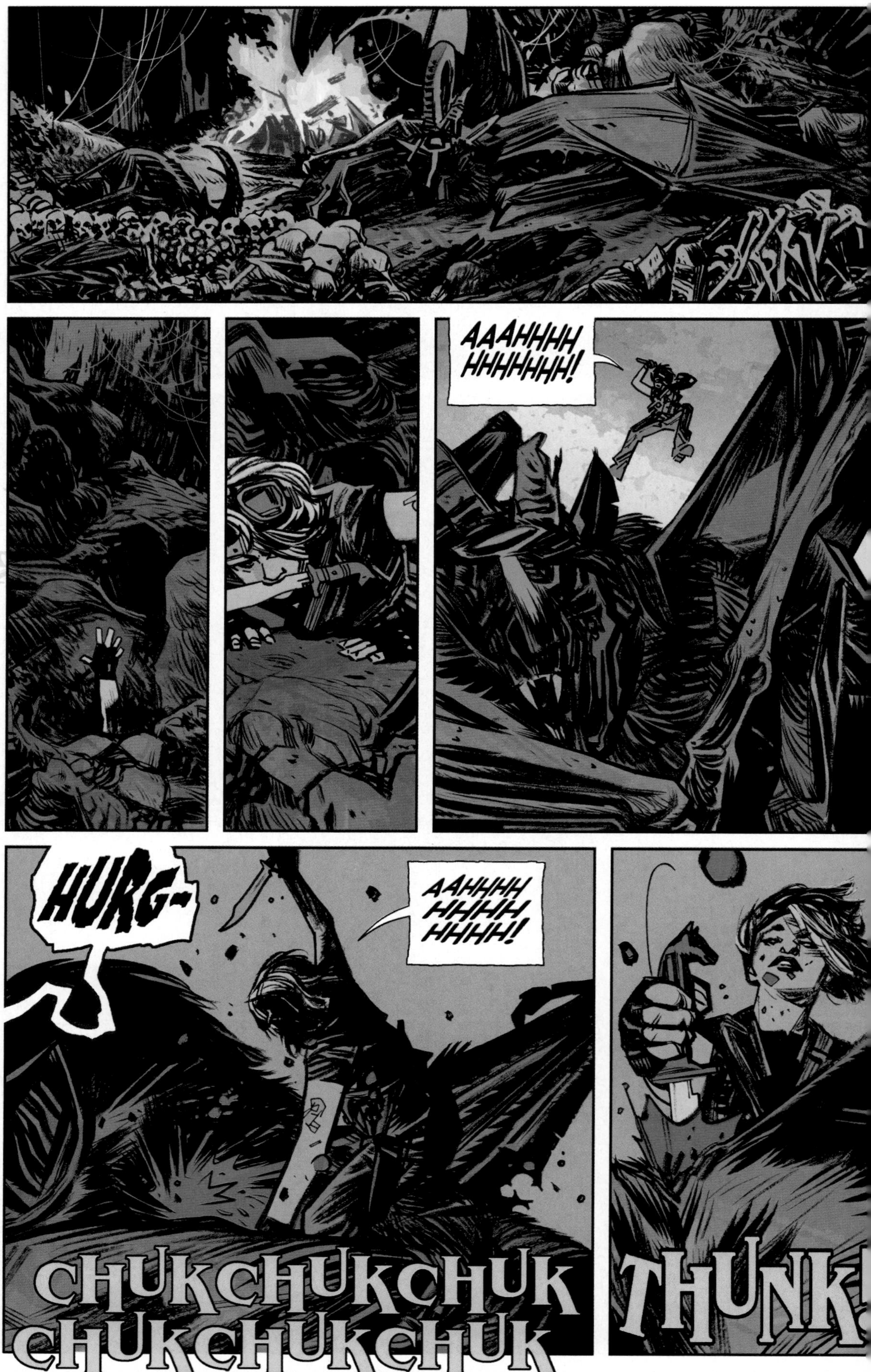
AAAHHHH
HHHHHHH!
HURG-
AAHHHH
HHHH
HHHH!
CHUKCHUKCHUK
CHUKCHUKCHUK
THUNK!

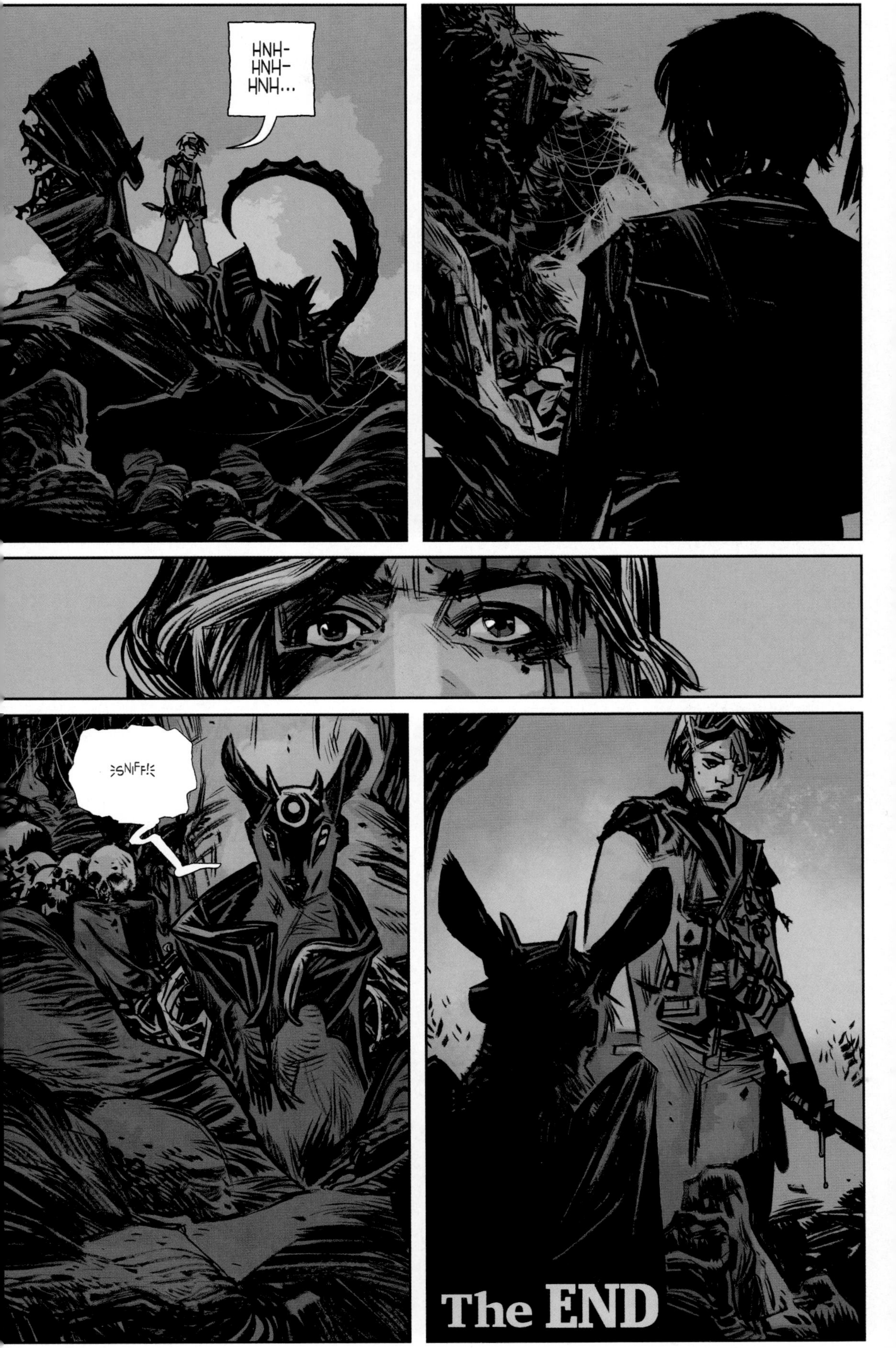
HNH-
HNH-
HNH...
SNIFF!
The END

# Greetings from GRENDEL

When reading *Beowulf* during the early days of writing *Grendel, Kentucky,* something jumped out at me that I hadn't known, or had known and long forgotten. Grendel attacks King Hrothgar's magnificent shield hall because he's jealous of the fellowship and the prosperity of the people gathered there.

What did he want?

It was this point that stuck with me and eventually formed into the story *Grendel, Kentucky.*

In Grendel I imagined a town that exists as an island of sorts in Kentucky coal country. Grendel, we learn, had long ago turned their local econ-

**Jeff McComsey**

omy to farming, specifically marijuana farming. The weed business and the town are completely intertwined, and are happy to be so. The business has kept two generations of Grendel men out of the

mines. Our King Hrothgar is Randall "Pap" Wallace. The pot business is a family business for the Wallaces. A responsibility they take very seriously. It's through him and his family that we learn it's not just luck that makes the grass grow in his little fiefdom.

Our Beowulf is Marnie, a 6'3" biker. She's captain of a rowdy club, THE HARLOTS, and as we learn, she has some unfinished family business in Grendel. The Harlots are in a tough spot. Marnie's relatively strong moral code keeps the club from indulging in some of the nastier ways to make a living as an outlaw.

When originally discussing the project with Axel and Mike, I said I wanted to do a Southern fried retelling of *Beowulf.* "Grindhouse" was a word we used a lot. I wanted Beowulf and his band of warriors to be an all-female outlaw motorcycle club (later named The Harlots) from Hickory Hills, Pennsylvania.

We were thinking outlaws, motorcycles, monsters, big gnarly trucks, and old-school cop cruisers. Naturally our first

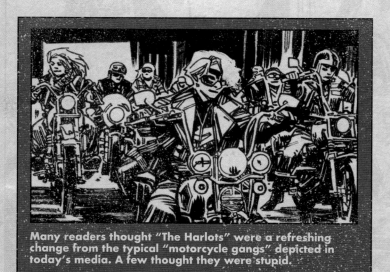

Many readers thought "The Harlots" were a refreshing change from the typical "motorcycle gangs" depicted in today's media. A few thought they were stupid.

choice to draw all this was Tommy Lee Edwards.

Watching Tommy's art come in is awesome. I've been a fan of his work for a long time and was admittedly very excited to work on a project with him that I knew he would nail. I know Tommy is a guy who restores engines and has ridden a few motorcycles in his day. All those details and elements that really sell a period piece are there in loving detail. He's done *Grendel* in traditional inks, which are a real treat to see raw scans of. I am a cartoonist in addition to writing, and seeing Tommy's process (thumbs to colors!) has been like getting a masters in that sweet science of making comics.

Finishing off the look of *Grendel, Kentucky* are letters by John Workman, another gent who I am thrilled to work with. Tommy and John work together often and start blocking out SFX and balloon placement before finished art gets started, a luxury not always available during production. It's made for some great storytelling opportunities. As comic creators, sound is not a tool we can use to tell stories (which hurts as a music lover). Luckily, we have John to make up for all that!

**JEFF MCCOMSEY**
**Lancaster, Penn.**

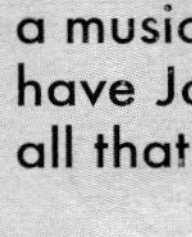

**Wow, that was long-winded, Jeff. You should be a comic-book writer or some shit. Let's see what our next reader has to say.**

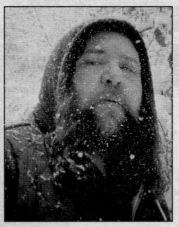

**Tommy Lee Edwards**

Lots of memories have been swirling around in my brain lately. Childhood "snapshots" of growing up in Detroit. Weekends spent watching TV20's *Thriller Double Feature*, Channel 50's *Count Scary*, and reading Warren magazines like *Creepy* and *Eerie*. My uncle Craig would drive me to the newsstand in his 1977 Firebird Trans-Am. He got me hooked on *Hot Rod Comics* and *CARtoons* magazine. My uncle Jeff was a motorcycle nut who scored me old copies of DC's *House of Mystery* and *The Witching Hour* at a local garage sale. My friends and I traded Hot Wheels cars and made monster masks. Sometimes I got to visit my mom's office at the GM proving grounds and feel like a top secret VIP. My dad restored a 1952 Chevy pickup in our garage. Grandpa, Aunt Marilyn, and everyone else worked at either Chevy, Ford, Cadillac, or Chrysler. My first high school job was as a forklift operator at a stamping plant.

Anyway...

I blame most of this nostalgia on creating *Grendel, Kentucky* with Jeff McComsey.

As an adult, I ride motorcycles, drive a 1966 Plymouth, and spend my weekends working on old cars. Now I just need to grow some weed and find some monsters to fight.

**TOMMY LEE EDWARDS**
**Pittsboro, N.C.**

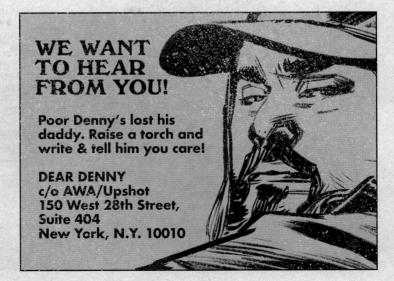

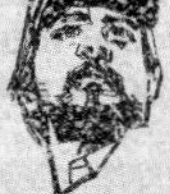

**I reckon none of your kin were killed by a bear or nothin', so sounds like you had a pretty good childhood.**

WE WANT TO HEAR FROM YOU!
Poor Denny's lost his daddy. Raise a torch and write & tell him you care!
DEAR DENNY
c/o AWA/Upshot
150 West 28th Street,
Suite 404
New York, N.Y. 10010

# Behind the SCENES

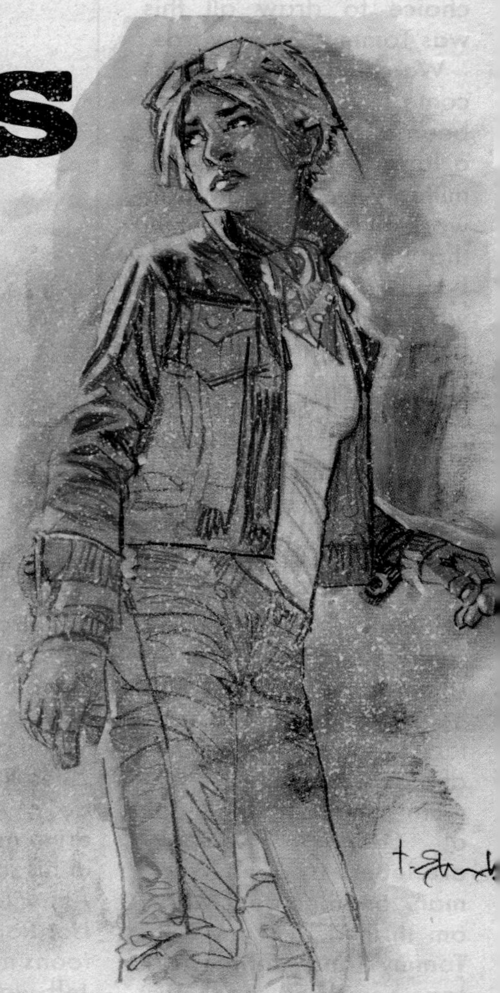

**Right: Artist Tommy Lee Edwards' first illustration of Marnie, the lead character of *Grendel, Kentucky*. Below: Concept illustration of Mike's police car.**

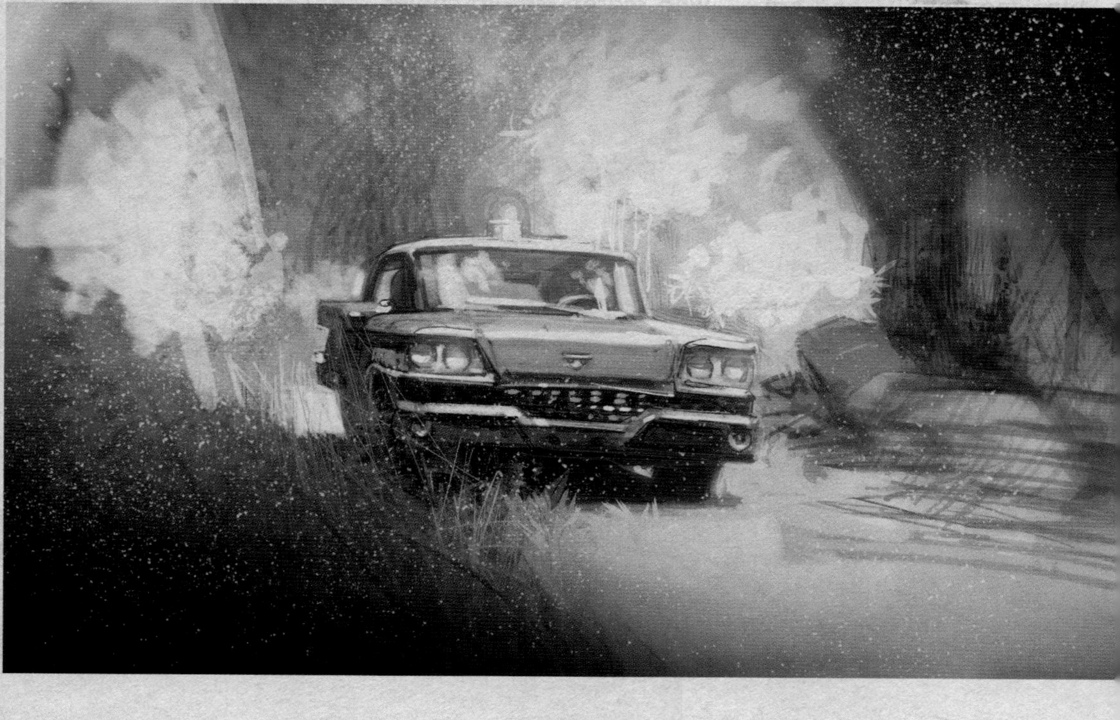

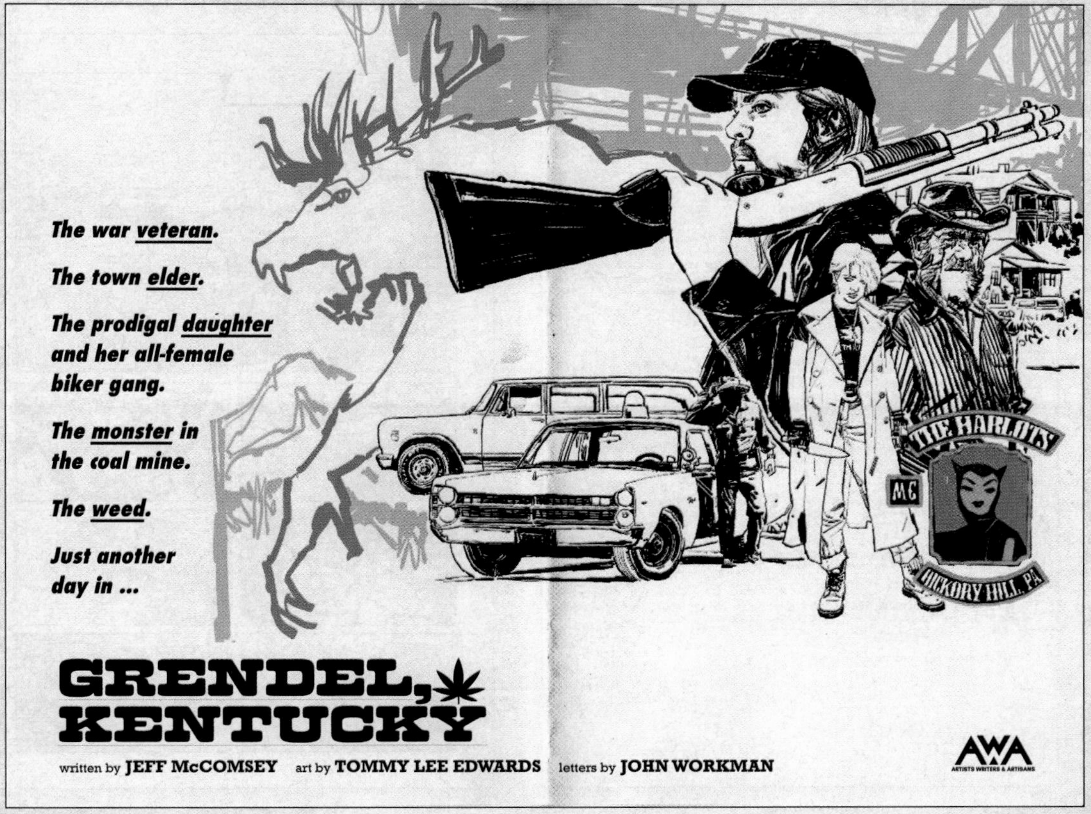
The war veteran.
The town elder.
The prodigal daughter and her all-female biker gang.
The monster in the coal mine.
The weed.
Just another day in ...
THE HARLOTS
MC
HICKORY HILL, PA
GRENDEL, KENTUCKY
written by JEFF McCOMSEY
art by TOMMY LEE EDWARDS
letters by JOHN WORKMAN
AWA

**Edwards and designer Chris Ferguson wanted to give *Grendel, Kentucky* a 1970s grindhouse/biker gang movie aesthetic, as evident in this work-in-progress versions of the promotional poster (above) and covers to issues #1 and #3. Note the early versions of the *Grendel* logo.**

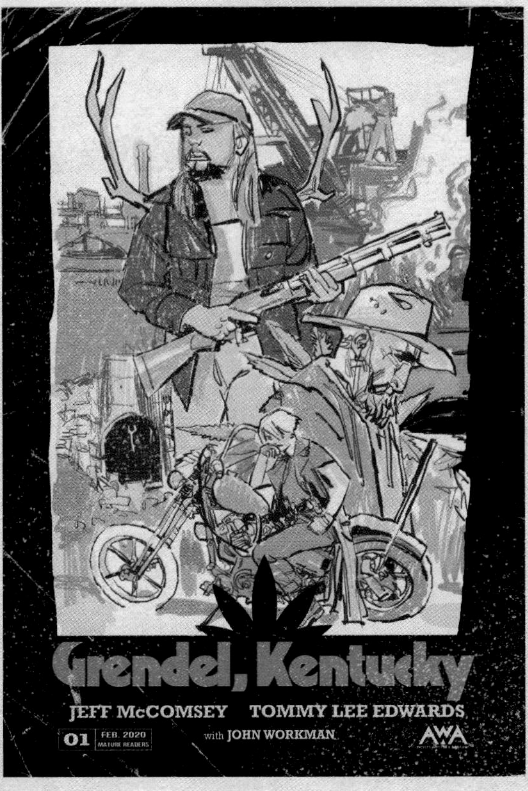
Grendel, Kentucky
JEFF McCOMSEY
TOMMY LEE EDWARDS
01
FEB. 2020
MATURE READERS
with JOHN WORKMAN
AWA

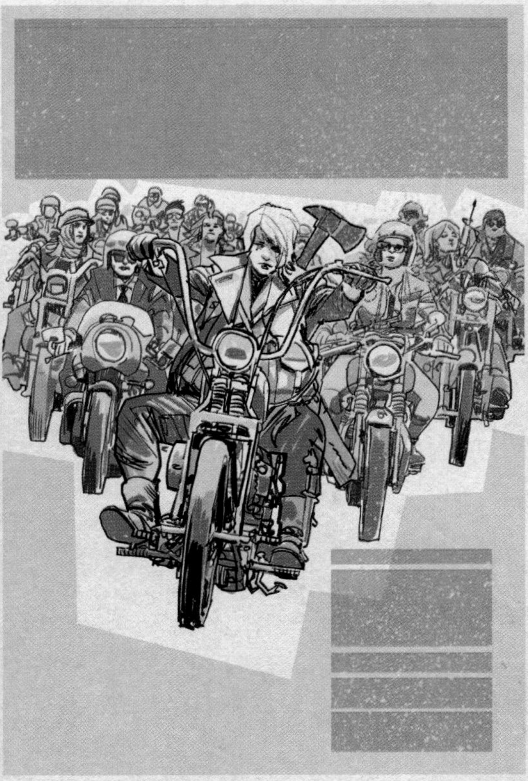

## Issue #1, page 1 ▼

**GRENDEL, KENTUCKY #1**
**Chapter 1: Here lies a man**
**Story by Jeff McComsey**

**PAGE ONE**

1
Daytime exterior a large old style abandoned coal mine entrance carved out of the side of a mountain. A 1962 Ford pick up truck sits a distance away from the mouth of the mine. A man is at the rear of the truck with the tailgate down. At this distance we can't quite make out him or what he's doing. The entrance to this mine is something we'll return to a few times throughout the course of the story. I imagine it a relic from the 1920's with various old warning signs. Disused since then, but still open. (River, rocks, tree-line, etc)

01. CAPTION Grendel, Kentucky. Fall, 1971.

2
One of a series of six POV panels. I imagine it like the bottom 6 of a 9 panel grid.
A large hand that we'll discover belongs to Clyde Wallace, but for now it's just a burly hands wrap black tape around a small bundle of dynamite sticks, whose fuses have already been similarly wrapped.

3
POV shot of the same hands Now duct taping a catcher's chest guard, with shoulder plates in place on his chest. (Make more gnarly. He's going into BATTLE.)

4
POV shot of the hands filling the gas tank up on a large chainsaw that sits on the tailgate. On top of the hand guard to the chainsaw, a flashlight has been duct taped.

5
POV shot of hands as they secure catcher's shin guards in place over jeans and big work boots. (maybe instead loading 'nam-era grenade launcher)

6
Shot of the hands loading the taped up bundle of dynamite into the open duffel where we see a sawed off and one or two other similarly taped bundles of dynamite.

7
Shot of the hands zipping up the duffel.

1
Truck bed
SHUMP
FOOMP
ZZZIP


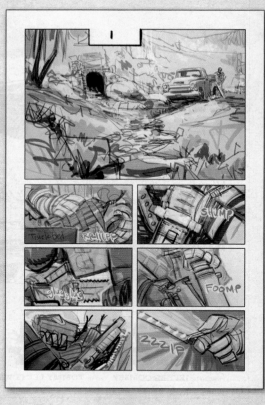

**The page process for *Grendel, Kentucky* begins with a detailed script from writer Jeff McComsey.**

**Illustrator Tommy Lee Edwards then sketches out the page layout on his Cintiq tablet, noting caption/sound effect/dialog placement.**

## Issue #3, page 18 ▼

**PAGE EIGHTEEN**
1
Match cut to the severed arm displayed on a makeshift "shrine" on display in the Hall. Mostly beer bottles/cans, liquor bottles. Maybe Marnie's bloody axe.

VOICE You know what this means?

2
Wide interior establishing shot inside the Hall. The Harlots, Denny and Deputy Mike are all present and partying. I imagine there's a group of Harlots gathered around the tap with giant glass beer steins, slugging them back. Denny and Elvis help Mike hit some giant bong elsewhere. Everybody seems elated about the victory. Marnie is drinking by herself, maybe she's looking at the shrine.

HARLOT 1 If monsters are real, there could also be **mermaids**.

HARLOT 1 Mermaids, Jess. Think about it.

HARLOT 2 Vampires could be real. Maybe even dinosaurs too.

3
Denny sidles up next to Marnie. He's got a bottle in his hand that he's put a serious dent in. Denny's pretty drunk.

DENNY Hey. How'd you know It'd take the bait.

4
Marnie looks at him. Denny is offering his bottle.

MARNIE Figured he hasn't done much huntin' for himself in a good long while.

MARNIE I was hoping he'd be hungry and sloppy.

5
Marnie takes a big swig.

DENNY You think if you'd have stayed here instead of running off, you coulda done what Pap and Daddy did?

6
Marnie hands the bottle back to Denny, who's seated now

MARNIE Fuck no.
MARNIE You don't kill people for money **or** whatever the fuck this was.

USMC
1
2
3
4
keg
5
6
7
8
9
10
sits

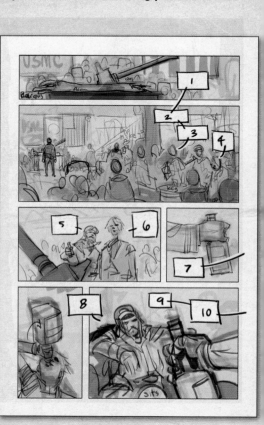

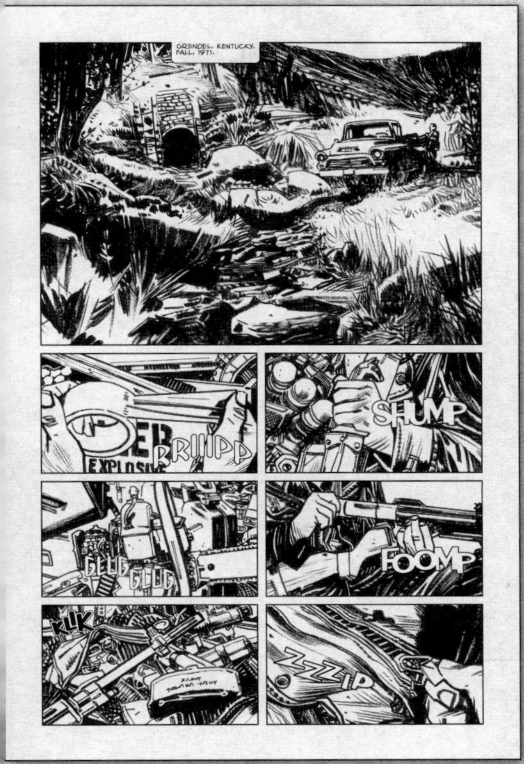
GRENDEL, KENTUCKY.
FALL, 1971.
BRIIIPP
SHUMP
GLUG GLUG
FOOMP
KLIK
ZZZIP

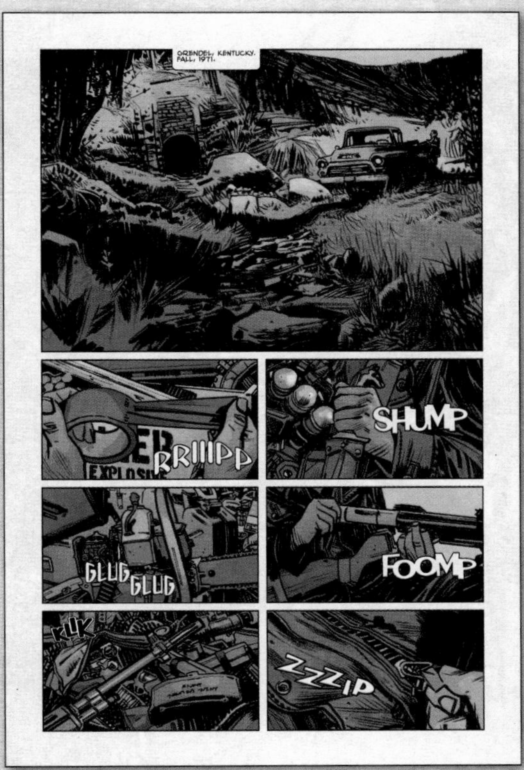
GRENDEL, KENTUCKY.
FALL, 1971.
BRIIIPP
SHUMP
GLUG GLUG
FOOMP
KLIK
ZZZIP

**After John Workman provides lettering based on the script/placement, Edwards then goes to the illustration stage and does the final inks.**

**Finally, the coloring is done digitally. Issues #1 and #2 were colored by Edwards, and the final two issues were done by Giovanna Niro.**

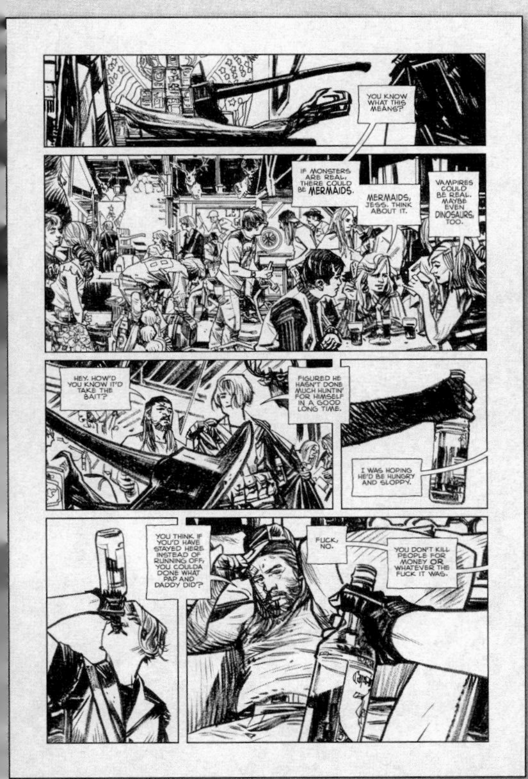
YOU KNOW WHAT THIS MEANS?
IF MONSTERS ARE REAL, THERE COULD BE MERMAIDS.
MERMAIDS, JESS. THINK ABOUT IT.
VAMPIRES COULD BE REAL. MAYBE EVEN DINOSAURS, TOO.
HEY. HOW'D YOU KNOW IT'D TAKE THE BAIT?
FIGURED HE HASN'T DONE MUCH HUNTIN' IN A GOOD LONG TIME.
I WAS HOPING HE'D BE HUNGRY AND SLOPPY.
YOU THINK, IF YOU'D HAVE STAYED HERE INSTEAD OF RUNNING OFF, YOU COULDA DONE WHAT PAP AND DADDY DID?
FUCK, NO.
YOU DON'T KILL PEOPLE FOR MONEY OR WHATEVER THE FUCK IT WAS.

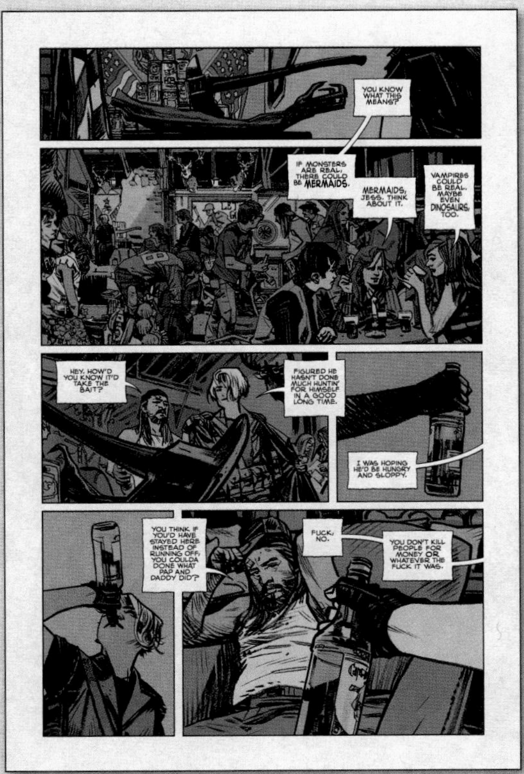
YOU KNOW WHAT THIS MEANS?
IF MONSTERS ARE REAL, THERE COULD BE MERMAIDS.
MERMAIDS, JESS. THINK ABOUT IT.
VAMPIRES COULD BE REAL. MAYBE EVEN DINOSAURS, TOO.
HEY. HOW'D YOU KNOW IT'D TAKE THE BAIT?
FIGURED HE HASN'T DONE MUCH HUNTIN' IN A GOOD LONG TIME.
I WAS HOPING HE'D BE HUNGRY AND SLOPPY.
YOU THINK, IF YOU'D HAVE STAYED HERE INSTEAD OF RUNNING OFF, YOU COULDA DONE WHAT PAP AND DADDY DID?
FUCK, NO.
YOU DON'T KILL PEOPLE FOR MONEY OR WHATEVER THE FUCK IT WAS.

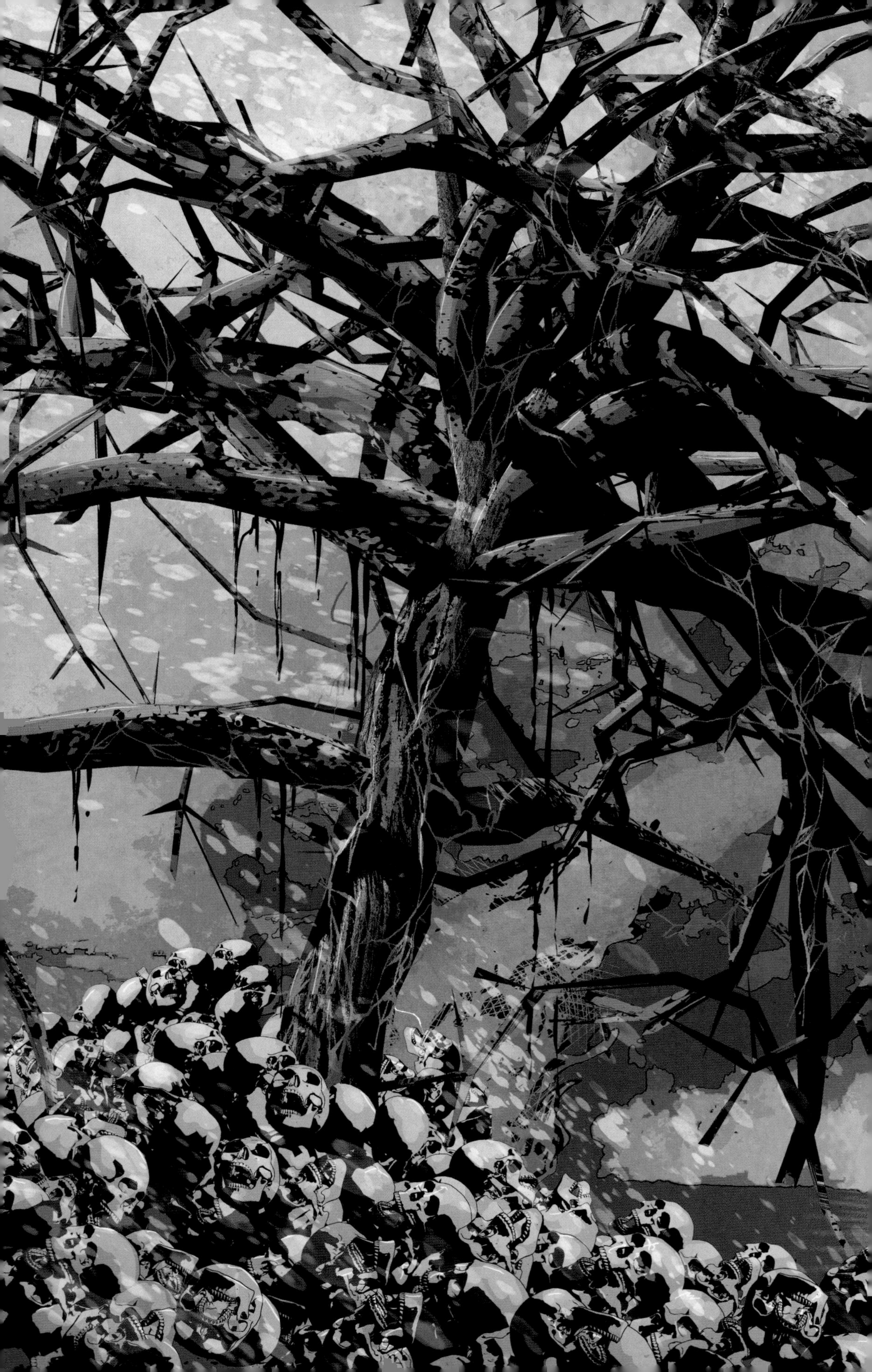

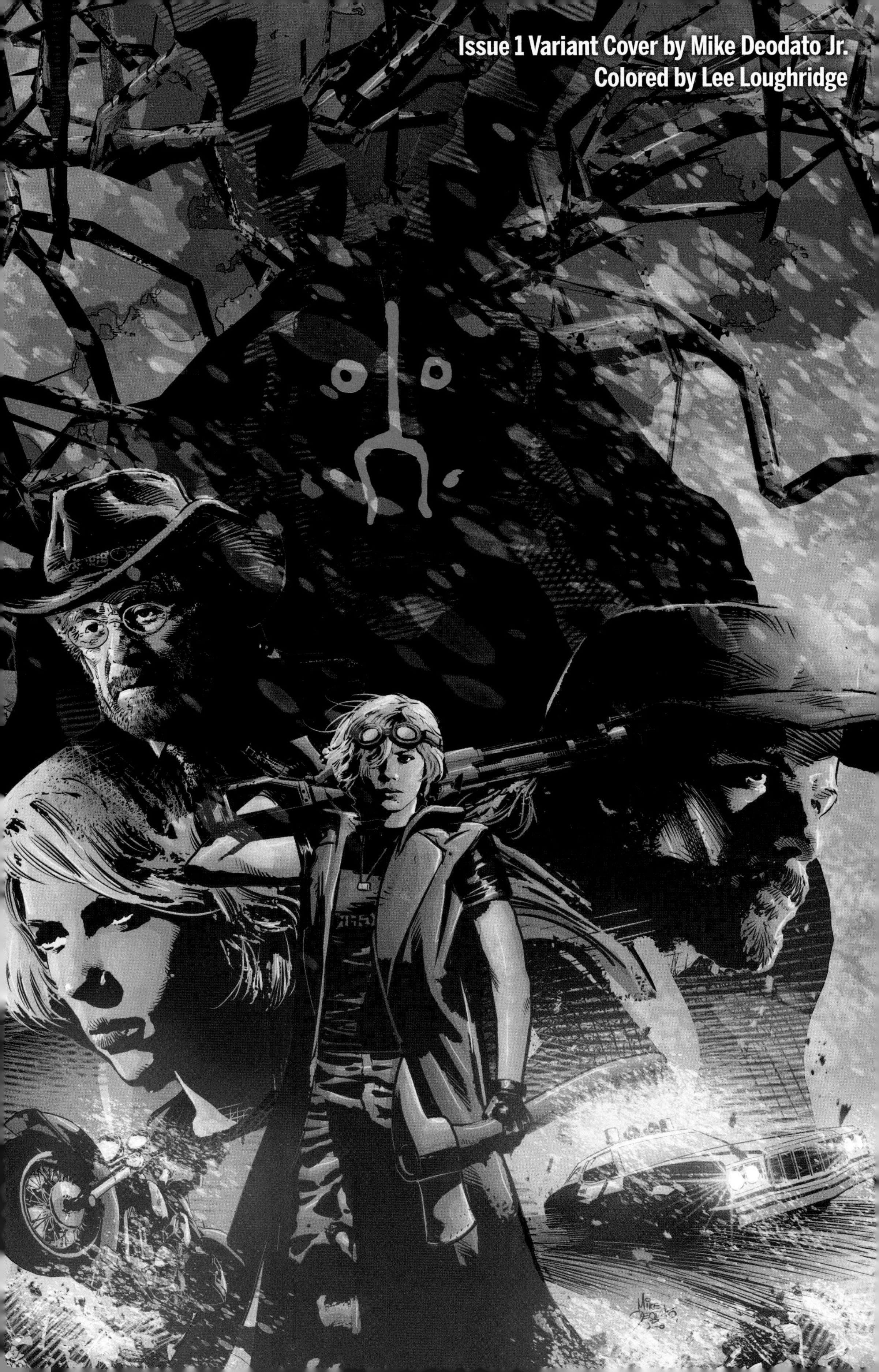

Issue 1 Variant Cover by Mike Deodato Jr.
Colored by Lee Loughridge

**Issue 4 Variant Cover by Dave Johns**

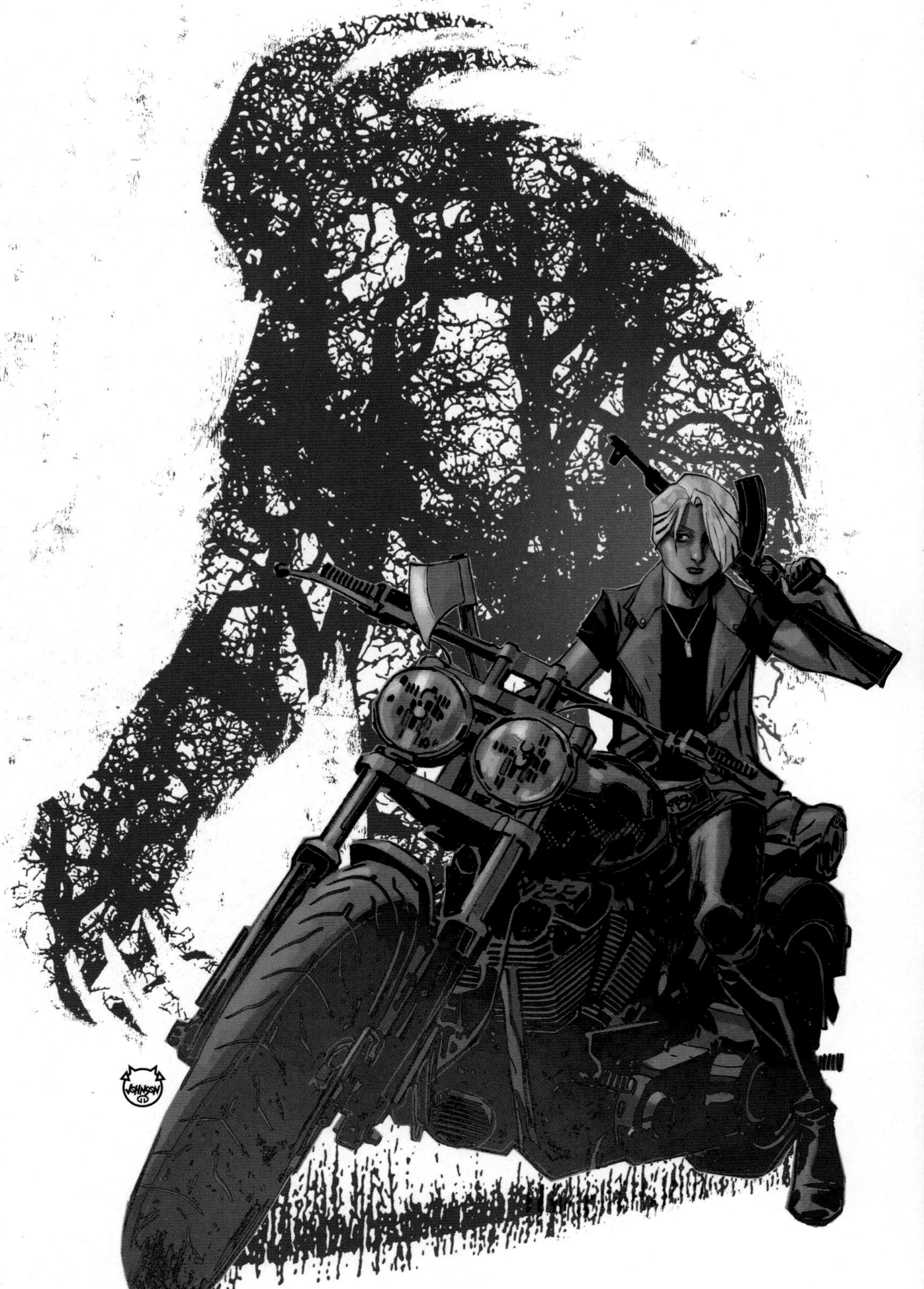